"Victoria Thompson shines . . .
Anne Perry and Caleb Carr fans rejoice!"
—Tamar Myers

Praise for the Edgar® Award-nominated
Gaslight Mysteries

MURDER ON ASTOR PLACE

Nominated for the Best First Mystery Award by
Romantic Times *magazine*

"Victoria Thompson is off to a blazing start with Sarah Brandt and Frank Malloy in *Murder on Astor Place* . . . [A] tantalizing mystery."
—Catherine Coulter, *New York Times* bestselling author

"Sprinkled with fascinating details of turn-of-the-century New York City . . . Sarah and Frank are appealing characters, and the author develops their rapport subtly and believably."
—*Publishers Weekly*

"The corrupt, vibrant, crowded world of late nineteenth–century New York fills the pages . . . The mystery is solid . . . The best part of *Murder in Astor Place* was the shifting relationship between Sarah and Malloy . . . [I] can't wait until they share another adventure."
—*The Mystery Reader*

"Excellent characterization and sense of place . . . A very good read in every respect."
—*Books 'n' Bytes*

"Reminiscent of Anne Perry . . . Spellbinding . . . The setting is beautifully drawn, and Thompson shows a steady hand at creating human drama. The sexual tension between Malloy and Brandt is palpable. This is a bravura performance."
—*Romantic Times*

continued . . .

MURDER ON BANK STREET

"The story line is fast-paced, especially the last quarter, while also providing insight to 1890s New York . . . Terrific."　　　　　　　　　　*—Genre Go Round Reviews*

"Thompson serves up another Gilded Age page-turner . . . Highly entertaining . . . [She] proves once again that she is an absolute master of first-class historical mysteries."
　　　　　　　　　　　　　　　　　　　—Fresh Fiction

MURDER IN CHINATOWN

"Thought-provoking . . . Vivid."　　　　*—Publishers Weekly*

"The unexpected climax adds to the impact of this first-class historical mystery."　　　　　　　　　　*—Booklist*

MURDER ON LENOX HILL

"Ms. Thompson is skilled at dialogue . . . and this dialogue moves the book along quickly. [*Murder on Lenox Hill*] grabs one's interest early, especially since the crimes seem so unsolvable."　　　　　　　*—The Washington Times*

"Well-crafted . . . Good plot twists and a highly satisfactory wrap-up mark this as the work of a master of the period mystery."　　　　　　　　　*—Publishers Weekly*

"Transports the reader back in time . . . Victoria Thompson's Gaslight Mysteries are first rate with a vivid historical setting and a hero and heroine that will keep readers eagerly returning to Sarah Brandt's New York City."
　　　　　　　　　　　　　　　—The Mystery Reader

"A tremendous entry in one of the best historical series."
　　　　　　　　　　　　　　—Midwest Book Review

MURDER ON MARBLE ROW

"Engaging characters . . . An enjoyable read."
—Margaret Frazer, author of *The Apostate's Tale*

"Victoria Thompson has a knack for putting the reader inside her character's heads, and her detailed descriptions of New York at the turn of the century bring the setting vividly to life."
—Kate Kingsbury, author of *Ringing in Murder*

MURDER ON MULBERRY BEND

"An exciting intrigue of murder, deception, and bigotry. *Gangs of New York,* eat your heart out—this book is the real thing."
—*Mystery Scene*

"A thrilling, informative, challenging mystery."
—*The Drood Review*

MURDER ON WASHINGTON SQUARE

"Victoria Thompson's Gaslight Mysteries are always . . . exciting treats to read."
—*Midwest Book Review*

MURDER ON GRAMERCY PARK

"This series is so well written. The characters are so real and the time period laid out so well . . . The darkness of New York really adds to this series. Her writing of the time and the way she lays out the story without giving the killer away is terrific . . . This cozy mystery is great. I highly recommend this book as well as the whole series."
—*Books 'n' Bytes*

MURDER ON ST. MARK'S PLACE

Nominated for the Edgar® Award

"Lovers of history, mystery, and romance won't be disappointed. Exciting . . . Will hold the reader in thrall."
—*Romantic Times*

MURDER ON ASTOR PLACE

Victoria Thompson

BERKLEY PRIME CRIME, NEW YORK

THE BERKLEY PUBLISHING GROUP
Published by the Penguin Group
Penguin Group (USA) Inc.
375 Hudson Street, New York, New York 10014, USA
Penguin Group (Canada), 90 Eglinton Avenue East, Suite 700, Toronto, Ontario M4P 2Y3, Canada
(a division of Pearson Penguin Canada Inc.)
Penguin Books Ltd., 80 Strand, London WC2R 0RL, England
Penguin Group Ireland, 25 St. Stephen's Green, Dublin 2, Ireland (a division of Penguin Books Ltd.)
Penguin Group (Australia), 250 Camberwell Road, Camberwell, Victoria 3124, Australia
(a division of Pearson Australia Group Pty. Ltd.)
Penguin Books India Pvt. Ltd., 11 Community Centre, Panchsheel Park, New Delhi—110 017, India
Penguin Group (NZ), 67 Apollo Drive, Rosedale, North Shore 0632, New Zealand
(a division of Pearson New Zealand Ltd.)
Penguin Books (South Africa) (Pty.) Ltd., 24 Sturdee Avenue, Rosebank, Johannesburg 2196,
South Africa

Penguin Books Ltd., Registered Offices: 80 Strand, London WC2R 0RL, England

This book is an original publication of The Berkley Publishing Group.

This is a work of fiction. Names, characters, places, and incidents either are the product of the author's imagination or are used fictitiously, and any resemblance to actual persons, living or dead, business establishments, events, or locales is entirely coincidental. The publisher does not have any control over and does not assume any responsibility for author or third-party websites or their content.

PRINTING HISTORY
Berkley Prime Crime mass-market edition / May 1999
Berkley Prime Crime trade paperback edition / September 2009

Berkley Prime Crime trade paperback ISBN: 978-0-425-22972-9

PRINTED IN THE UNITED STATES OF AMERICA

10 9 8 7 6 5 4 3 2 1

To my agent Nancy Yost, who never stopped believing and who always makes me laugh, even when the news is bad. And to my dear husband Jim, who eased the load so I'd have the time and energy to write this.

I

Aᴛ ꜰɪʀꜱᴛ Sᴀʀᴀʜ ᴛʜᴏᴜɢʜᴛ ᴛʜᴇ ᴛɪɴᴋʟɪɴɢ ᴏꜰ ᴛʜᴇ bell was part of her dream. It sounded so sweet and soothing, and she was following it across a sunlit meadow, as if it were a golden butterfly. But then the pounding started, and she knew this wasn't a dream at all. Dragging herself away from the meadow and out of the depths of sleep, she forced her reluctant eyelids open. Sure enough, someone was pounding on her office door.

"Hold your horses," she muttered as she threw off her covers. The night air was chilly for early April, and Sarah recalled the freak storm that had struck yesterday, dropping several inches of snow on the city. Shivering, she felt around in the dark for her slippers but failed to locate them. Padding barefoot through the darkness toward where she knew the bedroom door to be, she snatched her robe from the foot of the bed and shrugged into it as she went. "Coming!" she called, wondering if whoever was knocking could hear her over the racket he was making.

What she really wanted to say was, "Calm down! Babies usually take their own sweet time, so there probably isn't any rush." In the three years she'd been delivering babies for a living, Sarah could count on the fingers of one hand the times that had truly been an emergency.

Usually those were the cases where she was summoned to some hovel on the Lower East Side to a woman too poor to pay her fee but whose delivery had gone horribly wrong. Left with no choice, the family summoned her in the often-vain hope that she would be able to save either the mother or the child.

Shaking off the last vestiges of sleep as she moved through the frigid front room of her flat, which also served as her office, Sarah offered a silent prayer that this wasn't one of those calls. The gaslights on the street outside reflecting off the newly fallen snow cast enough light through her curtained windows that she was able to pick her way through the room without colliding with any of her equipment.

"Who's there?" she called when she reached the front door. A woman living alone in New York City couldn't be too careful, even if she lived in the relatively civilized section known as Greenwich Village.

"It's Ham Fisher. I just started boarding with Mrs. Higgins. It's her time, and they sent me to—"

"I'll be right there. Just give me a minute." Sarah let herself feel some relief as she hurried back to her bedroom to dress. Mrs. Higgins should be an easy case, barring some unforeseen complication. This would be her sixth child, and her other births had gone easily. Sarah herself had delivered number five not quite two years ago. And she didn't have to go into the Lower East Side in the middle of the night, where any woman walking on the street after dark would automatically be considered a prostitute, even if she had an escort. She assumed Ham had been chosen for his ability to ensure her safe arrival, but she would have needed more than one bodyguard to protect her over among the tenements.

Tonight, however, she'd only have to go a few blocks through the Village to Mrs. Higgins's boardinghouse, which was a mercy because the snow was still deep in places. Who, Sarah wondered idly, would do the cooking for the lodgers while Mrs. Higgins was laid up? Sarah would have to be very firm about making sure the new mother didn't get up and back to work too soon, no matter what the temptation. Six children in less than ten years took a toll, and if Sarah couldn't prevent the children from being conceived, she could at least make sure the mother's health didn't suffer any more than necessary.

Hastily, as much from the cold as from the urgency of her mission, Sarah put on the requisite undergarments and what she considered her "birthing clothes"—her oldest skirt and shirtwaist, which couldn't be ruined by the stray spatter of blood or whatever other bodily fluids might be splashing around during the birthing process. When she was ready, just a few short minutes later, she threw her heavy cape over her shoulders to protect her from the wintry winds and grabbed her medical bag. Tom's medical bag, that is. The one she'd given him when he officially became a doctor. The one still engraved with his name, Dr. Thomas Brandt. She always felt close to him when she carried it. Ruthlessly banishing the memories, she hurried out the door.

Ham Fisher was waiting for her. He was a strapping youth with a pockmarked face, a mouthful of bucked teeth and eyes that were, at the moment, unnaturally wide with terror. "We gotta hurry, Mrs. Brandt." As it did most men, the mere hint that a baby might be on the way had sent him into a panic.

Sarah knew it was useless to argue with him. "Of course," she said and followed as he started off at a brisk trot. At least the storm was over, and the clouds had cleared. The snow in the street had turned to slush where wagon wheels and horses' hooves had passed but the sidewalk was still ankle deep, except where other footsteps had smashed it down. Sarah felt the dampness already seeping through her boots, and she followed carefully in the trail Ham was blazing.

She'd only gone a few steps when she heard a window being raised in the house next door to hers, and a familiar voice called, "Mrs. Brandt, is that you?"

"Yes, Mrs. Elsworth," Sarah called back, smiling because she knew it was too dark for Mrs. Elsworth to see her amusement. She should have known she couldn't slip away without her neighbor noticing, even if it *was* the middle of the night. Sometimes she wondered if the old woman ever slept at all.

"Oh, my, is a baby coming on a terrible night like this?"

"That's right!" Sarah hoped all this shouting wouldn't wake the entire neighborhood. "I've got to be on my way," she added, seeing Ham Fisher had stopped to wait for her but with obvious impatience.

"Oh, dear, and here it is, the tenth day after the new moon. You know what that means, don't you? Anyone born on the tenth day after the new moon is bound to be restless and a wanderer. Do you think you could hold off the birth just one more day? No sense in dooming the poor child to a life of—"

"I'll do my best, Mrs. Elsworth," Sarah promised, shaking her head because she knew Mrs. Elsworth couldn't see her disgust. The old woman had a superstition for every occasion. Sarah had heard literally hundreds of them in the years she'd lived next door, but Mrs. Elsworth was still surprising her with new ones all the time. There seemed to be an endless supply.

"Mrs. Brandt, *please.*" Ham entreated desperately.

"I'll see you in the morning, Mrs. Elsworth," Sarah called, hurrying to catch up with her escort, who had already set off again.

"I hope you're carrying a pinch of salt to protect you from disaster, going out on a night like this!" Mrs. Elsworth shouted after her.

"Yes, I am!" Sarah lied without a trace of guilt.

When Ham realized, half a block away, that she couldn't keep up with his pace, he slowed and waited for her, although his entire body fairly quivered with his eagerness to run. He pulled off his battered cap and ran long, bony fingers through his sleep-tousled hair instead.

"Who's that?" another familiar voice called from the shadows across the deserted street. Ham looked up in fright, but Sarah called, "It's Mrs. Brandt, Officer Murphy!"

The policeman, who had been checking all the doors along his beat to make sure they were locked, stepped into the glow of the gaslit streetlamp and squinted over at them. "On a call, are you?"

"That's right."

"Not going far at this hour, I hope."

"Oh, no, just to Mrs. Higgins's house."

He nodded, the light winking off the star on his domed helmet. "Get along with you then."

She knew better than to expect an offer of safe escort. The New York police were notoriously corrupt, in spite of recent attempts at reform, and Sarah couldn't afford to pay for their protection. She had to satisfy herself with winning their goodwill with small gifts for their children and the occasional sweet, baked in her makeshift kitchen. All she could hope was that if she ever truly needed help, they would come to her aid.

Obviously, Ham Fisher had no desire for a police escort. He was already hurrying away, pulling his cap back down over his head when Sarah reached him. She wondered for a moment if he had some reason to avoid notice by the police, but the thought was gone as soon as it formed. No one poor and powerless wanted to be noticed by the police, who might arrest you simply because they felt like it and might then beat a confession out of you for some crime you hadn't committed but for which they needed a suspect.

Sarah had long since denied herself the luxury of outrage over such things. One woman couldn't change the world. She could just make small parts of it better. That's what she was doing tonight.

She was fairly running to keep up with her companion now, and they reached the wide, snow-covered sidewalks of Fifth Avenue in mere minutes. Checking for traffic,

Sarah glanced down the street toward Washington Square where she could see the outline of the enormous arch they'd built there recently, practically on the doorstep of the house where she'd grown up. It's edges were dulled by the mounds of snow, but it's distinctive shape was still plainly visible against the night sky. Then she glanced up the street, toward where her parents had moved a few years ago, escaping the influx of artists and freethinkers who had changed Greenwich Village from an enclave of the rich to a community of bohemians. The same street, but what a change it made in the fifty blocks that lay between her old home and the brownstone town house where they now lived.

Sarah wondered if they ever appreciated the irony. She could have asked her mother, of course, except she hadn't spoken to either of her parents since Tom's funeral. The fifty city blocks that separated her humble office—formerly Tom's doctor's office and now hers—might as well have been an ocean since she and her parents now lived worlds apart from each other.

Sarah turned her attention to crossing the cobblestone avenue. In the daylight, crossing against the flow of carriages, hansom cabs, and motor cars would be a dangerous and nearly impossible proposition, but because of the storm, even the prostitutes and their clients had retired for the evening. All Sarah had to worry about was picking her way through the piles of horse manure and garbage that the street cleaners hadn't yet carried away and which were now hidden beneath the snow.

A few more blocks, then they cut across Broadway to the tiny zig that was Astor Place and the quiet residential neighborhood beyond where Mrs. Higgins's boarding-house lay. It had once been home to only her and her family, but when her husband's eyes had failed and he'd lost his prosperous tailoring business, they'd had to move their growing family into two back rooms and let the others out to lodgers.

Fortunately, one of the rooms was vacant at the moment, so Mrs. Higgins was laboring in relative privacy with the assistance of one of her neighbors. After shedding her cloak and stamping the snow off her boots, Sarah joined them.

"I'm glad to see you didn't start without me," Sarah said cheerfully as she quickly surveyed the situation. The room was spartan and bare, but perfectly clean, as were the bedclothes. Many doctors and midwives didn't see the need for cleanliness, but Sarah had long since observed that mothers who gave birth on laundered sheets did much better than those who did not.

The neighbor woman smiled, but Mrs. Higgins saw no humor in the situation. "The pains is coming one on top of the other. I don't think this one's gonna wait 'til morning. Oh, here it comes again!"

Sarah saw immediately that Mrs. Higgins was already pushing, a sure sign of advanced labor. She was right, this one wasn't going to wait until morning. Mrs. Elsworth would be very disappointed.

Sarah glanced at the gold watch she had pinned to her bodice, a Christmas gift from her parents in some year long past, to time the contractions. "I'll wait until you're finished before I examine you," Sarah said, "but I'm glad your lodger made me hurry. How long has she been pushing?" she asked the neighbor.

The woman opened her mouth to reply, but an anguished wail from the doorway startled them both. Sarah turned to find a young girl standing there. She could not have been more than sixteen or seventeen, her beauty still fragile and unformed, although unmistakable. Her golden hair lay in silken ringlets to her shoulders, and her hastily-donned gown gave proof that she had been awakened and had come to see what the commotion was. Plainly, she was horrified by what she saw. Her china-blue eyes were even wider than Ham Fisher's had been, and she had covered her mouth with the back of her hand, as if afraid she might be sick.

Sarah knew she'd never seen the girl before—she

would have remembered such a lovely creature—but still, a name came to her lips. "Mina?" she asked before she could think better of it.

The girl's glance shifted instantly from the woman writhing on the bed to Sarah, and the horror in her beautiful eyes turned to sheer terror.

"Get her out of here," Mrs. Higgins gasped as her pain subsided. "This ain't no place for her."

"Come along now, dear," the neighbor woman said, hurrying to do Mrs. Higgins's bidding. "We don't want to put you off having children of your own, now do we?"

At that, the girl's naturally pale face grew chalk white, and Sarah knew a moment's fear that she might actually faint. But the other woman was shooing her out. If she fainted in the hallway, she wasn't Sarah's problem. Banishing all thoughts of the girl from her mind, she turned back to her patient.

"Now let's see what's going on in there," she said, unbuttoning her cuff to roll up her sleeve for the examination.

SARAH DIDN'T THINK of the girl again until a day and a half later when she was paying her first postpartum visit to Mrs. Higgins and her new son. Ordinarily, she went the very next day, but since the baby hadn't actually been born until nearly the next day, Sarah had waited until another night had passed to pay her usual call.

The city was very different this morning than it had been the other night. All traces of the snow had been shoveled into carts and dumped into the river, and with it had gone the silence of that night. The roar of the elevated trains over on Sixth Avenue was a constant backdrop to the usual sounds of urban activity. Wagon wheels and horseshoes clattering over cobblestone streets, drivers shouting to their animals or to other drivers, street vendors hawking their wares, women calling for children or to neighbors. Sarah might dream of peaceful meadows, but this was what she truly loved, the vibrant sounds of city life.

While she walked, she replayed the events of the other night and recalled the girl she'd called "Mina." Sarah knew exactly who she'd been thinking of. Mina Van-Damm had been a classmate of hers at the exclusive private girls' school she'd attended. They'd also traveled in the same social circles, something that Sarah had once considered important, but which she now knew mattered not a wit. Perhaps Mina VanDamm had looked like that girl back when they were sixteen, but she certainly didn't look like that any longer. Mina was Sarah's age, over thirty now, and probably a plump matron with a houseful of children of her own.

As this girl would be, before long. Because Sarah knew something else about her, too. Something she hadn't realized until this moment. She was still mulling over her realization when she rounded the corner and saw the crowd gathered in front of the Higgins's boardinghouse. Several women, still in their plain housedresses beneath their heavy shawls, were huddled together on the sidewalk, which meant an emergency had called them out. Otherwise, they would have changed into their street clothes.

The women talked quietly while children ran around, playing games and rolling hoops, oblivious to whatever unfortunate event had brought their mothers together. Sarah thought of Mrs. Higgins and her new baby inside the house. If there was trouble, why hadn't they sent for her?

She hurried up to the nearest woman, Bertha Peabody. Sarah had delivered her of the fat baby now perched on her hip and contentedly sucking on his middle two fingers.

"What's happened?" she asked Bertha.

"There's been a murder," Bertha said, her shock obvious.

"Mrs. Higgins?" Sarah gasped in horror.

"Oh, no," Bertha hastily assured her. "One of her

lodgers. A young girl. Hadn't been there long, only a few
weeks, and this morning she turns up dead. One of the
children found her when she didn't come down for breakfast.''

"A girl with blonde hair?'' Sarah didn't want to believe
it.

"Yes, that's her.''

"Terrible thing, just terrible,'' another woman declared, and the others murmured their assent.

Sarah couldn't have agreed more. People died every
day in the city, often by violent means, but hardly ever
did someone in this neighborhood die by another's hand,
and certainly not someone as young and innocent as this
girl had been. And if Sarah was upset, imagine how Mrs.
Higgins must be affected. "I've got to check on Mrs.
Higgins. All this trouble can't be good for her or the
baby.''

"They ain't letting anybody inside,'' Bertha warned
her, but Sarah was already climbing the front steps to
where a portly police officer stood guard at the door.

"Can we take her out now?'' the fellow from the medical examiner's office wanted to know.

Detective Sergeant Frank Malloy took one last look at
the crumpled body of the girl and nodded wearily. This
wasn't the way he had planned on spending his morning,
not today or any other day. Finding out who murdered
this slip of a girl wasn't going to accomplish anything,
and it certainly wouldn't help advance Frank Malloy in
the world one little bit.

He'd seen hundreds of girls just like this, new in town,
trying in vain to find honest work that would support them
until their money ran out and then being forced onto the
streets—or into a bawdy house if they were lucky. This
one would've been lucky. She was pretty enough to go
into one of the better houses on Fifth Avenue. She might
even have caught the eye of some rich man looking for a
mistress, someone who would've set her up in style.

Maybe she would've been smart and saved her money and eventually opened a house of her own. That was the mark of success for a woman of pleasure, although few whores ever achieved it. Most of them ended up dead in a gutter somewhere, the victim of disease or a dissatisfied customer.

Instead, this one had ended up dead on a boardinghouse floor. And a respectable boardinghouse, too, not one simply calling itself that but functioning as a brothel in reality. And this girl never would've become the successful whore of Frank's fantasy. She wasn't smart enough. He knew because she'd apparently just begun to engage in the flesh trade and no sooner had she started than she'd chosen the wrong man and gotten herself killed.

It was a pity, a pretty girl like that, but Frank couldn't afford the luxury of pity. He had a job to do. And responsibilities. He needed to make Captain, and he was carefully saving his money to bribe his way up to that exalted position—the only method of advancement that had ever been possible in the New York City police force until the recent wave of reform had swept the city. Of course, Frank figured the wave would pass, just like every other attempt to change the system that had been in place for centuries. He'd continued to save in the meantime so he'd be ready when the reformers gave up and went back to their gentlemen's clubs. No one was going to give him a little extra under the table for solving this girl's murder, though, and solving it would take up valuable time that could better be spent serving people who were willing to show their appreciation in a practical manner.

"There's a lady on the stoop trying to get in. Says she has to see Mrs. Higgins," the officer he'd left guarding the front door reported as Frank made his way down the stairs into the front hall. This wasn't unusual. There was always at least one old biddy in the neighborhood who felt compelled to get some firsthand knowledge when a crime had been committed.

"Who is she?"

"A Mrs. Brandt."

"Does she know anything about the dead girl?"

"I didn't ask her."

Frank sighed. He'd reached the bottom of the steps. "Let her in. I'll talk to her in the parlor." The old biddies also usually knew all the gossip. Whatever he could learn might help get this case over with sooner.

The officer nodded and opened the front door. Frank was surprised at the woman who entered. He wasn't sure what he'd been expecting, but certainly not this. Mrs. Brandt was a handsome woman whose fine figure was encased in clothes that, while a little shabby, had once been expensive and well-made, and she was carrying what looked like a black medical bag. She was also much younger than the type of harridan who usually insisted on being admitted to a crime scene, much too young at least to have acquired the kind of brass it took to challenge the police. And most certainly too young to be quite as sure of herself as she appeared to be. Her amazing blue-gray eyes met his with the kind of defiance that set Frank's teeth on edge. This was the last thing he needed. She was probably one of those suffragettes, intent on making every man's life miserable just on general principles.

"This here's Detective Sergeant Malloy," the officer was saying. "He wants to talk to you."

"I'm Sarah Brandt," she told Frank without being asked. "I'm the midwife who delivered Mrs. Higgins's baby yesterday, and I need to make sure she's all right."

Midwife? No one had told him about this. Higgins had simply explained that his wife was indisposed and hadn't seen or heard a thing, so Frank hadn't bothered to question her yet. But she wasn't really ill; she'd just had a baby. A baby this Sarah Brandt had delivered. The knowledge tore at the old wound in his soul, bringing a pain he couldn't allow himself to feel while at the same time sparking a rage he didn't dare express. From habit, however, he managed to keep his reaction to himself.

At least he'd be prepared when he had to meet Mrs. Higgins. Or as prepared as he could be.

He forced himself not to sigh. "Step into the parlor for a minute, Mrs. Brandt. I'd like to ask you a few questions."

"About what?"

Now Frank was sure she was one of those suffragettes. Imagine questioning an officer of the law. "A young girl was murdered here last night."

"I know that," Mrs. Brandt assured him impatiently. "That's why I need to see my patient, to make sure she's all right. A shock like this can sometimes cause problems."

Yeah, well, we all have our own problems, don't we? he thought, and Sarah Brandt was going to be his. Ordinarily, Frank knew exactly how to handle a reluctant witness—a little shake, a slap or a punch, then the nightstick if all else failed—but he didn't think the usual methods would work on Sarah Brandt, as tempted as he might be to try them. He certainly couldn't be blamed for wanting to, even if he didn't dare raise a hand to a respectable female, and no one would fault him for being short with her. "Your patient will wait a few minutes while you answer my questions."

She widened her eyes at his tone—out of amazement, not fright, he couldn't help noticing with annoyance—but at least she went into the parlor when he indicated she should, leaving her black bag in the hall. She wasn't happy about it, though. She made him understand that without saying a single word.

Maybe he ought to try a different tack with her, much as it might gall him to do so. Butting his head against a wall would just give him a headache.

"Have a seat, Mrs. Brandt," he said, trying to muster up some civility. He hadn't used it in a long time and was very much afraid he'd lost the knack.

Apparently he had, because Mrs. Brandt didn't sit down. "I don't know what you think I can tell you."

"I don't either, so why don't we find out?" Frank said without even grinding his teeth. He was amazing himself with his patience. "Did you know the dead girl?"

"No."

This was going to be even harder than he'd thought.

Frank closed his eyes, summoning up more patience, and tried again. "Did you know anything about the dead girl? Her name was . . ." He consulted his notes. "Alice Smith."

Sarah Brandt sighed with obvious exasperation. "I only saw her once in my life, the night before last when I was here to deliver Mrs. Higgins's baby. She came into the room for a moment and . . ."

"What is it?" Frank prodded when she hesitated. Plainly, she knew more than she was telling. Perhaps she even knew more than she realized.

"Nothing. I was mistaken."

Frank figured Sarah Brandt was hardly ever mistaken about anything.

"Come on, Mrs. Brandt. A girl has been murdered. Anything you can tell me will help catch her killer. You don't want a killer running loose, do you? A woman like you who makes her living traveling around the city, going to strange places—"

She sighed again to let him know how put-upon she felt. "I thought she looked like someone I used to know," she admitted. "An old friend."

"An old friend here in the city?"

She nodded grudgingly.

"Could she have actually been who you thought she was?"

"No. She resembled an old schoolmate of mine, a woman my own age, so I know this girl couldn't have been the same person."

"What part of the city are you from, Mrs. Brandt?"

"Right here in Greenwich Village."

Frank looked her over again in the better light of the parlor windows. She stiffened at his effrontery. She probably figured he was sizing up her figure, which was even better than he'd originally thought, but actually, he was sizing up her clothes. Just as he'd thought, they were quality, although she'd been wearing them for a long time. "You came from money, didn't you?"

"I don't think my background is any of your business, Detective Sergeant Malloy," she said coldly.

Oh, yes, she came from money, all right. Only a rich person knew how to use that tone to put an underling in his place. But Frank wasn't her underling, not in this situation. "At the moment, everything is my business, Mrs. Brandt. And for your information, the dead girl came from money, too."

"How can you know that?"

"The same way I can tell about you, her clothes."

The sound of footsteps on the stairs distracted them both, and Frank looked toward the open parlor door to see the orderlies carrying the sheet-covered body out on a stretcher. He heard Sarah Brandt's gasp and smiled at his good fortune. Nothing like a little shock to soften up a reluctant witness. He waited until they had carried the body out of the house. The bloom had noticeably faded from Sarah Brandt's smooth cheeks.

By then Frank had decided he would use Sarah Brandt a little, and possibly get back at her in the bargain. "Maybe you'd help me out by going up to her room and looking around. Since Mrs. Higgins is, uh, indisposed, I mean. See if anything looks out of place, and give me your opinion of her things. Maybe I'm wrong about her background after all."

He'd figured Sarah Brandt would jump at the chance to prove him wrong about anything, but her natural reserve was apparently stronger than her need to prevail. "I couldn't."

"Couldn't what? Snoop through her things? Make judgments about her? Mrs. Brandt, when a person is murdered, they don't have a right to privacy anymore. Or maybe you'd rather I took you down to the station house to finish questioning you,'' he added, forgetting his plan to be civil.

"Why?" she challenged, anger flashing in those marvelous eyes of hers. "So you can beat me into confessing to her murder? That would save you a lot of time, wouldn't it? Then you wouldn't even have to conduct an investigation."

Frank felt a flash of anger himself. How dare she judge him like that? How dare she assume he was something he wasn't? Understanding instinctively, however, that any attempt to defend himself would only make her more certain she was right about him—and consequently make her more obstinate—he somehow managed to swallow his own fury and sound reasonable again. "No, so I can get you to tell me what you know about this girl. What you may not even realize that you know about her," he amended quickly when she would have protested.

"I really need to see Mrs. Higgins," she insisted.

"As soon as we're finished in the girl's room. And just to put your mind at ease, I'm pretty sure you didn't kill Alice Smith, so I won't bother trying to beat a confession out of you," he added.

She didn't smile.

"You want me to catch the killer, don't you?" he tried.

Plainly, it galled her to admit it. "All right, I'll give you a few minutes, but then I must see Mrs. Higgins."

"Sure," Frank agreed amiably. A few minutes was probably all he'd be able to stand of Mrs. High-and-Mighty anyway. "Her room's upstairs, on the right."

She didn't wait for a second invitation. He watched her go, wondering how a woman could convey so many opinions without uttering a word. Well, if she could give him any information at all, he would forgive her just about anything.

Frank followed her up the stairs, resisting with difficulty the temptation to fall far enough behind to possibly catch a glimpse of her ankles beneath her swishing skirt.

He already knew way too much about Sarah Brandt's figure for his own peace of mind.

Sarah couldn't believe she was doing this. Going into a dead girl's bedroom to give the police information about her. And what could she possibly tell them? Besides being able to look at the girl's clothes and know if they were expensive or not. And what would that prove? Countless young women from good families found themselves suddenly penniless every day because the man who provided for them—be he husband or father—died or otherwise abandoned them. If this girl still had a family or any means of providing for herself, she would not have taken a room at the Higgins's house.

The door to the girl's bedroom stood open, and Sarah stopped in the opening, looking around. Everything seemed unnaturally quiet here, as if the girl's death had muffled even the ordinary sounds of the city. The room was oddly neat for being the scene of a murder, too. Somehow Sarah had pictured overturned furniture and smashed and broken crockery. But nothing here had been disturbed at all except the plain, iron bed. The coverlet was rumpled, as if someone had laid down on it, and what appeared to be a red shawl lay casually discarded at the foot of it. Other than the bed, there was little else in the room to disturb. A stuffed chair, a dresser and a cabinet for clothes. It looked, in fact, hardly more inhabited than the unoccupied room downstairs where Sarah had delivered Mrs. Higgins's baby the morning before.

"Go on in," Malloy said.

Sarah bit back a sharp retort. Good breeding forbade her from speaking rudely to anyone, but good sense played a part in her self-control as well. He might not have been bluffing about taking her down to the station house. She entered the room.

The first thing she noticed was the smell. Could there be an uncovered chamber pot in here? But then she remembered that sudden death loosened control over bodily functions, adding one final humiliation to the process. She thought of the girl she had seen, dying in her own excrement, and she shuddered.

"You all right?" Malloy asked.

Sarah bristled at his feigned concern. "How did she die?" she asked, looking around reluctantly for any evidence of foul play. Mercifully, she saw no blood.

"Strangled."

"Was it someone who broke into the house?"

"No sign of a break-in."

The top drawer of the dresser was half-opened, as if someone had already been rummaging through it. Probably Malloy. Unable to bring herself to rummage, Sarah went over and examined the articles that were readily visible. At first she couldn't believe her eyes, and without meaning to, she reached down and fingered the topmost garment. She hadn't been mistaken, she realized as she rubbed the fabric between her thumb and fingers and noted the fine hand-stitching. Silk. For an instant, she pictured the cloth lying against the girl's flawless skin and snatched her hand away.

"She's dead," Malloy reminded her crudely. "You can't offend her."

Sarah gave him what she hoped was a quelling glare. He was the kind of man her mother would have called common. A man who lacked education and refinement. Even his body seemed designed for manual labor with its broad chest and powerful shoulders. She thought of her father and the other men she'd known in her old life, slightly built men whose power came from wealth and knowledge. They were dangerous, able to crush anyone who stood in their way, but Detective Malloy was dangerous, too, in a very different way. Sarah would do well to remember that.

She glanced back at the dresser. Nothing on it but a brush, a comb and some stray hairpins. Except that the brush, when Sarah turned it over, had a silver back, and the comb was tortoiseshell.

Something was very wrong here. Very wrong indeed.

Forgetting Detective Malloy, who still watched her from the bedroom doorway, Sarah pushed the top drawer shut and opened the next one. It was empty.

"All the others are empty, too," Malloy said.

Sarah didn't even acknowledge him. She was too busy trying to make sense of something. She went to the clothespress and pulled the doors open. Only a few garments hung inside. "Was she in her nightclothes when she died?" Sarah asked.

"No. She was still completely dressed. Even had her shoes on."

Only two spare shirtwaists and a jacket in the clothespress, and just enough underclothes to fill one drawer. Those details told her something, although she wasn't yet sure what. The waists were simply made, but Sarah instantly recognized the work of a skilled seamstress in the delicate tucks across the bodice of one. She reached for the jacket, trying not to think of the girl who had so recently worn it. Sarah could still catch what must have been the girl's scent in the folds of the finely woven wool, and for a moment her head swam. She fought off the momentary weakness and examined the jacket. Mother-of-pearl buttons and intricate braiding down the front. She turned the garment in her hands, knowing what she would find or at least what she *should* find, unless the girl had been clever enough to remove it. But she hadn't, and there it was, embroidered into the lining by the seamstress who had custom made it, the name of the person for whom it had been designed.

Alicia VanDamm.

With a cry, she dropped the jacket as if it had burned her.

"What is it? What's the matter?" Malloy demanded, crossing the room with long strides.

Sarah hardly heard him. She was too lost in memories, visions of a tiny girl with long, golden curls and enormous blue eyes. A girl of delicate beauty who always seemed much older than her years and who hardly ever smiled. Mina's baby sister.

"Sit down," Malloy was saying, and he put his big, workman's hands on her and forced her down into the chair. "Don't go fainting on me now. Put your head down."

Before she could stop him, he'd forced her head down almost to her knees.

"Let go of me!" she cried with as much dignity as she could muster with her face practically in her lap. She had to twist her head from side to side to dislodge his grip, losing her hat in the process, but finally he released her.

Sputtering in outrage, she sat upright and glared at him again. If she'd been a man, she would've punched him, policeman or not. As if guessing her thoughts, he backed up a step and put up his hands as if to ward her off. Or maybe he was just letting her know he was finished man-handling her.

"Good, you've got your color back," he said. "For a minute there, I thought you was gonna go all vaporish on me."

"I don't get the vapors, Detective," she informed him.

"If you say so," he replied, unconvinced. He picked up the jacket from where she'd dropped it. "What did you see on this?"

Sarah swallowed against the dryness in her throat. "Inside, in the lining."

He turned the jacket and found the embroidery. "This her name?"

Sarah nodded.

"You know her? Is that why . . . ? But you said you didn't know her," he recalled.

"I said I thought she looked like an old friend. The old friend is Mina VanDamm. Alicia is her baby sister. Or was."

"Unless the girl stole the jacket."

Sarah only wished that were true. She shook her head. "No, I'm sure it was she. I haven't seen her since she

was a child, but she looks . . . *looked*," she corrected herself, "too much like Mina for there to be any mistake."

"What would she have been doing here all by herself,
then?" he asked, staring at the jacket as if it would give
him the answer. "Did the father die? The family break
up? Lose all their money?"

"Not that I know of." Indeed, she was certain Cornelius VanDamm was very much alive and well and still a
millionaire. Suddenly, Sarah had to get out of that room.
She rose to her feet. Where was her hat?

She saw where it had rolled over beside the bed. She
went for it in the same instant Detective Sergeant Malloy
guessed her purpose and went for it as well. He beat her
there, and in his haste, brushed against the shawl that lay
at the foot of the bed. It slid to the floor and something
metal tumbled from its folds, clanging to the uncarpeted
floor between them.

"What's this?" he asked of no one in particular. Since
he still held the jacket in one hand and had picked up her
hat with the other, he shoved the hat at her and bent to
pick up the long, slender object. When he rose, he held it
up to examine it.

Sarah couldn't contain her surprise.

"Do you know what it is?" he asked.

Sarah was very much afraid she did. "It's a curette."

"A what?"

"A medical instrument." She had a set of them, although she had no use for them now. They had belonged
to Tom.

"Why would the girl have had it?"

"I don't think she did." Everything was making sense
now, or at least a little bit of sense. Sarah remembered
her impressions of the girl in those brief moments when
their paths had crossed yesterday, and the realization she'd
had this morning on her way over here. "I think someone
must have brought it here."

"Why?" His eyes were dark, almost black, and he suddenly seemed very large and dangerous again. She didn't

want him to know this about Alicia, but she had no other choice. He would find out soon enough anyway.

"Because . . . It's an instrument that . . . Well, it can be used for other things, but it's what an abortionist uses."

He didn't say a word, but his very silence was a force, compelling her to continue.

"I thought when I saw her yesterday . . . it was just an impression, but sometimes you can tell just by looking at a woman. Something in the eyes . . . And that would explain why she was here, why she'd left her family. I think . . . I think you'll find that Alicia was with child."

2

FRANK COULDN'T BELIEVE THIS. HE'D LOOKED AT the girl's body long and hard, and he hadn't seen anything to indicate she was in a family way. If she was, this Sarah Brandt must be a witch to have divined it. Still, if this really *was* a tool used by an abortionist . . .

"You seem pretty sure of yourself. Maybe you do a little of that on the side yourself," he tried. Performing abortions was illegal, although the authorities hardly ever prosecuted anyone for carrying out what many believed was a service to humanity. And maybe it was, if it was a service to prevent children who would grow up poor and hungry from ever being born.

But if Frank had hoped to rattle Sarah Brandt, he failed. She simply stared right back at him, her blue-gray eyes as cold and still as glass. "I'm not trained to perform abortions."

"Then how do you know what this is?" he challenged, holding the instrument up to her face.

She didn't flinch. "My husband was a physician. I . . . sometimes assisted him in certain procedures. When a pregnancy goes wrong . . ." She hesitated, probably seeing what Frank was feeling reflected on his face. "But perhaps you'd rather not hear the details."

She was right about that. She probably thought he was squeamish or maybe that he was embarrassed by this frank discussion of female problems. Let her think that. He'd humble himself a lot before he'd reveal the true reason for his discomfort with the subject of pregnancies gone wrong.

"So you think an abortionist came here to her room. Someone she hired to get her out of a tough spot," he said, trying out the theory to see how it sounded.

"I don't think anything," she corrected him. "I'm a midwife. You're the detective."

He ignored her. "That would explain why there was no break-in. She let the abortionist in. Late at night, after everyone was asleep. And then . . . what? She decided not to go through with it and refused to pay and . . ."

"And the abortionist strangled her?" Mrs. Brandt supplied, her skepticism obvious.

Frank had to agree. It didn't sound very logical. In his experience, abortionists did very well for themselves. The prospect of losing a fee didn't seem likely to inspire one of them to murder.

But Frank had another idea. A very clear idea, and one he suddenly realized he didn't need to share with Sarah Brandt. He didn't really need her for anything else now. Bringing her up here had just been a whim, and—he had to admit—a rather juvenile way of imposing his will on a woman who looked as if she didn't get imposed upon very often.

But he'd had his fun—if you could call it that—and he was finished with her.

"You can go now," he told her.

She widened her eyes at him again. This time she was amazed at his rudeness. Unfortunately, she wasn't the least bit humbled by it. "Detective Sergeant Malloy, Alicia's family is very wealthy and influential, and I'm sure they'll be extremely, uh, *grateful* to whoever finds the person who murdered her."

Frank bristled at her implication, all the more offended

because the implication—that he'd work harder to solve a case for someone rich—was true. "I'm sure I don't care if they're grateful or not, Mrs. Brandt. I've got my job to do, and I'll do it."

She didn't snort in derision—ladies of her class didn't snort—but she gave every indication that's how she felt about his assertion. Frank told himself he didn't care. He'd given up caring about other people's opinion of him a long time ago.

At least she didn't argue with him. He watched her turn and start out, but then she remembered the hat she was still carrying, the silly thing with flowers and ribbon all over it. She stopped in front of the dead girl's mirror and took a moment to put it back on, silently telling him she would do just what she wanted, when she wanted to do it, and detective sergeant or not, he couldn't rush her.

She smoothed her blonde hair with one hand where the hat pin had pulled it loose of the fancy roll she'd done it up into. Then she removed the hat pin, placed the hat on her head, just so, and reattached it with the long pin.

Memories stirred to life, memories he hadn't allowed himself for years. How long since he'd been in a bedroom and watched a woman smooth her hair? How long since he'd been alone like this with a woman at all?

He knew exactly: three years and three months in another week. The night he'd sat at Kathleen's bedside and held her hand while the life's blood drained out of her. All because of a woman like Sarah Brandt.

But just as he felt the old rage building, she turned to face him. Her expression couldn't be called humble. Sarah Brandt would never wear such an expression. But this was as close as she probably ever came.

"Please, Mr. Malloy, find Alicia's killer," she begged him.

She didn't wait for his reply, probably knowing he had none to give.

•   •   •

SARAH WANTED TO go straight back home and lock herself in her bedroom and give vent to all the terrible emotions roiling inside of her. She wanted to weep and wail and rant against the injustices of the world, against the ruthless forces that snatched the good and the innocent and left the evil and the corrupt behind. She wanted to mourn Tom's death anew while she mourned sweet little Alicia for the first time. She wanted to announce to the gods how much she hated the way they ran the world. She wanted to tell them how things should really be.

But Sarah didn't have time for such an indulgence at the moment. She had a patient to see.

The officer in the foyer nodded politely when she came down the stairs and retrieved her medical bag. And he didn't stop her when she went down the hall to the cramped and cluttered rooms where the Higgins family lived. Someone had sent the older children outside, thank heavens, because Mrs. Higgins was nearly hysterical with fear and fury.

"Did you hear, Mrs. Brandt? Did they tell you?" she demanded tearfully the instant Sarah entered her room. She lay in the plain, iron bed, propped up on some bundles of rags that passed for pillows. "That girl was murdered right here in my own house! We could have all been killed in our beds! And my dear little ones sleeping like angels, and who could protect them with Mr. Higgins not being able to see his hand in front of his face or just about?"

"How are you feeling?" Sarah asked solicitously, pulling up the only chair in the room, a straight-backed chair with a hole in the caning. The Higginses saved their good furniture for the paying guests.

"How do you think I feel? There was a woman murdered in my own house!"

The newborn babe lay on the bed beside his mother, fretting but not really crying yet. Sarah picked him up and unwrapped him carefully, lovingly. The sight of new life always awed her, this promise of tomorrow, a promise she herself would never fulfill.

Fortunately, the baby looked healthy enough. No sign of dehydration. But if Mrs. Higgins's milk dried up, he wouldn't do nearly as well as if she was able to feed him. And the Higginses probably couldn't afford canned milk, either. While Sarah's main job was to get the babies safely delivered, she also took great pride in making sure they thrived afterwards, too.

"This is a terrible thing, I know, and you must be very upset, but try to remember that none of your family was harmed. Whatever happened, you and yours were spared. And now you have a baby to think of. He needs you to be calm."

As if to prove her point, the baby began to wail. Mrs. Higgins frowned, probably annoyed by having her diatribe interrupted, but she took the baby when Sarah handed him over and bared a swollen breast for him. This was her sixth child, after all, and she knew exactly what to do.

He latched onto the engorged nipple greedily, but after a few moments of avid sucking, he let go of it and wailed again.

"My milk won't let down," Mrs. Higgins said, wailing, too. "And is it any wonder? I'm beside myself!"

"There now, just relax. Lean back against the pillow, take some deep breaths and let them out slowly. Close your eyes, that's right."

As Mrs. Higgins did as Sarah instructed, she also coaxed the now-screaming baby to take the nipple again. After only a few more moments of frustration, he was rewarded with a gush of milk that had him gulping to keep up with it.

When the baby had settled in, Mrs. Higgins opened her eyes. Sarah realized she looked unutterably weary and a lot older than Sarah knew her to be. And why shouldn't she? Burdened with a nearly blind husband and a houseful of children and the care and feeding of her lodgers, and

now a girl had been murdered in her house. She didn't
need to add an infant into the bargain, but she had one.
Sarah would see that they both weathered this storm and
came through all right.

"I'm going to prescribe beer for you, Mrs. Higgins,"
Sarah said. "Two big glasses a day." The brewer's yeast
would strengthen her and the alcohol would relax her.
"I'll send someone out for it right now. How about that
fellow who came for me the other night? Is he around?"

Mrs. Higgins moaned in anguish. "He's gone! Moved
out in the night! Without a word! One room already
empty, and now two more, and who will live here, where
there's been a murder? And with no lodgers, we'll starve
to death! All of us! What's to become of us now?"

Postpartum depression, Sarah judged, although anyone
in Mrs. Higgins's circumstances could be excused for being depressed. She would bear close watching to ensure
she didn't do something untoward. Women in her condition sometimes harmed themselves or others, even their
newborns. She'd have a talk with Mr. Higgins and make
sure some of the neighbor women came in to help. And
she'd come by often to check the baby for signs he was
failing to thrive. Short of removing Mrs. Higgins's problems, it was all Sarah could do.

Only after she left the house, once she'd gotten Mrs.
Higgins to drink her glass of beer and extracted promises
from her husband and neighbors, did Sarah recall one vital
piece of information Mrs. Higgins had given her: Ham
Fisher had moved out. In the night. The night in which
Alicia VanDamm was murdered.

For a moment she considered going back to tell Detective Malloy. He'd probably be very interested in that bit
of news. But then she remembered his arrogance and his
rudeness, and she knew he wouldn't thank her for helping
him do his job. No, surely he'd find out for himself that
Fisher had moved out. And he'd probably also figure, as
Sarah had, that his sudden departure was too coincidental
not to have some relation to Alicia's murder.

No, she'd leave Detective Malloy to his investigation. And meanwhile, she'd do a little investigating of her own.

FRANK WALKED OVER the one block from the Sixth Avenue elevated train station to Fifth. The trains, which ran on elevated tracks along various avenues in the city, were a godsend for getting from one end of the congested city to the other in a reasonable time. Traffic in the unregulated streets clogged to impassability at major intersections during busy times of the day, so a trip uptown could take hours by cab or trolley. Of course the noise the trains caused and the dirt and cinders they dropped on hapless pedestrians below were a scourge of major proportions, too, inspiring talk of building a railroad underground instead. Frank agreed with those who claimed the only people who would ride such a thing were those who didn't want to be seen riding a train.

As he studied the enormous mansions that graced Fifth Avenue at its northern end, he could hardly believe they existed in the same city as the Lower East Side with its crowded, filthy tenements. Up here in the fifties, the rich lived in houses that sometimes filled entire city blocks and which probably contained enough treasure to support the whole population of the ghettos for years. Another block farther up stood the elegant Plaza Hotel, named for the plaza on which it was built, and across the street from it was one of the Vanderbilt mansions. Frank thought the place looked like a museum, but people rarely asked his opinion about such things.

Frank could remember when this whole area was open ground. When he was a boy, the only people living at this end of Manhattan Island were vagrants and bums who had constructed a shantytown on the outskirts of the park some city fathers with foresight had begun up here. But when the park was finished, they ran off the bums and sold the lots to millionaires who wanted to live away from the noise and smells and heat of the city itself. Now the city had spread upward to meet them, so if they really wanted to get away, they had to escape the city altogether, to mansions in the country. The poor, of course, had Coney Island.

But Frank had given up railing against the inequities of the world. Now he concentrated on getting as much of those treasures for himself as he could. Other people were depending on him.

The VanDamm house was only slightly less pretentious than some of the others, a stately town house on the block of Fifth Avenue between Fifty-Seventh and Fifty-Eighth streets called "Marble Row." It had marble steps, of course, and a shiny brass door knocker. A butler in a uniform that probably cost as much as Frank earned in a month opened the door for him. It was clear he thought Frank should have used the service entrance.

"Detective Sergeant Frank Malloy," he told the butler before the man could order him around to the back. "I'd like to see Mr. and Mrs. VanDamm. It's about their daughter."

There, if that didn't get him in to see the girl's parents, he'd need dynamite.

Frank figured the butler was trained not to show any emotion, but he'd also probably never had a policeman come to the door, either. He seemed to blanche a little at the mention of the girl.

"Please wait in the front parlor," the butler instructed stiffly as he grudgingly allowed Frank to enter. "I'll see if Mr. VanDamm is at home."

Nice trick the rich had, Frank mused. If they didn't want to see somebody, they'd just tell the servant to report that they weren't at home. Frank had a feeling the VanDamms would be home to him, though, at least for today.

Frank's opinion of the rich dropped a notch or two as he looked around the front parlor (which meant they probably had a back parlor, too; what in God's name did they need two parlors for?). Frank decided he'd been in classier whorehouses. This place was a disaster of ostentation, with red velvet everywhere, draped in enormous folds over the windows and covering all the plush furniture. The walls were covered with dark paper in a hideous design. A palm tree in the corner and potted plants on every flat surface. Tables adorned with lace doilies and cluttered with figurines of every description. And they were all ugly.

He found himself wondering what Kathleen would have said. Too much stuff to dust, probably. Kathleen had always been practical.

When the parlor doors opened twenty minutes later, Frank was examining the covers someone had put on the piano's legs. He'd heard about people who were so modest that they never uttered the word "leg" and even clothed the legs of their furniture. He'd never expected to actually see such a thing, however.

The man who entered the room was obviously the master of the house. He was dressed for the street, in an impeccably tailored suit of the finest wool and a shirt so white it could blind a man. Frank noticed his tie was slightly askew, however, telling him VanDamm had made himself presentable in a hell of a hurry.

"Detective, I'm Cornelius VanDamm," he said, in case there could be any doubt. Frank noticed he didn't offer his hand. Probably he didn't shake hands with messenger boys, either. "I understand you have something to tell me about my daughter."

VanDamm was a man trained never to show a trace of weakness. Men who moved in the circles he did, where millions were made or lost on a man's word, couldn't afford to reveal any vulnerability without risking attack. VanDamm would be very good at hiding his true feelings, but Frank figured he was about to put him to the ultimate test.

"Is your wife available?" he asked. "I told your man I had to see you both." He wanted to tell them together— so he would be sure of seeing their initial reactions, which would reveal a lot about a lot of things. How they felt about their daughter and about each other and about her death. And whether they knew more than they intended to tell him, information he might have to get from other sources.

"I'm afraid my wife is indisposed at the moment," VanDamm said without the slightest trace of apology. "What is it you've come to tell us? I know it can't be good news, Detective, so out with it."

Frank hadn't yet decided whether to obey or not when the doors opened again and a woman appeared. She was a fragile, birdlike creature dressed in a filmy gown with flowers printed all over it that swirled around her and made her seem almost ethereal. She must have been a beauty in her day, but that beauty had faded with the years, along with her once-golden hair which was now almost entirely gray. Her pale cheeks were sunken, her eyes hollow, and her skin had turned crepey, even though she probably wasn't even as old as her husband, who was still a fine figure of a man.

"Cornelius, what's going on? Bridgett said the police were here, something about Alicia." Her eyes seemed slightly unfocused, and at first Frank wasn't sure she even noticed he was in the room. Then he realized she was simply not acknowledging him. She looked at her husband, waiting for him to explain.

"Alicia? Don't be ridiculous, Francisca, go back to your room. I'll take care of this," he told her sternly, as if speaking to a recalcitrant child.

"I think this is something you should both hear," Frank contradicted him, watching as Mrs. VanDamm finally looked directly at him. Even her eyes were faded, to a washed-out blue, and they watered slightly as she blinked at him curiously. Maybe she was just short-sighted, he couldn't help thinking.

She turned back to her husband. "What could he have to tell us about Alicia? She's at Greentree. If anything had happened, Mrs. Hightower would have sent word."

Her husband spared her only a bored glance. "Of

course she would. This isn't about Alicia at all, and don't say I didn't warn you, Francisca. All right,'' he said to Frank. ''What have you come to tell us?''

Now Frank was the one who was confused. Obviously, VanDamm was expecting bad news, but not about Alicia. If she'd been away at this Greentree place, maybe he didn't even know she was missing, although that seemed difficult to believe. And if he was expecting bad news about his other daughter, he didn't seem too upset about it. Ordinarily, a parent in this situation would be bracing himself for something horrible, but VanDamm didn't seem to require bracing.

The woman knew nothing, of that Frank was certain.

''Maybe you better sit down, Mrs. VanDamm.''

The vagueness in her eyes turned to confusion. ''I do feel a little strange,'' she admitted. ''It's that weakness I was telling you about, Cornelius. It comes on me at the oddest times, I never know when. And then sometimes I can't get my breath—''

''*Sit down*, Francisca,'' VanDamm said firmly, this time the way you'd would speak to a slow-witted child. Frank understood about that only too well.

''Well, if you think it's best,'' she murmured as she moved like a wraith to the nearest of the several ornately carved sofas in the room and perched on it, back ramrod straight the way a proper lady was taught to sit. Her hands fluttered restlessly in her lap, though, as if she thought she should be doing something but couldn't remember exactly what.

VanDamm simply stood where he was, arms down to his sides, hands relaxed, showing Frank no more than common courtesy. The way he would if Frank had come to sell him tickets to the policeman's ball. Or the way he would if Frank's news wasn't going to be a surprise. But whatever VanDamm was expecting to hear, Frank was pretty sure it wasn't what he'd come to tell them.

''Mr. and Mrs. VanDamm,'' he began, looking at each of them in turn. ''It is my sad duty to inform you that your daughter Alicia has been the victim of a crime. I'm sorry to tell you that she has been murdered.''

VanDamm's face went chalk white, but he never so much as flinched. *"Murdered?"* He repeated the word as if he'd never heard it before. He may have been expecting something, but Frank was pretty sure this wasn't it. *"Alicia? Are you certain?"*

"I'm afraid so. We found her name embroidered in her jacket, and someone identified her. An old family friend.''

"What on earth is he talking about, Cornelius?'' Mrs. VanDamm asked plaintively.

VanDamm continued to ignore her. Frank figured he probably usually did. "Where? What happened to her?'' he demanded.

"We found her in a rooming house in Greenwich Village. She'd been living there for several weeks.''

"That's impossible," Mrs. VanDamm insisted. "Alicia is at Greentree. Tell the man there's been some mistake, Cornelius.''

When Cornelius said nothing, his face as blank and stiff as if it had been carved from stone, she turned to Frank with a weary sigh.

"Our daughter is at our country home in Mamoraneck, Officer,'' she explained patiently. "She's been there for over a month, and if anything had happened to her, our housekeeper would have sent us word immediately. We have a telephone for just such emergencies, so you see, the girl you found couldn't possibly be Alicia. You've wasted a trip and bothered us for nothing, and I must say, I plan to complain to Teddy about this. That's Police Commissioner Roosevelt to you. His mother is a dear friend of mine, and I used to dandle him on my knee when he was a boy. He'll be most interested in the way you have inconvenienced us, I'm sure. Imagine, coming into a person's house and telling such outrageous—''

"Francisca, that's enough.''

The rebuke was mild, in Frank's opinion, but it was enough to make her stop and gape at her husband in confusion. He didn't even spare her a glance. The color was coming back to his face, which meant that he was over whatever shock he'd felt at his daughter's death.

"Detective," he said in a perfectly reasonable voice, the one he probably used to seal million-dollar business deals. "As you've no doubt guessed, my daughter really isn't at our country house." His wife sputtered in protest, but neither man paid her any heed. "Although we sent her there, she ran away a few weeks ago, disappeared completely. Alicia has always been a willful girl—"

"*Willful?*" his wife echoed incredulously. "Alicia is the most sweet tempered girl alive! Never a harsh word to say to anyone. And obedient! I can't remember the last time I had to scold her. If anything, she's too agreeable. I always tell her—"

VanDamm seemed not to even hear her protests, any more than he seemed to feel any emotion. His expression was still controlled, and even his flush had faded again. "How did she . . . ? Who did it?" he finally asked, interrupting his wife's ramblings.

He was saying all the right things, asking all the right questions, but Frank didn't like his steely reserve. Is that the way members of the Four Hundred handled tragedy? Frank had precious little experience breaking bad news to them, so he had no way of judging. Still, he knew how ordinary bereaved parents acted. Oddly, Mrs. VanDamm's behavior was the most normal. Shock invariably produced denial in most people.

"She was strangled," Frank said. "And we don't know who did it. Yet," he added, in case VanDamm was going to make assumptions about him the way Sarah Brandt had. "I was hoping you could help me there. Do you have any idea why your daughter ran away? Did she have a lover—?"

"A lover?" Mrs. VanDamm echoed in outrage. "Alicia most certainly does *not* have a lover! She isn't even out yet!"

For a minute, Frank couldn't think what she might have

been out of, but then he realized she meant the girl hadn't made her debut into society yet.

"Alicia is just sixteen!" Mrs. VanDamm was saying. "She has no suitors. She's never even been alone with a young man! A lover, indeed! Cornelius, why are you standing there listening to this rubbish?"

"Francisca, go back to your room," VanDamm said coldly. "I'll explain everything to you later."

"I certainly hope so. And I fully intend to complain to your superiors," she told Frank as she floated and fluttered her way out of the room, murmuring her outrage at Frank's effrontery.

Frank couldn't help wishing she really would complain to Commissioner Roosevelt about him. Everyone on the force hated the playboy-turned-reformer who had gotten himself appointed to the Police Commission with an eye toward cleaning up the corruption in the department. A rebuke from Roosevelt would likely propel him to Captain even without paying the requisite bribes as soon as Roosevelt got bored and went back to his old life and things in the department returned to normal.

"I'm afraid I can't be of any assistance to you, Detective," VanDamm said when she was gone. The only sign of whatever emotional distress he was experiencing was the way he idly fingered his gold watch chain. "I have no idea why my daughter chose to run away from the safety and comfort of her home and family. And my wife is right, Alicia doesn't know any young men, certainly no one who could have lured her away."

He was lying, of course. Parents always lied at first. Either they didn't want their children to look bad or they didn't want to look like irresponsible parents. Frank figured a cold fish like VanDamm would be more worried about his own reputation.

And VanDamm hadn't seemed the least bit surprised that his daughter was living in a rooming house in Greenwich Village. Hadn't even questioned the identification of the body, as most parents did. As his wife had done. She was sure Frank had made some mistake.

VanDamm didn't think Frank had made a mistake. He'd known where she was. Certainly he knew her condition, which was why she'd been banished to the country house in the first place, and he might also know with whom she'd run away. He wouldn't tell Frank, though, at least not today.

Frank was just about to suggest that VanDamm go with him to the morgue to identify the girl's body when once again the parlor doors opened. This time a younger woman entered. She must have just come in from outside, because she was still wearing her hat. She was large-boned and tall for a female, almost as tall as Frank's five feet, eight inches, and she was dressed in the most outlandish outfit Frank had ever seen. Probably considered the height of fashion, the bold plaid of her skirt and matching jacket made him dizzy. Or maybe it was the woman herself, who came in with the force of a whirlwind.

"What's going on here, Father? Alfred said the police are here!"

VanDamm didn't seem too happy to see his daughter, although with VanDamm it was a little hard to tell exactly what he was feeling. Frank figured this must be the one Sarah Brandt knew, the one she'd mistaken Alicia for. The one VanDamm obviously thought Frank had come to tell him about. Frank could imagine this one getting into some kind of scrape. She looked like one of those suffragettes, always looking to cause trouble. He tried to see the resemblance Mrs. Brandt had noticed, but if this woman had ever looked like the dead girl, it was a long time ago.

"Mina, I'm afraid Alicia has been murdered." There it was, bald and brutal, but Mina VanDamm could obviously take it.

"I knew it!" she declared, pulling off her gloves with

furious motions. "I knew she'd come to no good. Didn't I tell you that when she ran away?"

So much for sisterly affection, Frank thought. So much for any normal human reaction at all. The mother, whom Frank had pretty much decided was crazy as a bedbug, was the most regular person in the bunch.

"Do you know why your sister ran away?" Frank asked her, hoping to catch her off guard.

But Mina VanDamm was never off guard. She looked at him as if he was something that had just crawled out from under a rock for having dared to speak to her directly without benefit of a formal introduction.

"Mina, this is Detective . . ." VanDamm realized he hadn't bothered to get Frank's name.

"Detective Sergeant Malloy," Frank supplied. If he'd hoped to impress them with his title, he failed.

Mina simply stared at him in acknowledgment.

"Mina doesn't know the reason Alicia ran away either. It's a mystery to us all," VanDamm assured him.

"She ran away because she's an ungrateful little baggage," Mina said, making her father a liar. "After all Father has done for her, this is the way she repays us. Running away, getting herself murdered and bringing disgrace down on all our heads. How will we ever go out in polite society again?"

"I doubt she got herself murdered just to ruin your social life," Frank tried, unable to resist. But it was obviously impossible to insult the VanDamms, at least by criticizing their finer feelings. They merely stared back at him blankly. He sighed in defeat. "Mr. VanDamm, I'll need for you to go down to the morgue and identify the body."

He frowned at that, but Mina was positively outraged. "How dare you ask my father to go to a place like that? Don't you know who he is?"

"He's the father of a murdered girl," Frank said. "We need positive identification of the victim. You wouldn't want to bury some stranger, would you?"

"I'm afraid the officer is right, Mina," VanDamm said reasonably. "We must be sure it's Alicia."

Mina opened her mouth, but she must have changed her mind about whatever she'd been about to say. She closed it again with a snap and took a moment to collect herself. Then she smiled a queer little smile that gave Frank gooseflesh because it looked so forced, and she said, "You mustn't do this," using a voice that surprised Frank. Suddenly, she was kind and gentle, as if speaking to someone infirm. "No one will blame you for not wanting to see her like that. No one can expect you to put yourself through such an ordeal."

VanDamm considered this for a moment, wanting to agree with her, and then he remembered something. "I thought you said someone already identified her," he said to Frank. "An old family friend."

Mina looked shocked, as well she might. "A family friend?" she echoed incredulously.

"She didn't exactly identify her. Your daughter's name was sewn into her jacket, and this woman said she'd thought the girl looked like Miss Mina VanDamm. She knew you, she said."

"Who is she?" Mina asked skeptically.

"Sarah Brandt. She's a midwife."

Mina widened her eyes at him. "I know no such person, although I suppose it's possible she may know *of* me. We're one of the oldest Knickerbocker families in New York."

She didn't have to tell Frank, of course. Everybody knew the Dutch families—dubbed Knickerbockers ages ago because of the knee britches the early arrivals had worn—had been the first to settle in what was then New Amsterdam. Frank didn't think that made them particularly special, just because their ancestors had fled persecution a hundred and fifty years before his had, but that was the way of the world. Mina VanDamm seemed intent on making the most of it, too.

"In any case," Frank explained doggedly, "Mrs.

Brandt hadn't seen Alicia in a number of years, so she couldn't make a positive identification.''

Mina VanDamm sighed to show her impatience, then she had another thought. ''Alfred can go, then,'' she told her father. ''He'll recognize Alicia as well as any of us.''

VanDamm nodded sagely, as if this were the only logical solution.

''Who's Alfred?'' Frank asked, thinking for an instant he might have discovered Alicia's lover.

''Alfred is the servant who admitted you,'' VanDamm said.

Frank couldn't believe it. They were going to send a damned *butler* to identify a member of their own family.

And just when Frank thought nothing could shock him more, Mina VanDamm turned to him and said, ''I think you've bothered my father quite enough for one day. You may leave now.''

SARAH LOOKED UP at the tall town house on what was known as ''Marble Row'' and hesitated. All during the long elevated train ride up from Greenwich Village this morning, she had debated the wisdom of calling on her old friend. She hadn't seen Mina VanDamm in a decade, and likely, Mina no longer lived here anyway. She'd be married and gone. Sarah couldn't remember reading about her wedding in the *Times*, but that meant nothing. She hadn't followed the society column for years.

She could ask for Mrs. VanDamm, of course, but Sarah remembered her as one of those flighty, worthless women who never had a thing to say worth hearing. She wouldn't learn much from Francisca VanDamm. And approaching Mr. VanDamm wasn't even worth considering. He was a man just like her own father, a man who considered females just one step above dogs in intelligence and who wasn't likely to give her the time of day, much less a hearing.

Well, maybe the servants would at least tell her where Mina lived now. Then she would seek her out and share with her what she knew about Alicia's last days. If the police couldn't find Alicia's killer—and Sarah had personal experience with their failures—then the VanDamms could hire their own investigators, which was the best way to solve a crime in any case, according to Sarah's understanding of the current police situation.

The police commissioners had made great strides in cleaning up the department in the past year, but in purging the corruption, they had decimated the ranks, leaving the entire force seriously under strength. Even the most dedicated officers were overwhelmed, and Sarah had no reason to believe this Detective Sergeant Malloy was particularly dedicated. So if Alicia's murder was solved, it would probably be only because her family hired someone to do it.

The butler who opened the door looked at her askance, probably judging her unworthy of entering. Indeed, she knew her appearance no longer marked her as a member of one of the elite families of New York, but fortunately, she recognized him from her visits here as a girl.

"Good afternoon, Alfred," she said, startling him. "I heard about the family's tragedy, and I was wondering if you could tell me where I can find Miss Mina to express my condolences."

"I'm sorry, madame, I don't . . ." He shook his head to express his confusion.

Sarah smiled. "It's been a long time. I'm Sarah Brandt. That is, that's my married name. When you knew me, I was Sarah Decker."

His eyes lightened with recognition. "It *has* been a long time, Miss Decker . . . I mean, Mrs. Brandt. These are very sad times for the family, and I don't know if Miss Mina is receiving this morning, but if you give me your card . . ."

Sarah shouldn't have been surprised to find Mina here after all. Naturally, she would be here with her parents in their time of grief. She stepped into the foyer and handed him her card after folding down the top right corner to indicate she was calling to pay her respects. There was a whole language to the business of calling cards, depending on which corners were folded over, but those cards were usually engraved with just the visitor's name on fine paper. Sarah's card was the kind that identified her as a midwife. Alfred frowned over it for a second, obviously wondering if he should even deliver such a thing to Mina.

"Please tell Miss Mina that I saw her sister, Alicia, the night before she died."

The butler's head came up in surprise, although his expression betrayed little. Then he offered her a seat and disappeared up the stairs, moving a little more quickly than propriety allowed, she couldn't help thinking.

Sarah wouldn't have been surprised at being turned away. Mina had probably forgotten all about her, and the two of them had never actually been friends in the first place. Mina was always a bit too self-important and conscious of her position in society for Sarah's tastes, even back when Sarah had been conscious of those things herself. But to her relief, Alfred soon returned and ushered her upstairs to one of the private suites where she found Mina swathed in black and reclining on a fainting couch. One hand clutched a lacy handkerchief into which she had apparently been weeping, and the other reached out limply in welcome.

"Sarah, dear, how good of you to come," she said, her voice faint and cracked with grief. "Have you heard the news? We've lost dear, sweet Alicia!"

3

"I'M SO SORRY," SARAH SAID, CROSSING THE ROOM to take Mina's hand in hers. Closer now, she realized that Mina didn't look as if she'd really been doing much crying into the crumpled handkerchief. Her eyes were clear and dry.

Her mourning gown looked rather fresh and unwrinkled, too. Every well-dressed lady had at least one such gown for attending funerals and for weathering the period of time between the unexpected loss of a loved one and the moment when one's dressmaker could deliver an entire new wardrobe of mourning apparel. Sarah had a feeling Mina had already ordered hers.

"I could hardly credit it when Alfred told me you were the one who found poor Alicia," Mina said, her pale blue eyes properly troubled and confused.

"I didn't find her," Sarah said. "In fact, I only saw her for a moment the other night, at the house where she'd been living. I was there to deliver a baby and—"

"Then it's true?" Mina exclaimed, glancing down at the hand in which she still clutched her handkerchief. Sarah saw Mina also held the business card she'd given to Alfred downstairs, the one that proclaimed her profession. "You're a *midwife*?"

She said it as if being a midwife was one step lower than being a grave robber, but Sarah chose not to be offended. Sometimes, she mused, good breeding was a curse. "Yes, I am."

"How awful for you! I had no idea! I thought you were married." She glanced at the card again. "Your name is different."

"I'm a widow," Sarah said, deciding not to mention that she'd probably be delivering babies even if Tom were still alive to support her. Mina would never understand such a thing, and neither would any other woman of her class.

"But that's still no reason for you to have a . . . a *trade*," she said, selecting the most demeaning term she could imagine. "Surely, your father would provide for you."

And just as surely, Mina couldn't imagine why he wasn't doing so. But if she was looking for gossip, Sarah wasn't going to oblige her. She hadn't come here to talk about herself anyway.

"I was a little surprised to find *you* still at home," she said, deftly changing the subject and looking pointedly around at the lavishly decorated chamber which was obviously still Mina's permanent abode. Apparently, Mina had found the new Moorish style of decorating to her liking. The place was furnished the way Sarah imagined a Pharaoh's tomb might be. Or perhaps a Pharaoh's harem, if Pharaohs *had* harems. "I was certain you'd be married yourself by now and living elsewhere."

Sarah had just returned her old friend's insult in kind, since finding one's self an old maid was perhaps even more humiliating than having to support one's self with a "trade." She thought she caught a glimpse of anger in Mina's pale eyes, sort of like the spark of stone striking flint, but only just that one flash. It was gone as quickly as a spark, and Mina managed to dredge up a pitying look.

"It was a sacrifice, as I'm sure you understand, but I simply couldn't marry and leave Father alone. You know how Mother was when we were girls, and she's only gotten worse through the years. Her mind is . . . well, she hasn't been herself for years, and her health has failed dreadfully as a result. Then Alicia . . . What can I say? She was always such a trial to us, and now—'' She quickly covered her mouth with her handkerchief, letting Sarah's card fall to the floor as she apparently fought for control of her emotions.

Sarah couldn't help wondering what those emotions were. As she recalled, Mina had never been particularly fond of Alicia. She'd been almost seventeen when the girl was born and positively mortified at this evidence of her parents' sexuality. Mina had left school when word got around, refusing even to discuss the rumors of her mother's pregnancy, although her pain—and probably her jealousy—had been patently obvious. She hadn't shown her face at a single social event for months before Alicia was born, and for a long time afterward had been unwilling even to acknowledge the child's existence. Apparently, time hadn't reconciled her to her younger sister.

After a moment, Mina was able to speak again, and when she did, she forced a pained smile and said, ''Where are my manners? I haven't even offered you a chair.''

She looked around, as if searching for one, and Sarah took it upon herself to pull up a stool so she could remain near enough to read every nuance of Mina's expressions. The stool's seat was upholstered with gold brocade and rested on a base made entirely of a gilt sphinx with grotesquely large and naked breasts. She thought even a Pharaoh's harem would have rejected such a piece.

When she was seated, she said, ''I can't help wondering what Alicia was doing in that boardinghouse.''

Mina collapsed back against the cushions as if merely considering the issue was more than she could endure, and she lifted her hand to her forehead in the classic ''tragic heroine'' pose. Sarah rolled her eyes, but of course Mina didn't notice.

''We had no idea she was there, of course. We had no

idea where she was at all! She was always unstable, but she'd begun behaving even more strangely these past few months. She'd taken to having hysterics over every little thing and weeping for no reason whatever. Finally, we had to send her to Greentree. That's our country home on the bay. We thought the country air might be good for her, and of course, the solitude. But then she ran away. One morning the servants went to waken her, and she was gone, as if she'd disappeared. We've feared the worst for weeks now. How could we not? A young girl alone in the world with no one to protect her, and Alicia was even more helpless than most. She was a wicked, evil girl to frighten us all like that, but then, she's always been hopelessly spoiled. Mother ruined her, and now we all must pay the price of the scandal she's brought down on us.''

Sarah would have thought the family would be more aware of their loss of a daughter than their loss of reputation because of the circumstances of her death, but Sarah had also not lived among the socially prominent in quite a while. She'd almost forgotten how callous and self-centered they could be. And she knew only too well how unforgiving a family could be when one of their members broke society's rigid code of conduct.

But she was wasting her time in judging the Van-Damms, time that could be better spent finding clues that would lead to Alicia's killer. ''Could someone have helped her run away?'' Sarah asked, aware that she was asking the kind of questions the police detective should have. Malloy wouldn't thank her for interfering, but if she found out something useful, she wouldn't worry about that. ''She couldn't have managed it on her own, could she?''

''I wouldn't be so sure,'' Mina said coldly. ''She was cunning enough to take her jewelry with her, probably to sell it so she would have money to live on. Heaven knows, she wouldn't have had any other means of support. So obviously, she planned the whole thing.''

''But how would she have known how and where to

sell it without being recognized?'' Sarah wondered aloud, remembering how naïve she herself had been at that age.

"I'm sure I have no idea,'' Mina snapped. "Alicia was very secretive, and she certainly never confided in me. If she had, I might have been able to stop her from making our family a laughingstock. But you saw her the night before she died. Perhaps she said something to you, something that would explain her behavior.''

This time Sarah could not mistake the calculating gleam in Mina's eyes. Sarah wasn't the only one interested in the circumstances of Alicia's death. Mina wanted every scrap of information Sarah could give her about her sister, and she wanted it now.

"I only saw her for a moment. We didn't really speak at all,'' Sarah admitted. Was Mina relieved or annoyed? Sarah couldn't be sure. "I didn't even know who she was then, except that she looked so much like you—like the way I remembered you when we were girls—that I actually called her Mina. That seemed to frighten her, but I suppose that's because she was afraid of being found out.''

"Of course she was, the stupid little baggage!'' Mina said angrily. "She was afraid we'd bring her back to the bosom of her family where she was doted upon and pampered. Where her every wish was instantly granted, and where she never had to turn her hand except to feed herself.''

"But something must have driven her away,'' Sarah prompted, recalling her own sister and how she, too, had run away from much the same situation. "Perhaps there was a young man—''

"What on earth makes you think that?'' Mina demanded, but then she remembered. "Oh, because of Maggie,'' she said knowingly, instantly tearing open old wounds that Sarah had thought long healed. "Well, Alicia wasn't a bit like *your* sister. She didn't have *ideals*.'' She said the word as if it left a bad taste in her mouth. "Alicia was just selfish and silly, and she certainly didn't run off out of love for some common laborer. Even if she'd known any young men—which she didn't—Alicia never loved anyone but herself."

Sarah bit back the urge to defend the two girls. Maggie was past caring, just as Alicia was. Still, she couldn't leave Mina basking in her self-righteousness, especially not if enlightening her might help find Alicia's killer.

Trying to pretend she took no pleasure in hurting Mina in return, Sarah said, "I think you must be mistaken about your sister, Mina. She most certainly knew at least one young man. You see, I'm fairly certain she was with child."

"*What?*" Mina's face went scarlet and her eyes blazed with outrage. "How dare you say such a thing!"

"Believe me, it gives me no pleasure to shame her like this, but I thought you should know. Your father can probably keep it from becoming public, but finding out who the father of her child was will undoubtedly help the police find her killer, since he probably—"

"The *police*?" Mina echoed scornfully. She was sitting bolt upright now, fairly quivering with fury. "You mean that horrible Irishman who came here to tell us Alicia was dead? Well, I won't have it! I won't have someone like that probing into our lives and spreading lies and gossip about us! Father will never allow it. He'll put a stop to this investigation immediately!"

"Then how will you find out who killed her?" Sarah asked.

"I don't care who killed her! Why should I when she never cared about any of us? And what good will finding her killer do anyway? It won't bring her back, and it will only ruin the lives of those of us she left behind, and we've suffered enough already!"

"But you can't—"

"Sarah, I think you'd better leave now. You've caused enough trouble for one day. And if I hear a word of these lies about Alicia being spread about, I'll know who's responsible. I can see to it that you are never again received by any respectable family in the city!''

It was a threat designed to terrify, one that would most certainly have terrified Mina, and Sarah didn't have the heart to tell her that she hadn't been received by any of those families for years already. Still cursed by her good breeding, she said instead, ''I'm sorry to have upset you, Mina. I know this is a painful ordeal for you. If there's anything I can do to help, please let me know. My address is on my card.''

Somewhat mollified by Sarah's apology, Mina nodded stiffly. ''I'm sure I can count on your discretion about all this, can't I?''

''Of course.'' At least Sarah had no intention of gossiping about Alicia.

Satisfied that she had done all she could, Sarah rose to leave, but just as she reached the door, Mina called after her.

''I don't suppose the police found her jewelry, did they? She had several very lovely pieces. One of them was a family heirloom.''

''I'm sure if they had, they would have returned them to you,'' Sarah said, sure of no such thing. If the jewels had been in Alicia's room when she was found, an underpaid police officer might well have slipped them into his pocket. But they could also have been stolen by Alicia's killer. Tracing them might help solve the case. She would have to make sure Detective Malloy at least knew they were missing. ''But if she needed money to live on, she might have already sold them.''

''She probably did,'' Mina mused. ''But perhaps we could offer a reward to have them returned.''

Sarah saw no reason to reply and let herself out, wondering what insanity had persuaded her that coming here would be a good idea. She'd really taken no pleasure in hurting Mina, regardless of how much she might have deserved it, and now she had to accept the fact that Mina cared more for her social standing and the missing jewelry than for finding out who killed her sister.

None of this should have come as a surprise to her, of course. She'd lived with people just like Mina most of her life. Her own sister had died because of people like Mina. Which of course didn't make her any more kindly disposed toward them. Alicia may well have been just like Mina, too, and unworthy of Sarah's concern. But Sarah couldn't believe that, not when she remembered the haunted look in the young girl's eyes that night before she died.

Alicia had been young and terrified and alone and pregnant, and someone had choked the life out of her, murdering not only her but her unborn child as well. Even if Alicia hadn't been worthy of Sarah's concern, the innocent child certainly was, and she couldn't stand the thought that someone could snuff out two lives and never be held accountable. Sarah might have to deal with injustice every day, but she didn't have to like it. And if she could possibly defeat it, just this once, then she would.

Lost in her thoughts, she didn't realize that someone had been watching her as she descended the ornately carved staircase into the front hallway.

"Sarah?"

Startled, she looked up to find Cornelius VanDamm standing in the foyer below. He looked, she noticed with some relief, like a man who had just lost a child. His face was pale and his eyes haunted, although his clothing was immaculate and remarkably free of creases, as if he'd only just now put it on.

"Mr. VanDamm, I'm so very sorry about Alicia."

"It really is you, isn't it? Sarah Decker? I could hardly credit it when Alfred told me."

"I'm Sarah Brandt now."

"Oh, yes, of course. I thought I remembered that you'd married. I don't think I know your husband, though."

Of course he didn't. Tom hadn't wasted his time with society. Sarah decided not to mention that, though, or to explain that she was now a widow, either. The man had enough death on his mind at the moment. "I stopped by to pay my respects to Mina."

"Is it true you saw Alicia the night she died?"

"No, it was the night before, or rather, early the morning before. I'm a midwife, you see, and—"

"A midwife?" he echoed her, but without the contempt Mina had shown. He was merely puzzled. "How odd that your father would permit such a thing."

"My father has no say in the matter, I'm afraid," Sarah informed him, shocking him thoroughly. Before he could pursue the subject further, she said, "I already told Mina that I didn't really speak with Alicia that night. I didn't even know who she was until . . . Well, the police asked my help in going through her things, and I found her name embroidered in her jacket."

He nodded and looked away, his face carefully expressionless—men of his class considered any display of emotion vulgar—but his eyes were haunted with a pain Sarah could only imagine.

"Mr. VanDamm, I hate to mention this, but I spoke with the detective who is investigating Alicia's death, and . . . Well, perhaps you aren't aware of it, but the police don't usually exert themselves to solve cases unless they stand to gain something from it."

His gaze swung back to her, the pain in his eyes replaced by the kind of amazement he might have expressed if his gardener had suddenly presumed to offer him advice.

Before he could stop her, Sarah hurried on, knowing she wouldn't have another chance like this one to state her case. "I don't know how capable this Detective Malloy is, but I'm sure he won't bother to find Alicia's killer unless he is compensated in some way. Even if he is, there's no guarantee he has the resources to succeed, either, so you might want to consider hiring a private investigator of your own to make sure the case is solved."

There. Mina might think finding Alicia's killer was a

waste of time, but she didn't make the decisions here. Cornelius VanDamm was the master of this house, and now he understood just what he had to do to ensure his daughter's killer was brought to justice.

Sarah would have felt better if he wasn't staring at her as if she'd just grown a second head. Most likely no female had ever presumed to advise him on anything, most certainly not on the handling of criminal investigations. She was awfully glad she hadn't mentioned that Alicia was pregnant. VanDamm probably would have had her thrown bodily from the house for being so shameless. Well, he'd find out soon enough, probably from Mina, but certainly from the authorities. If even they would dare reveal it to him. Or if he didn't already know.

"Thank you for the information, Sarah," VanDamm said. He had withdrawn completely, shutting off any indication of his true emotions, a trick she'd seen her father use when he no longer wanted to discuss something particularly painful. Like Maggie. "And thank you for stopping by. I'm sure Mina appreciated it."

Sarah could have contradicted him, but she decided to leave instead. Being in this house with these people was bringing back too many unpleasant memories. After murmuring the appropriate condolences, she made her escape out into the street.

What had ever made her think she could do any good in that house? If Cornelius VanDamm wanted his daughter's murder solved, it would be solved, even if that meant the police superintendent himself had to handle the case. And if he *didn't* want it solved . . . Well, there was nothing Sarah Brandt or anyone else could do about it. She'd already done all she could. Now she would just have to wait and see.

"BABY KILLER! BABY killer!"

The cry from the small boys in the street told Frank that the woman he sought must be approaching. He'd been sitting on the stoop of the comfortable house on

Gramercy Park for almost an hour, using the time to mull over the facts in the case of Alicia VanDamm's murder. He hadn't reached any enlightening conclusions, but perhaps the woman for whom he was waiting would be able to help.

Emma Petrovka was a middle-aged woman of substantial girth who made her way laboriously down the street using a silver-headed cane for support. Such canes had come into fashion when Queen Victoria started using one in her old age, but Frank suspected Mrs. Petrovka didn't use one because it was stylish. More likely, her knees had given out under the strain of supporting her enormous weight, and she needed the extra support.

At first Frank thought her hearing must have gone, too, because she seemed oblivious to the chanting of the hoard of street Arabs who descended upon her. They were the filthy, ragged, barefoot urchins who sold newspapers or shoe shines to earn their daily bread and who slept in culverts and alleys because their own families had turned them out to fend for themselves.

"Baby killer! Baby killer!" they cried.

They had, it seemed, found someone lower than themselves whom they were free to torment. Because in spite of her rich gown, which she held up in the typically feminine "skirt clutch" with her free hand to protect it from the dirt of the street, and her luxurious home, Emma Petrovka was socially no better than these homeless waifs.

But if Frank thought she couldn't hear the taunts, he was wrong. She was simply ignoring them. As she reached the house, she stopped, patiently opened her purse and withdrew something in her clenched fist. For an instant, Frank thought she meant to harm her tormentors, although what she could have thrown at them to hurt them, he couldn't imagine. But when she cocked her arm and threw, she released a shower of pennies that clattered musically onto the cobblestones.

In an instant the guttersnipes were scrambling and pushing and shoving, trying to snatch up as many coins as they could before their fellows got to them. Forgotten, Emma Petrovka turned and started up her front steps.

Only then did she notice Frank, who rose to meet her.

"That only encourages them to taunt you again," he pointed out mildly.

"No, it prevents them from doing even worse," she said, heaving her weight up first one step and then another. "Who are you and what do you want? I don't talk to no newspaper reporters, so if that's who you are—"

"I'm with the police," Frank said, showing her his badge. "I'm Detective Sergeant Malloy."

If she was afraid—as well she might have been, since her profession was patently illegal—she gave no indication. Instead she sniffed in derision. "I pay my protection money every month. You ask the captain. He will tell you not to bother me."

"I'm not here to bother you. I want to ask you some questions. About a girl you may have seen."

"I have seen many girls, Mr. Detective Sergeant. That is the nature of my profession." She had reached the front door, her sheer bulk forcing Malloy to step aside, and she was fitting a key into the lock.

"This girl was murdered."

Emma Petrovka looked up at him. Her eyes were the color of mud, peering out like two dull marbles from the folds of fat that made up her face. She had a large mole on her cheek with several long hairs growing out of it, and her small mouth was pursed into a frown. "If a girl dies after one of my procedures, that is not murder," she informed him, and returned to the task of unlocking her front door.

"That's not how she died. Someone strangled her. But we know she was going to have a baby and an abortionist visited her the night she was killed."

Emma Petrovka pushed open her front door, then gave Frank a pitying look. "Do you think I killed this girl?"

Plainly, such a thing was impossible, so Frank didn't even consider replying. "I think whoever sent you there killed her. Her name was Alicia VanDamm.''

She raised her bushy, black eyebrows but gave no other indication that she recognized the name. "I do not know this person, Mr. Detective Sergeant. I cannot help you."

Before Frank could pose another question, Emma Petrovka had passed through the doorway, and now she slammed the door shut in his face. For an instant he stood staring at the lace curtains swinging on the other side of the glass and considered forcing his way inside. Except he wasn't really that interested in talking to her anymore. She was an ugly, unpleasant old woman. If he wanted to talk to an ugly, unpleasant old woman, he'd go home.

Sighing wearily, he turned and sauntered down her steps. The boys who had been tormenting her were gone now, scattered after cleaning the coins from the street to find other sources of amusement. Frank reached into his coat pocket and pulled out the list of names he had culled from various sources. The list was surprisingly short. He would have thought a city the size of New York could provide work for hundreds of abortionists, and he would have thought they'd all be willing to cooperate with the police on any matter. He would've been wrong on both counts. The half dozen women he had visited today had all been as tight-lipped as Emma Petrovka.

He was wasting his time, of course. No one was going to admit having attempted an illegal procedure on a girl who was later murdered. But as thin as this thread was, it was the only one he had. Checking the next address on the list, he headed off downtown.

Sarah was pleased to see that the "Room for Rent" sign was gone from the front window of the Higgins's house. Several of the Higgins children were playing on the front stoop. Sarah greeted them by name.

"How do you like your new baby brother?" she asked them.

"He sleeps all the time," Mary Grace informed her disdainfully. As the eldest, Mary Grace apparently felt it

was her responsibility to speak first. Her brown eyes were
large in her delicate face and much too serious for a girl
who had only known ten summers.

"He's too little to play," Robert complained. Robert
was only five but much sturdier than his slender sister.

"He'll grow," Sarah said. "But he'll never catch up
with you. You'll always be bigger than he is."

"I will?" Plainly, this idea delighted Robert.

Eight-year-old Sally looked up from rocking her rag
doll and said, "But you'll never be as big as me and Mary
Grace. You'll always be our *baby* brother."

"I'm not a baby!" Robert cried in outrage and began
to howl.

Sarah would have comforted him, but Mary Grace was
apparently used to such outbursts and wrapped her frail
arms around his husky body and patted his shoulder for
a few seconds until he'd forgotten why he was crying and
ran off to find something else to do.

"Is your mother staying in bed?" Sarah asked Mary
Grace, figuring the girl would tell the truth while the
mother might lie.

"Most of the time," Mary Grace said. "I try to make
her rest."

"Remind her that if she gets sick she'll make double
work, because then the rest of you will have to take care
of her on top of doing her work for her. Maybe that will
help."

Mary Grace nodded solemnly. "I'll do that. Thank you,
Mrs. Brandt."

Sarah wished Mary Grace would smile. She looked far
too old for her years. Just the way she remembered Alicia
VanDamm. She knew why Mary Grace was so serious.
Her mother was overwhelmed, and a lot of her burdens
fell on the child. But Sarah couldn't imagine why Alicia
VanDamm, a child of wealth and privilege, had seemed
so troubled. Now she might never find out.

Inside, in the cluttered family quarters, she discovered
Mrs. Higgins in bed, just where she should have been,

and looking better than the last time Sarah had seen her.

"Oh, Mrs. Brandt, you don't know the trouble we've had. The police were here asking everybody questions and going door to door on the street, asking did anybody see or hear anything. As if they'd tell the police if they had! And then we packed up that poor girl's things because we had to rent out her room—had to charge a dollar a week less because somebody was murdered there! Can you imagine?—and then a man came to collect her belongings. He was the strangest creature. So formal and polite. I asked was he a relative, but he said no, just an employee of the family. Did you ever hear of such a thing? Sending the hired help to collect her things? What kind of people are they? Everybody says they're rich, that her father owns a bank or something. Could that be true? But why was she living here? I mean, she always paid her rent on time every week, but she never went out or acted like she had anything extra to spend. If her family was rich, why was she on her own?"

"How's the baby doing?" Sarah asked, determined not to spread any gossip about Alicia VanDamm and her sad history. The infant was sleeping on the bed beside his mother, and Sarah carefully unwrapped his blanket to examine him. She was pleased to note that he had filled out nicely. His little cheeks were rounding, and his arms and legs were growing plump. He stirred a little, his small mouth making sucking motions, as if he dreamed he was suckling, and Sarah quickly re-covered him before he could awaken. "He seems to be doing well," she remarked. "Have you decided on a name?"

"Harry after Mr. Higgins's father," Mrs. Higgins said almost absently. "But that wasn't the worst of it. That man—that *employee*—he wanted to know if we'd stolen Alicia's jewels! Can you imagine? He practically accused us to our faces! This is a respectable house, I told him. If she had any jewels, I never knew anything about them, and if they're gone missing, he'd do better to be asking the police about it."

"I'm sure he didn't really think you'd taken them," Sarah soothed her. Sarah could just see the VanDamm's butler looking down his nose at the Higginses and telling them they'd better turn over Alicia's jewelry or else.

"If anybody took them, it was that Hamilton Fisher. From the day he moved in, he was always hanging around her room. Not that she ever left it, except to eat, mind you. I used to wonder what she found to do all alone up there all day. Just stared out the window, I expect. But whenever she did come out, he was right there, trying to make her talk to him. Or just notice him, I expect. Never saw a young man so taken with a girl. He'd sit at the table with her and say all kinds of wild things, trying to make her smile. She never did, though. I think she was a little afraid of him. And who could blame her? She just wanted to mind her own business, and there he was, bothering her all the time. But maybe it wasn't her he was after at all. Maybe he really wanted to steal her things. Do you think that was it, Mrs. Brandt? Do you think he might've finally decided just to go into her room and take what he wanted, and when she put up a fuss, he—"

"I'm sure that wasn't it at all. Please, Mrs. Higgins, you mustn't upset yourself. It's not good for you or the baby. I'm very glad you were able to rent out your rooms after all."

Mrs. Higgins sniffed derisively. "Not to the kind of lodgers I'm used to. They're a very rough sort of men, I can tell you. That's what happens when I leave things to Mr. Higgins. He can't see what people look like, so he isn't as careful as I would be. But I doubt they'll be here long. That kind never stays anywhere very long. And when they leave, I'll be sure to get a better class of lodgers. For full price, too."

Sarah was hardly listening. She was too busy thinking about Hamilton Fisher and wondering why he'd been so intent on making the acquaintance of Alicia VanDamm. It could be as simple as a young man wanting to be noticed by a pretty girl. But it seemed like more than that, from what Mrs. Higgins described. And of course, he'd vanished the night she died. Had Malloy asked about him? Did he know how interested Fisher had been in Alicia? "Did that young man, that Mr. Fisher, did he have a job?"

"Not that I ever knew," Mrs. Higgins said, apparently undisturbed by the change of subject. "I was worried he might not be able to pay, but he gave me a month's rent in advance, so I couldn't complain, now could I?"

"And then he ran off after Alicia was killed, after only living here a week, when his room was paid for a month?"

"Makes him sound guilty, don't it?" Mrs. Higgins said, with a worried frown.

"Have you told the police all this?"

Mrs. Higgins gave her a pitying look. "That fellow they sent over, that detective, he hardly asked me any questions at all. Acted like he couldn't be bothered. Oh, I know nobody's going to care if some orphan girl gets herself murdered, but if Alicia's family is really rich, wouldn't they at least offer a reward? Something to get the police interested?"

"I'm sure they will," Sarah said, mentally cursing Frank Malloy. Well, he might not appreciate her help in the case, but she had far too much information now to even consider keeping it to herself. Like it or not, she'd have to track him down and make him listen to her. And then she'd have to find out if the VanDamms were going to offer a reward. And if they weren't . . .

Well, she'd decide what to do next when she found out. If Alicia's own family didn't care enough to find her killer, Sarah wasn't sure what she could do, but she would do something. Or die trying.

SARAH LOOKED OUT of the hansom cab and frowned up at the slightly tawdry, marble-fronted building on Mulberry Street that served as police headquarters for the city of New York.

"Here you are, ma'am," the driver called down from his perch above her. Quickly, she paid him through the window overhead and climbed out. The driver wasted no time in clucking his horse into motion again and moving out into the early morning traffic, leaving her standing alone on the sidewalk. Oddly enough, police headquarters was located in a rather rough neighborhood, one in which Sarah didn't feel comfortable walking unescorted, which was why she'd taken a cab. The hansoms, which were one-seated carriages with the driver mounted above and behind the passenger compartment, were a relatively new addition to the streets of New York, although they had been popular in England for over fifty years. Sarah had felt perfectly safe inside the cab, but as she watched it pull away, her sense of well-being evaporated, and she began to regret her decision to confront Detective Malloy.

She shouldn't have felt so very uneasy. The tenement buildings around her were just the kind of buildings she frequently visited to deliver babies. The women hanging out of the windows, gossiping and arguing, were the kinds of women who had those babies. And the children playing in the streets, the vendors pushing their cards and shouting for customers, and all the other sights and smells of poverty were only too familiar. No, it wasn't the neighborhood that worried her, but rather the building that should have provided a sanctuary amid the squalor of the tenements.

Well, what was the worst that could happen to her? Malloy had already said he didn't consider her a suspect, so she most likely wouldn't be arrested. Smiling grimly at this small comfort, she looked up at the fanlight window over the green, double entry doors and read the words, "New-York Police Headquarters." Pretty forbidding. Walking in and brazenly asking for Malloy would also be embarrassing, but Sarah had been embarrassed before and survived. Thinking of poor Alicia renewed her courage, and ignoring the stares of the suspicious looking characters loafing nearby, she made her way up the steep stairs to the front door. Then she had to explain her mission to the doorkeeper who only grudgingly admitted her.

The place smelled of unwashed bodies and tobacco juice. The floor was littered with battered spittoons, but no one seemed able to hit them with their streams of juice because the floor was brown with it. Before her stood a high desk, and behind it sat an enormously fat man in a police uniform. His bald head gleamed brightly in the early morning sunlight.

Sarah tried to ignore the men seated on the benches that lined the walls, all of whom were shackled and some of whom bore signs of a recent beating, but they had most certainly noticed her.

"Hey, O'Shaughnessy, you got the whores making house calls now?" one hollered.

"Is this one of them reforms that Roosevelt's making?" another cried. "No wonder he wanted to get rid of Byrnes," he added, naming the recently resigned chief of police.

"If I gotta get measured, I want *her* to do it!" another called, making reference to the newly instituted Bertillion system of identifying criminals by taking measurements of various body parts and keeping them on file along with their photographs for identification purposes.

"Shaddup," the desk sergeant commanded, but the suggestive banter kept on anyway. Sarah simply ignored it.

"I'd like to see Detective Sergeant Malloy, if he's in," she told the desk sergeant over the din.

"Malloy, is it?" He peered down at her, turning his double chin into a triple. "He expecting you?"

Not likely, she thought, but she said, "Yes, I have some information for him about a case he's working on."

He didn't seem to believe her. Probably, the usual police informants looked nothing like Sarah. "I ain't sure he's here," he said skeptically.

"Perhaps you could check and see. Or send someone to find him. My information is very important. He won't want to miss it.'' There, if that didn't make Malloy furious with her, nothing would. Sarah didn't particularly care, however, so long as he listened to what she had to tell him when he got here.

The desk sergeant was scowling at her now, his face a lot redder than it had been, and it had been pretty red before. Plainly, he didn't like having a woman tell him what to do, no matter how gently she phrased it.

For a moment, she thought he was going to vent his wrath on her, but suddenly, his fury faded into something more sinister. ''*O'Brien!*'' he shouted without warning, startling her.

A scrawny young man who hardly looked old enough to shave but who nevertheless wore a police uniform, appeared from a nearby doorway. ''Yes, Sergeant?''

''Take this here *lady* downstairs to one of the *waiting rooms*.'' He used the word ''lady'' as if he didn't really mean it.

O'Brien looked Sarah over in surprise. His eyes were very blue and a little frightened, and his pale blond hair was plastered to his skull with hair tonic. ''*Downstairs?*'' he echoed uncertainly.

''That's right, O'Brien, downstairs. She's waiting for Malloy. Maybe when you're done, you can go find him for her.''

''Where is he?''

''How the hell . . . ? Oh, sorry, ma'am,'' the sergeant said, not sounding sorry at all. ''How should *I* know? If he's expecting her like she says, he won't be far now, will he? And in the meantime, the *lady* can wait for him downstairs.''

Sarah wasn't sure she wanted to find out what was ''downstairs,'' but she also didn't want to leave without seeing Malloy since she had no illusions he would ever come to her, no matter how much information she promised him.

''I'll be happy to wait, Officer O'Brien,'' she assured him.

For a long moment, O'Brien seemed torn between doing his duty and obeying some higher instinct, but in the end, duty won. Or perhaps the Sergeant won. He certainly looked intimidating. Sarah wouldn't want him angry with *her*, or at least no angrier than he already was.

"Come with me, then," Officer O'Brien said, not letting himself look at Sarah again. Sarah knew she was probably making a terrible mistake by going with him, but she'd already come this far. Her chances of getting Malloy to her place were probably nil, she reminded herself, unless she killed someone herself, so this was her only option.

Determined not to show any hesitation, she followed Officer O'Brien down the long, dingy hallway. The walls were painted dark green beneath layers of dirt, and even though the sun shone brightly outside the many windows, the exterior awnings kept the interior dim.

O'Brien led her down some rickety stairs that were littered with decades of dirt and refuse. Holding the rail, Sarah was glad she'd kept her gloves on. As they reached the basement, new and fouler odors assailed her, the origins of which she didn't want to know. She was beginning to understand why O'Brien hadn't wanted to bring her down here.

Through another hall, this one dirtier than the one upstairs, past several doors. Sarah thought she heard the sound of moaning coming from behind one, but she didn't let herself think about it. Finally, they reached a door that Officer O'Brien opened and indicated she should enter. Unfurnished except for a small table and several wooden chairs, the brick-walled room was illuminated by a single gas jet that cast strange shadows into the corners. Although the sergeant had called this a "waiting room," Sarah was pretty sure it wasn't typically used for waiting.

"I'll try to find him quick as I can," O'Brien told her apologetically. "And I'd better lock you in. So nobody can bother you," he added when Sarah widened her eyes in alarm.

Before she could change her mind and beg him to take her back outside where she could hail a cab and flee, forgetting the insane impulse that had brought her here in the first place, he was turning the key in the lock outside.

4

THIS WAS A MISTAKE, A TERRIBLE MISTAKE. SARAH knew that now. Her only hope was that Malloy wasn't so furious with her that he'd leave her here to rot. Or that the desk sergeant upstairs wasn't so annoyed that he didn't bother to send for Malloy at all. But surely, someone would come for her sooner or later. This was a police station, after all, and she was an honest citizen who was only trying to help.

If only she didn't know how little good that would do her if they simply decided to forget about her entirely.

But it was now too late to change her mind. Forcing herself to sit in the cleanest of the chairs, she drew a few deep breaths and managed not to panic. Once she had her control back, she concentrated on her surroundings. This must be one of the rooms they used to interrogate prisoners, she decided. To give them the "third degree," a term developed by Thomas Byrnes, the longtime chief of the Detective Bureau and until recently the superintendent, whose methods of questioning prisoners were equally violent and effective. He had, they said, actually invented the "third degree."

As awful as this room was, however, Sarah knew that those on the floor below would be even worse. There, prisoners were held in dank cellar rooms a floor below street level where no ray of sunlight or breath of fresh air ever permeated. They said that after a few hours in one of those cells, a man would confess to anything just to get out.

Until recently, the cellar had also provided housing to the homeless who were too poor even to manage the few cents required for floor space sleeping in a Bowery flophouse. So awful was this space that few people ever actually took advantage of the free lodging except in the worst weather. Still, it was the only place in town where a homeless woman who was not actively engaged in prostitution could stay. But Police Commissioner Theodore Roosevelt had closed the police department homeless shelters a few months ago, on the advice of newspaper reporter and self-appointed reformer Jacob Riis. Riis seemed to think the shelters were a breeding ground for vice and sin. Sarah wondered if he realized that the people who had once used the shelters now had to sleep in the very streets instead. What kind of a breeding ground would that be?

Having satisfied herself that she had adequately proved Riis wrong, for a while Sarah passed the time by imagining what Malloy would say when he found her here, assuming he ever did. She could even picture the expression he'd have on his face when he came through the door, please God, let him come through very soon. He'd be furious and impatient and even a little smug, thinking she'd gotten herself into a fine fix and wasn't it just what she deserved for sticking her nose into things that weren't her business?

When she was finished with that, she rehearsed what she'd say to him, refining and clarifying what she had to tell him, so he wouldn't have time to cut her off before he'd heard the most important information. He could be a little short, and she was certain he wouldn't be in the mood for lengthy explanations when he finally arrived, which had better be soon. And when she was satisfied that her speech was perfect, she simply waited, imagining she heard rats scurrying and men moaning and cursing, and trying not to imagine that the spots she saw on the far wall were blood.

More than an hour passed before she finally heard a key turning in the lock, and the door was flung open to reveal Detective Sergeant Frank Malloy. He looked exactly the way she'd expected, which was not at all happy to see her.

"What the hell are you doing here?" he demanded.

Thank heaven he had no idea how genuinely thrilled she was to see him. To see *anybody*, in fact, who might rescue her from this hellhole. Resisting the impulse to jump up and throw her arms around him in gratitude and carefully keeping all trace of elation from her voice, she said, "Didn't they tell you? I have some information about Alicia VanDamm's murder."

Malloy ran his fingers through his hair in a gesture of exasperation. Hair, Sarah noticed, that appeared to be uncombed. Just as his cheeks appeared to be unshaven. And his tie was crooked. Indeed, he looked as if he'd just gotten up and had dressed in a very big hurry. It *was* early in the morning, but not *that* early.

"This better be something really important," he warned her, closing the door behind him with a decisive slam.

Frank couldn't believe it. Sarah Brandt was sitting in an interrogation room. Had actually been *locked* in an interrogation room, and for quite a while, if what O'Brien told him was true. O'Brien was an idiot. He'd been looking all over town for Frank when he'd been right here in the building, sleeping in the officer's dormitory upstairs after having been up half the night investigating a warehouse robbery. A warehouse robbery that promised to add substantially to Frank's savings, if he played it right, and he most certainly would.

By the time O'Brien had found him, Frank realized Mrs. Brandt had been locked in the basement for quite a while, more than long enough to reduce a normal female to hysterics, which was how he'd expected to find her. Not that he was looking forward to dealing with an hysterical female, but finding her sitting here looking perfectly calm was even more unsettling. The woman was positively unnatural.

"I'm sure you'll at least find what I have to tell you interesting," she said, just as prim and proper as you please. As if she was sitting in her own parlor instead of right where countless criminals had endured countless beatings, all in the cause of justice. He should've left her here for another hour before coming to rescue her. Maybe by then she would've started acting like a normal woman.

"All right," he said grudgingly, pulling up a chair to the opposite side of the table and sinking down into it. "What is it, and be quick." He rubbed his gritty eyes, half hoping that when he opened them again she'd be gone. But she wasn't. "I've been awake all night, and I'd like to get a little more sleep before I get called on another case," he warned.

"Oh, dear, they should've told me. I could come back another time," she offered, annoying him even more. He didn't want her to be thoughtful. He wanted her to be gone.

"Just spit it out and get it over with," he snapped, wondering what evil he'd done to deserve having Sarah Brandt enter his life.

"I'll try to hurry," she said, folding her hands on the table in that prissy way she had that set his teeth on edge. "I called on the VanDamm family yesterday. To express my condolences," she added when Frank scowled his disapproval. "Mina and I are old friends."

Well, he supposed he couldn't stop her from calling on an old friend.

"At any rate," she continued, "she told me something that might be useful. It seems that when Alicia ran away, she took some valuable jewelry with her."

"We didn't find any jewelry in her room." Frank absently began to rub the bridge of his nose. His head was starting to ache, and his eyelids felt like they were lined with gravel.

"It may have been stolen, and the thief may have been the person who killed her."

Frank frowned again, this time because he was annoyed he hadn't thought of that himself. He would have in another minute, of course. He was just tired. "You know what this jewelry looked like?"

"No, but I'm sure the family can give you a description. They may even have paste copies of the pieces. People sometimes have their jewelry copied so they can wear the fakes and keep the real ones safely locked up. If you find out who pawned her jewelry, you'll probably find her killer."

"Unless . . ." Frank muttered, thinking aloud.

"Unless what?"

Frank didn't particularly want to share his thoughts with her, but he was too tired to get into an argument about it. "Unless she sold them herself. To get money to live on. Would she have had any money of her own otherwise?"

"I can't know for sure, of course, but she probably wouldn't have. Mina didn't think so, and in fact, she thought Alicia had probably taken the jewelry to sell since she had no other source of money. Girls of that class don't usually need access to money. Their families provide everything for them."

"Even when they go shopping?"

"The family would have accounts at all the stores. And if she ever did need to buy something, she'd have a servant along to handle the transaction. It's considered vulgar for a female to carry cash."

The more Frank learned about the upper classes, the less he liked them, and he hadn't liked them very much to begin with. "Which means her sister was right, she probably took the jewelry to sell, so it was probably long gone by the time she was killed."

"Except that I also can't imagine Alicia would have known where to sell the jewelry herself or how to go about it even if she did. Girls of her class don't go to pawnshops, Mr. Malloy. If she did sell the jewelry, someone would have had to help her."

"I'll check it out," he said, "in case she hadn't sold all the pieces yet. If her killer did steal something, at least that would give us a reason why she was killed."

"I think I may know who her killer was, too, Detective."

Frank seriously doubted this, but he could use a good laugh. "And who was it?" he asked with exaggerated patience.

She bristled a little at his tone, but she said, "Hamilton Fisher. He was a lodger at the Higgins's house, too, and—"

"And he disappeared the night she was killed," he finished for her. Did she really think he wouldn't know this most basic piece of information? Now Frank was bristling, too.

"Did you know that he'd been paying her particular attention?" she asked.

"A natural enough thing. She was a pretty girl."

"And did you know he didn't have a job? Yet he'd paid his rent a month in advance, and he moved in just a few days before she died. And he started paying Alicia marked attentions from the moment he—"

"So?" Frank's patience was wearing dangerously thin.

"So, he was probably a cadet," she said as blandly as if she'd just accused the fellow of being a Methodist.

"A *cadet*?" Frank didn't know what was more shocking, that he hadn't thought of it himself or that Sarah Brandt even knew what a cadet was. "What makes you think so?"

"Didn't I already explain that?" she shot back.

Actually, she had. A "cadet" was a young man who used his charms to seduce naïve or desperate young women into prostitution. The laws of supply and demand required a constant supply of fresh, young females to satisfy the enormous demand of a profession that used them up at an alarming rate. Young men supplemented their meager incomes by working as cadets and helping the pimps fill their need for replacements in the brothels and on the streets.

A girl as lovely and alone as Alicia VanDamm would have seemed a logical target. Maybe Fisher had grown frustrated with his failure to attract her attentions and gone to her room and been a little more forceful than he'd intended in trying to recruit her.

Not wanting to admit he'd missed all the clues, Frank said, "We're already looking for Mr. Fisher."

She didn't seem cheered by that information. Maybe she guessed that Frank hadn't exactly made Hamilton Fisher a priority in this investigation. "Perhaps now you'll be looking for him in some different places."

He probably would, but he didn't want to admit it to Mrs. Brandt. "Do you think the VanDamms will offer a reward for the missing jewelry?"

"Mina seemed very anxious to get it back. Is it absolutely necessary to have a reward, though?"

Oh, yes, Frank wanted to say, but instead he said, "Without it, I doubt we'll see the jewelry again. If it was pawned, the pawnbroker will want his investment back. Even though it's illegal to buy stolen goods, I won't be able to prove he did unless he tells me. Since he's not likely to do that, I can't arrest him for it."

"So if he's not afraid of being arrested, your only leverage is to bribe him," she guessed. She didn't approve, but Frank couldn't help that. That's the way the world worked. Sarah Brandt could reform it on someone else's time.

"I do what I have to do." He only hoped she didn't know that the customary arrangement was for the pawnbroker to split the reward with the police, too. Which, of course, gave the police an incentive for finding missing property in the first place. In fact, some thieves didn't bother with fences at all. They just held onto the stolen goods until the reward was offered, then turned it in and split the proceeds with the cops. Easy work, but a little too uncertain for Frank's taste.

"Has Mr. VanDamm offered a reward for the murderer?" she asked.

"I haven't actually approached him about it yet," Frank admitted. He didn't like to rush into something so delicate. If you asked too soon, people thought you were unfeeling, and the VanDamms seemed like just the kind of folks who could get offended.

"I suggested he offer one," she said, thoroughly shocking him. "I saw him when I called on Mina, and I tried to explain to him why it's necessary. You won't find her killer without one, will you?"

Frank didn't think the answer to that question would do him credit, so he ignored it. "A man like that, with plenty of money, I guess he'll do whatever it takes to catch the killer."

To Frank's surprise, she frowned as if she didn't agree.

"You don't think so?"

"He didn't say anything, one way or the other, when I mentioned it to him," she admitted, "and I didn't want to press him. He was still very upset."

"How could you tell?" Frank asked, honestly wanting to know.

She shrugged one shoulder, a distinctively feminine gesture that Frank found far more appealing than he should have. "He's very reserved by nature. Most men are, I think, but men in his position must be even more so. Cornelius VanDamm probably wouldn't shout if his house was on fire, but when I saw him the other day, he looked as if he hadn't been sleeping at all, and his eyes were . . . well, they were haunted. There's no other word for it."

"Then he'll pay whatever it takes to find the man responsible."

"I'm not so sure."

"Why?" Frank challenged, not liking her theories at all. "You can't think he doesn't want the killer found."

To his surprise, she didn't protest. "It's not that so much as . . . He might be afraid of the scandal."

"How much more scandal could there be? His kid was murdered."

"Does anyone know that? Anyone except you and I and the police, I mean? I haven't seen anything about it in the papers, have you?"

Frank really hadn't had time to look. "So?"

"So he's been able to keep the circumstances of her death a secret. He probably has a story he's been telling to explain her death, a tragic accident perhaps, since the truth would be too awful to admit. The funeral will be private and no one will ever know the truth . . . unless the killer is caught."

This made absolutely no sense to Frank. "What's the shame in getting murdered?"

"The shame is in the circumstances. She had run away from her home, which is bad enough, but the reason she ran away is even worse. I'm assuming that she really was with child."

Frank nodded grudgingly. The medical examiner had confirmed that at once.

"How far gone was she?"

Frank shifted uneasily in his chair. He'd never get used to discussing such topics with a female he hardly knew. "Almost six months, they said."

"Then her family must have known. That's why they sent her to Long Island, to keep her out of sight since her condition would soon be obvious."

"But they wouldn't've been able to keep it a secret once she had the baby," Frank pointed out.

"Of course they would. They'd simply spirit the child away someplace and return Alicia to society as if nothing had happened."

"Their own grandchild?" Frank scoffed. Nobody could be that heartless. "What would become of it?"

"Maybe a servant would adopt it, or maybe they would give out some story about a distant relative who died and left her child in their care. Who knows? The important thing is that no one would ever know the truth. Alicia's reputation would be safe so she'd still be able to marry well, and the family wouldn't lose their place in society. But with her running away, they'd have a much more difficult time making up a story. They'd have to invent excuses for her disappearance, which would be hard to explain, and now with her death, the situation is even more delicate. If the truth came out, that she was pregnant and living in a boardinghouse alone and her parents didn't even know where she was, they'd become a laughing-stock. I'm very much afraid they might think that was too high a price to pay for justice."

"Are you saying they'd let their daughter's killer go free just to protect their reputation?" *She must be exaggerating,* he thought. "I know rich people are a little strange, but that's not human."

For a long moment, she didn't speak, and Frank thought his skepticism must have shown her how ridiculous her theories were, but then she said, "In some ways, rich people *aren't* human, at least some of them aren't."

"You know this for a fact?" He very much doubted it, but she nodded.

"From my own personal experience. With my own father. He's a close friend of Cornelius VanDamm."

Well, he'd known she came from money. He'd known she and Mina VanDamm were friends. This shouldn't be a surprise, but still, he had a difficult time believing she'd come from the same stock as the VanDamms. "What's his name?"

"Felix Decker."

Frank tried not to show his surprise. Felix Decker was definitely one of the Four Hundred socially elite in the city. His family had been here since before the flood, and he was probably richer than God. Was it possible Decker's daughter could be sitting here with him in a filthy room in the basement of police headquarters? "Felix Decker's daughter is a *midwife*?" he asked in disbelief. Surely, that alone proved the lie.

She leaned back in her chair and smiled at him. It was a bitter smile, full of pain and wisdom dearly earned, and suddenly, Frank knew things about Sarah Brandt he had no desire to know.

"I had a sister," she began, telling him a story he knew he didn't want to hear. "Her name was Maggie. She was three years older than I, and I adored her. She was beautiful and smart and so strong. Too strong, as it turned out. She didn't approve of the way our father treated his workers. He was too cruel, she thought, but she couldn't convince him to adopt more humane methods. She began spending time at the shipyards. She was especially interested in proving to my father that it would be in his own best interest financially to treat his workers better. Since my father's only concern was his financial best interest, she stood a good chance of changing his mind if she could prove her theories. But while she was going over his books, she met one of the clerks and fell in love with him.

"Peter was a beautiful young man, and I think he truly loved my sister in return. He must have, because he stayed with her even after . . . But I'm getting ahead of myself. Maggie and Peter fell in love, and they wanted to marry, but of course my father refused to allow it. His daughter would never be allowed to marry a penniless clerk. She was to be the bride of some millionaire's son or perhaps even of an English Lord. My father had great hopes. He simply failed to realize that Maggie could be as stubborn as he.

"She refused to stop seeing Peter, so my father fired him, turned him out without a reference and blackened his name everywhere, so the only work he could find was as a common laborer. He thought this would be the last he'd hear of Peter, but Maggie had conceived a child. She thought when she told our father about the baby, he would relent and allow her to marry, but instead, he tried to send her off to Europe. In fact, we thought she did go to France, but she'd manage to escape from the ship before it sailed, and she found Peter. They were married, and by the time we discovered what had happened, she'd vanished.

"I begged my father to find her and at least help Peter find a decent job, but he said she'd made her choice, and she could live with it. I think he expected that once Maggie had a taste of poverty, she would come crawling back to him and beg forgiveness, but of course, she didn't. The next we heard was one night when Peter sent us word to come to her because she was dying. My parents were out for the evening, but I went. They were living in a rear tenement on the Lower East Side. On the fifth floor."

Frank winced. This would be about the cheapest lodging available. The rear tenements were built in the courtyards behind the regular tenements, cut off even from what little light and air were available in the crowded streets of the city.

"I found her in a back bedroom, a room with no windows, hardly bigger than a closet. She was lying on a straw mattress on the floor, and she was bleeding to death."

For a moment, Frank thought he was going to be sick, but he swallowed down the bitter bile and forced himself to listen to the rest of Mrs. Brandt's story without betraying his weakness.

"The baby had come, but they were too poor for a doctor or even a midwife. Most of the time Peter couldn't find work, so they were surviving by renting out the other room of their tiny flat to lodgers who slept in rows on the floor. Five of them. They were all there that night, snoring in the front room while Maggie died in the back. I don't know how she stood it, the filth and the grinding poverty and the lack of privacy. Nothing in her life had prepared her for that, but she bore it all somehow. Perhaps it was her pride that kept her going.

"But even her pride couldn't protect her anymore. I

was just a girl then, only seventeen, so I didn't know how to help her or what to do. Nothing would have helped by then, though. She was so weak, she could hardly speak, but she begged me to take care of her baby. I promised I would, even though her baby was already dead. And then she was gone, too.''

Frank didn't like the way her eyes shone. If she started crying, he wasn't exactly sure what he should do. Fortunately, she blinked several times and regained her composure.

''Detective, Malloy, my sister died because my father didn't want to be embarrassed. He thought more of his good name than her happiness, and when he couldn't force her to his will, he abandoned her. I don't think he planned to lose her forever, or at least I hope that's true, but that's what happened nevertheless.''

''And was his good name ruined when word of her death got out?''

Mrs. Brandt gave him a pitying look. ''Don't you understand yet? Word *didn't* get out. He made up a story about her catching a fever in France. He said she died over there and was buried there, too. Oh, some people knew. There was gossip, but because my family told them a story they could pretend to believe, no hint of scandal ever touched us. My father didn't even put her in the family plot. She and the baby are buried in an unmarked grave in a cemetery on Long Island. And Peter, too. He hanged himself the day after she died.''

''Good God.'' Why had Frank assumed that having money would encourage finer feelings in people? Felix Decker was one of the wealthiest men in the city, and yet he had treated his daughter as cruelly as the drunken immigrant who sends his daughters out to prostitute themselves so he won't have to work.

''So you see, Detective, the VanDamms might decide they don't want the killer found. It won't bring their daughter back and will only cause them harm.''

''If they don't want the killer caught, why should *you*

care? You said yourself, you hardly even knew the girl.''

She thought this over for a few seconds. "I want to see justice done, Detective. I want someone punished for snuffing out Alicia's life and the life of her child. I don't want to watch another young woman vanish into a web of secrets and lies."

Frank's head was throbbing now. "But if her own family doesn't want her murder solved . . ."

"The police force is changing Mr. Malloy. I know what's going on, how men are finally being promoted on merit rather than on how big a bribe they can afford. If you bring this killer to justice, you'll be noticed. Noticed for something good. Don't you want to be Superintendent someday?"

"I'm not that ambitious, Mrs. Brandt," he assured her sourly. "Captain is all I'm aiming for."

"I have friends in government, Mr. Malloy. I'll make sure they notice you."

Frank wished he believed this. "The reformers won't last long. Don't you read the papers? Roosevelt's stupid plan to enforce the law and keep the saloons closed on Sunday is already making all the wrong people mad. He won't last, and when he's gone, things will be the way they've always been."

"Then I'll pay you a reward," she said, startling him yet again. "I have some money of my own, and I can't think of a better way to use it."

The thought of taking Sarah Brandt's money was unsettling, and Frank didn't like the feeling one bit. Since when had he gotten so particular? Money was money, and that's what he needed if he ever wanted to make Captain, Teddy Roosevelt and his reforms be damned. And he had to make Captain, because he had a story of his own, a story just as awful as Sarah Brandt's, but one that he had no intention of ever telling her or anyone else.

"If the VanDamms don't cooperate, I won't get very far, no matter how big the reward is or who pays it. Nobody else is likely to tell me anything useful or even *know* anything useful,'' he pointed out.

''The servants will know. The servants know more than anyone. And if you need to bribe them, I'll be happy to provide the funds for that, too.''

Frank was pretty sure he would've thought of the servants eventually. He was just groggy from not enough sleep. And maybe that was why he said, ''Keep your money, Mrs. Brandt. I won't be needing it.'' He couldn't think of any other reason why he would say something so foolish.

''But you *will* try to find Alicia's killer, won't you?''

Frank knew he shouldn't make the promise, but he said, ''I'll find him.''

And he wasn't sure if he was terrified or grateful when he saw that Sarah Brandt believed him.

CORNELIUS VANDAMM DID offer a reward for his daughter's jewelry. When Frank explained that stolen goods could often be recovered this way, VanDamm was only too happy to oblige. The sapphire necklace had belonged to his mother, he said. Frank hadn't mentioned that the trail of the pawned jewelry might also lead to Alicia's killer. He didn't want to ruin the deal, especially when VanDamm hadn't mentioned anything about a reward for the killer yet and Frank wasn't yet sure he even wanted the killer found.

The pawnshop was on Catherine Street, amid the slums of the Bowery. All the pawnshops in the city were located in the Bowery. The shop was small and crowded with a strange assortment of goods, ranging from gold watches to eyeglasses. Overcoats hung along one wall, and musical instruments of various ages and stages of repair were piled in a corner. There was even a rack of umbrellas. People in need would sell anything for a few cents.

The proprietor, a sly character known only as Slippery Joe, greeted him warmly. ''Detective Malloy, as I live and breathe, and how are you this fine day?''

It was gray and drizzling a bit outside, but Frank didn't bother to mention this. "I've got a little problem, Joe, and I thought you might be able to help me with it."

"Anything I can do for the police, you know I always try to help." Joe was a slender man of indeterminate age, with watery eyes and thinning gray hair and an ingratiating smile for detectives. Frank had no idea how he treated his customers since they always made themselves scarce when the coppers were around.

"I'm trying to trace some jewelry. Would've been sold sometime in the last month."

"You know I don't deal in stolen articles, Detective," Joe reminded him unctuously. To give him credit, few pawnbrokers served as fences. The risks were too great, and besides, they made enough money already simply doing their regular work.

Frank gave him a conspiratorial smile. "You probably didn't know they were stolen. And I doubt the person who had them would've gone to a fence." He was still going on the theory that Alicia VanDamm had sold the jewels herself to finance her escape. "They're nice pieces, and there aren't many places that would handle them. Not many other brokers would recognize the quality."

Joe had to agree. He rubbed this stubbled chin thoughtfully and nodded. "What did they look like?"

Sarah Brandt had been right about the VanDamms having a paste copy of the jewelry. Frank pulled the imitation sapphire necklace from his pocket and laid it on the scratched counter. Joe's eyes grew wide, and Frank had to agree, it was a shocking sight, so much beauty amid the squalor of the shop's other contents.

"Yes, I think I might have seen something like that come through here. I'd have to check my safe, of course. Is there a . . . a reward being offered for its return?"

"Two hundred dollars."

A princely sum, to be sure, but only a fraction of what VanDamm had really offered. Frank wanted to leave some room for negotiation.

Joe studied the necklace and nodded. "Yes, yes, I think I may have seen just this very piece."

"There were other pieces that may have been sold with it. I've got the description of them, too. The owner wants all of it back. There's a pair of earrings, diamonds set in the shape of stars, and another pair that's pearls. A pearl necklace, too, and a brooch shaped like a spider with a ruby in the center."

Joe nodded again. "So many beautiful things. I couldn't possibly have given less than five hundred for them," he assured Frank.

Frank doubted this very much, but he was willing to dicker a bit to get what he wanted. "I'm sure the victim will go as high as three hundred, but that's probably all. She's a widow of limited means. The jewelry is all she has left in the world."

Plainly, Joe didn't believe Frank any more than Frank believed him, but he said, "I'll see if my memory is as good as it used to be. Please, make yourself at home, Detective, while I check my safe."

Just as Frank had suspected, Joe had all the pieces he was looking for. This meant they'd probably been sold as a group. If his luck was good, this meant they'd all been stolen from Alicia's room the night she was killed and pawned by her murderer. If his luck was bad, as he suspected it probably was, Alicia herself had pawned the pieces and lived on the proceeds for the past month.

"When did these come in?" Frank asked.

Joe consulted his ledger. "Five weeks ago."

Frank frowned. This was even before Alicia had disappeared. "Do you remember who brought them in?"

"I have a name here," Joe said with a small smile. "John Smith."

Well, maybe this wasn't too bad. The fellow who sold Alicia's jewelry was obviously in her confidence. Which also meant he was probably the father of her child. If Frank could identify the fellow, he'd be very close to finding her killer. "I might be able to get the victim to

82   *Victoria Thompson*

raise the reward an extra fifty dollars if you could possibly recall what this John Smith looked like,'' Frank said.

Joe pretended to consider. Probably, he knew exactly without making any effort at all. Merchandise like this rarely found its way into his shop, and the seller would have made an indelible impression.

"If I recall correctly, he was a man about your age. Not a swell, you understand, but not someone from the neighborhood either. He had an air of quality about him, which is why I believed him when he said he was selling the jewels for a friend who'd fallen on hard times. I had no reason to doubt him, at least,'' he added in his own defense, in case Frank was thinking about prosecuting him for dealing in stolen merchandise.

"What did he look like?''

This time Joe really did consider. "Tall and well built. Looked almost like a football player, he was so fit, but he didn't look like no college boy, if you know what I mean. Black hair, very curly. Irish, I'm sure, but no accent. Oh, and he had a scar right here.'' Joe drew a line along his jaw on the right side.

That should make him easy to identify, Frank thought. Now all he had to do was locate the fellow out of the millions of men living in New York City.

SARAH SMILED AS she laid the carefully wrapped infant in her mother's arms. New life was always a cause for rejoicing, and this one especially. Dolly Yardley had lost two others before this one, even though she wasn't yet twenty years old. Her labor had been long and difficult, but both mother and child appeared to be fine now, if a bit weary from their ordeal. Sarah was weary herself, having been up most of the night. She had never been able to figure out why the most difficult births always occurred at night.

"Oh, look, Will, ain't she beautiful?'' the new mother demanded of her young husband, pulling the blanket back from the baby's face so he could admire her.

MURDER ON ASTOR PLACE

Will had spent the night drinking stale beer with his friends in the seedy bar located in the basement of their tenement, so he was hardly in any condition to judge. "Next time we'll have a boy," he said.

Sarah glared at him until her disapproval penetrated his alcoholic haze, and she said, "The baby looks just like Dolly, doesn't she?"

"Oh, yeah," Will agreed as hastily as he could, given his condition. "The spittin' image. She'll be a beauty just like her Ma."

Dolly smiled at that and nodded her approval.

"Have you decided on a name for her yet?" Sarah asked.

"I think I'll call her Edith, after my ma," Dolly said.

"You ain't naming her after that whore," Will protested.

Sarah wanted to jump to Dolly's defense, but Dolly was more than capable of defending herself. "Edith Rose, after both our mothers," she said, sticking out her chin defiantly.

"Rose ain't my mother. I told you that."

"Maybe you should discuss this later, when Dolly's had some time to rest," Sarah suggested as tactfully as she could.

Will seemed perfectly willing to wait. The new father stared at his wife and child for a long moment, as if he couldn't quite bring them into focus, but apparently he was not as drunk as Sarah had thought, because after a moment, he turned to her a little sheepishly and said, "About your fee, Mrs. Brandt. I ain't had much work lately, and I was wondering, could I owe it to you until things is better?"

Sarah knew exactly what kind of work Will Yardley did, and if there hadn't been much of it lately, it was because he'd been too lazy to climb into someone's window and relieve them of their valuables. Or else he'd simply spent all his money treating his friends tonight. She glanced around the comfortably furnished room and wondered how much of the furnishings had been carried down a fire escape in the middle of the night while the rightful owners were sleeping unawares.

"Will, I have a business proposition for you that will take care of whatever you owe me. Let's step into the other room so Dolly and the baby can rest."

Will looked a little uncertain as he followed her out of the bedroom. They lived on the first floor in the front, the choicest location. No need to stumble up steep and dirty flights of stairs in the unlighted stairwells to a higher floor, and whatever fresh air was available would make its way into their front windows.

Unfortunately, as in most tenements, only the front room of the apartment had windows, so the rear rooms were dim even on the sunniest days. Will pulled the bedroom door closed behind him, leaving Dolly and the baby in darkness except for the single gaslight on the wall. The kitchen, which was the middle room, was also dark except for the light coming in the other doorway. Sarah went through it into the front room, where she could see that the rain of the last few days had finally stopped and the sun was coming up strong and bright again.

She turned to Will, who looked a little worried. "What kind of business proposition you got for me, Mrs. Brandt? I know people say things about me in the streets, but I want you to know, I'm an honest man. I never done none of the things—"

"I just need some information, Will. I need to locate a person, and you might have the contacts to help me find him."

"What's this person done?" Will asked suspiciously.

"Nothing that I know of," Sarah lied. Actually, he *might* be perfectly innocent, although an innocent man wasn't likely to behave as this fellow had. "I'd just like to ask him some questions. About a friend of mine."

Will nodded wisely, as if he received requests like this all the time. "Who is this bugger you want to find?"

"His name is Hamilton Fisher. He's a tall fellow. Not

very handsome. His hair is blond and his teeth stick out in front. I think he might be a cadet.''

Will frowned. Plainly, he considered such work beneath him. ''And you want me to bring him to you?''

''Oh, no, nothing like that,'' Sarah assured him hastily. ''I just need to know where he is. Then I'll send someone to talk to him.''

Will nodded, sure he'd figured it out. ''I see it now. You're trying to find some girl he recruited.''

''Something like that,'' Sarah agreed. She was getting far too good at lying.

''And when I find him, I let you know, and we're square?''

''We're square for this baby, and the next one, too. The boy you want so much,'' Sarah added.

Will scratched his chest absently as his gaze drifted toward the back of the flat where his wife and child slept. ''Sure would like to get me a boy.''

''Girls are nice, too. You'll see. And you'll find this fellow for me?''

''I'll find him.''

Sarah hoped he could. Finding Hamilton Fisher would bring her one step closer to finding Alicia's killer.

In fact, it might bring her face to face with him.

5

Frank COULDN'T BELIEVE HE WAS STILL IN THE same state as Manhattan. The wagon he'd hired at the train station in the picturesque little village of Mamoraneck had carried him down winding country lanes through lush fields rampant with wildflowers and past stately lawns that graced enormous mansions. When he thought of the squalid tenements of the Lower East Side and the dives of the Bowery, Frank wondered that they could exist in the same *world* as this place that looked like something out of a fairy tale.

On the other hand, he knew that the rich must have a haven outside the city that the poor could never invade. In the city, no matter how wealthy you were, you couldn't be very far from those who weren't. Fifth Avenue had become home to the wealthy because it was as far as you could get from either of the island's waterfronts and the slums and the vice found there. Even still, it was only a few short blocks away from that vice and could go no farther. Blocks that anyone, no matter how poor or depraved, could walk in a matter of minutes. Trapped on the tiny island of Manhattan, the rich could never hope to have a world completely unto themselves.

This is why, for decades, the rich had been going north

to where the land opened wide and could be purchased in huge parcels that would ensure no encroachment by the unworthy. They had come here to escape the unhealthy air and the unhealthy inhabitants of the city and to live in stately splendor.

And here they could send their daughters when they wanted to hide them, as the VanDamms had wanted to hide Alicia.

Frank glanced at the fellow driving the wagon. He was dressed in rough clothes, obviously a farmer, except instead of being in the fields on this unseasonably warm spring day, he was driving Frank to the VanDamm's summer home.

"Do you farm?" Frank asked.

The fellow looked over at him suspiciously. He was past middle years, his hair white where it straggled out beneath his farmer's hat, and his face was as brown and withered as an old potato. "Used to," he offered.

"But you don't anymore?" Frank said by way of encouragement.

"I drive this wagon. Make more money carrying the swells from the train to their fancy houses than I ever did behind a plow."

This made sense to Frank. "Do you ever drive the VanDamms?"

The fellow shrugged his powerful shoulders. "Sometimes. Mostly, they get their own carriage."

"Did you ever drive their daughter? The younger one, Alicia?"

"Once or twice. She's a sweet little thing. Not like the other one. That one's got a tongue on her could raise a welt on a leather boot."

Frank thought this was probably true. "The VanDamm girl's dead, you know."

He looked surprised. "Is she now? Can't say I'm sorry." He spit a stream of tobacco juice over the side of the wagon. "What happened? Did she try that razor tongue of hers on the wrong man?"

"Not her," Frank said. "The younger one, Alicia. She's the one who's dead."

"The hell you say!" the driver exclaimed. "And her so young. Hardly more'n a babe. She get sick or something?"

Frank watched him carefully as he said, "No, someone murdered her."

The driver gaped at him, his shock almost painful to behold. For a long moment, the only sound was the clop, clop of the draft horse as he plodded on, but finally the driver was able to say, "What happened?"

"That's what I'm trying to find out."

The driver nodded wisely. "That's it, then. I been wondering what a copper's doing out here, asking for the VanDamm place."

Frank frowned. He hadn't told the man his profession, so he must have been able to tell just by looking at him. He wondered what gave him away, but he didn't ask. The man would only lie.

"You didn't, by chance, take her to the train station about a month ago, did you?" he tried. "She would've been alone, or maybe with a young man."

The driver shook his head. "Haven't even seen her in a couple years. They keep 'em close once they start getting ripe."

It took Frank a minute to figure out what he was saying. "They keep a close watch on the girls, you mean?"

"Always afraid they'll get in trouble. You know what young men're like. It ain't so long since you was one yourself."

Frank could hardly remember, but he nodded his agreement. "You ever hear of her getting in trouble? With a young man, I mean?"

But the driver shook his head. "Never heard nothin' about her at all. Like I say, they keep 'em pretty close."

Frank knew he shouldn't be disappointed. The odds that this fellow had driven Alicia and her lover to the train when she'd run away were pretty slim. She would've been much more circumspect. Probably, she stole away in the middle of the night. Maybe she didn't even take the train at all. It was a long carriage ride back to the city and the roads were poor, but she might not have wanted to risk being recognized on the train.

"That's it there," the driver said, pointing with his chin.

Frank looked up and gasped in surprise at the house sitting on a rise before him. It seemed enormous, large enough to accommodate the inhabitants of an entire block of tenements. Myriad windows glittered in the blinding sun and the red bricks glowed. The grounds rolled away gently on every side, the grass newly green in the warm spring sunshine. From a distance, everything looked perfectly peaceful and serene, and why shouldn't it? The murder had taken place far from here, in that other world he'd left behind this morning when he'd boarded the train at Grand Central Station.

This morning he'd imagined that he could come out here and learn more about Alicia VanDamm and why she had run away and with whom. Now, looking at the home from which she had fled, he couldn't even imagine why she had done such a thing. Who in her right mind would leave this beautiful house for the uncertainty of a life alone, hiding in a strange place among people she didn't know? To run away with a lover, that Frank could understand. He could still remember passion, although the memories were sadly dim. He could still remember love, no matter how much he wanted to forget. Without those motivations, Alicia VanDamm's flight made no sense at all.

So now he knew one thing at least: Alicia VanDamm *must* have fled with a lover—or at least *to* a lover—because she never would have simply run away from a place so utterly magnificent for any other reason.

The driver waited, as Frank had previously arranged, since he couldn't depend upon the VanDamm's servants to provide him transportation back. Because this was an unsanctioned visit—Sarah Brandt had warned him not to ask VanDamm's permission because he most likely would have refused or at the very least warned his servants against revealing anything—Frank was going to have to rely on his ability to either charm or intimidate. If it had to be the latter, he wanted a guaranteed method of escape if things got too unpleasant.

Up close the house looked even more impressive. The carved oak door appeared solid enough to withstand an onslaught of armed barbarians. Through the spotless windows Frank could see the lace curtains which his mother had always told him only "quality" folks had. He'd have to get his mother some lace curtains just to prove her wrong.

Frank didn't have to knock. This was the country, and his approach had probably been observed when he was still halfway down the lane. The front door swung open before he reached the top of the porch steps. A formidable looking woman glared out at him, probably ready to run him off. Her ample figure was encased in black, giving the impression of rigidly tucked upholstery. Frank wondered if she was in mourning or if she always wore black. Somehow, he thought it was the latter. Her hair was hidden beneath the white cap of a servant, but her face was set into an authoritative glare which told him she was no ordinary servant.

"Good morning," Frank said, trying out the manners he so seldom used. "I'm Detective Sergeant Frank Malloy of the New York City Police."

If he'd thought to cow her, he failed miserably. She simply raised her chin another notch and looked down her hawklike nose at him. "Then what are you doing out here?" she demanded.

"I'm trying to find out who killed Miss Alicia Van-Damm," he replied, hoping to strike some nerve.

Her face tightened for an instant in what might have been a spasm of grief, but she gave no other sign of weakness. "You'd best go back to the city then, since that's where she was killed. You won't find no murderers here.''

Frank hadn't expected to, of course. "I was hoping to get some information about her. Maybe that will help me find who killed her.''

"I'm sure nobody here will be gossiping about Miss Alicia, so if that's what you're hoping, you came a long way for nothing.''

Frank figured she'd make certain none of the servants told any tales about Alicia. "I don't want gossip. I need to know when she left and who she left with.''

"We don't know,'' the housekeeper insisted, her broad, homely face reddening. "I already explained everything to Mr. VanDamm. We just woke up one morning, and she was gone. We don't know nothing else. Leave us alone.''

"Mr. VanDamm said I could search her room and question all the servants, just in case,'' Frank lied.

"I don't believe you,'' she said, her small eyes widening in alarm.

"Do you want me to go back to the city and tell him you wouldn't cooperate with my investigation?''

He could see her inner struggle. She didn't want to risk VanDamm's disapproval, but she wasn't certain which decision would bring it. Refusing Frank admittance seemed the sensible course, since VanDamm was most certainly not in the habit of having the police search his home and interrogate his servants. On the other hand, Alicia had been murdered, not a common state of affairs to be sure. Would this render all the usual rules null and void?

"I'd have to be sure Mr. VanDamm gave you permission,'' she hedged.

Frank wasn't about to let a little thing like that stop him. "I didn't bring a letter of reference, if that's what you're after.''

She sniffed derisively at him. "I'll telephone to find out.''

Damn. Frank had forgotten that they had a telephone here. "Go ahead,'' he bluffed, "but be quick about it. I haven't got all day.''

The chances that VanDamm would be at home in the middle of the morning were probably small, and somehow he couldn't imagine the mighty man stooping to speak to a servant on the telephone in any case. Of course, there was that snooty butler, but would he take it upon himself to withhold permission for Frank to do his duty?

Left standing on the doorstep, Frank decided to make himself comfortable. Might as well let the old bat find him taking his ease like a regular guest, not holding his hat in his hand waiting anxiously for her return.

When she returned, he was lounging quite comfortably, sitting on the steps with his legs out in front of him, crossed at the ankles, and leaning back against one of the massive pillars, his hat tipped down over his eyes. As if he had all the time in the world and not a single worry that VanDamm was going to have him tossed out on his ear.

She glared at him again, but she said, "Mr. VanDamm was out."

Frank managed not to betray the surge of relief he felt. "Are you going to keep me waiting here on the porch until he comes back in?" he inquired with all the annoyance he could muster.

For an uncomfortable moment, he thought she was, so he took the really big gamble and rose to his feet, dusted off his seat and reached into his pocket, pulling out his notebook and pencil. "What's your name?" he demanded.

"Mrs. Hightower," she replied, nonplussed.

Frank nodded ominously and wrote it down. "I'll be sure to tell Mr. VanDamm it was you wouldn't let me in."

He was gratified to see a flash of fear in her close-set eyes. Fear always worked to his advantage.

"You're not to touch anything in her room," she said, as if it had been her decision all along to allow him inside. "You can look around, but you're to leave everything just as it is. That was Mr. VanDamm's orders. Nobody is to touch anything.''

"I'll want to talk to the servants, too. All of them. Alone." He didn't want her intimidating them into lying to protect Alicia's good name.

"They don't know anything. None of us knows anything."

"Then it's my time that's wasted, isn't it?" Frank replied, tucking his notebook back into his pocket but giving it a little pat to remind her that he had her name if she thought about giving him any more trouble.

She sniffed again and started into the house, surging ahead like a schooner at full mast. Frank had to assume she expected him to follow, which he did, but the instant he reached the doorway, she turned abruptly and snapped, "Wipe your feet before you come in here!"

Cow, he thought, but he wiped his feet. Didn't want her complaining to VanDamm about his manners. It would be bad enough when she complained about his visit.

The interior of the house was dim, since the windows were all heavily draped. The sun faded fabrics, as his mother had told him time and again, and the VanDamms had a lot of fabric to fade. It hung in lavish folds around each window and was upholstered onto numerous pieces of furniture. This Frank glimpsed through a series of doorways during his hasty trip through the entrance hall to the long staircase at its opposite end. The hallway was paneled in dark wainscoting and wallpaper so elaborately patterned it made him dizzy to stare at it. An amazingly large crystal chandelier hung down from the second story. He knew exactly what Kathleen would've said: *How in heaven's name do they clean it?*

He followed the housekeeper up the stairs and remembered when he'd followed Sarah Brandt up a similar set of stairs. He'd been tempted to look at her ankles, but he wasn't the least bit tempted to look at Mrs. Hightower's.

Upstairs, the hallway branched to the left and right,

seeming to go on forever in each direction. She turned right, still surging along like a ship at full sail, never even glancing back to make sure he was behind her. A thick carpet muffled their footsteps, and Frank was struck by how silent the house was. Silent and forlorn, as if it were mourning the loss of the girl who had lived here. Or maybe it was just the result of the place being uninhabited, Frank thought, because no one really lived here even when they were here.

A little astonished at such a profound thought, Frank almost didn't realize the housekeeper had stopped in front of one of the closed doors. Her hand was on the knob, but she hesitated for a long moment. Frank thought she was just being obstinate, making him wait so she could show her power over him. But then he noticed she was blinking furiously as she stared resolutely at the panel of the door. Good God, she was trying not to weep. For all her coldness, she must have genuinely cared for the dead girl.

Maybe Frank could use this to his advantage.

After waiting respectfully for her to regain her composure, he remarked, "You must've known her a long time."

"Since the day she was born, right here in this house." Her voice was thick with unshed tears, tears she was probably too proud to let Frank see.

"Mr. VanDamm said she'd been here a little over a month. I guess she hadn't been feeling too well."

Mrs. Hightower, fully recovered now, glared at him. "It was nerves, is all. That girl was never sick a day in her life."

"What did she have to be nervous about?"

Her thin lips thinned down even more, obviously because she realized she'd already told him more than she'd intended. "I'm sure it's not my place to know. Well-bred girls are all high strung."

"Like thoroughbred horses," Frank suggested.

Mrs. Hightower did not approve of his comparison.

"Miss Alicia was sensitive. She let things upset her."

Now if Frank could only find out what those things were. "She was like her mother, then?" he suggested.

"Her mother?" she echoed suspiciously.

"Mrs. VanDamm," Frank prodded, wondering if she could have actually forgotten her own mistress.

Her expression pinched with disapproval. "She's nothing like Mrs. VanDamm. She's an angel."

Frank watched as she realized the irony of her assertion. Her strong face sagged with despair as the reality of her loss struck her anew.

He gave her only a moment to absorb the impact before using her weakness to press his case. "Is the door locked?"

She glanced at it in surprise, as if she'd only just realized where she was. "No, of course not. Why would it be locked?"

"Then you can go about your work while I look around. I'll let you know when I'm ready to talk to the servants."

For a second he thought she would refuse to leave, but then she glanced at the door again, and he could see how painful it was for her to even consider opening it. Just as he'd suspected it would be.

After making him wait another few seconds, she nodded. "I'll be in the kitchen." And then a final, sharp, "Don't disturb anything," before she launched herself down the hallway again.

Frank waited until she was on her way down the stairs before he opened the door. It was solid oak and moved silently on its hinges. No squeaking here. The interior of the room was dark like the rest of the house, the drapes drawn against the glare of the sun. Giving his eyes a chance to adjust, Frank looked around, getting his bearings. Then he went to one of the windows on the far wall and pulled back the draperies. He needed a minute to figure out how the chords worked for tying it back, and when he had it secured, he looked around again.

The room was large, larger than his entire flat back in the city. And if he'd known nothing about Alicia Van-Damm before, he would know everything about her from simply seeing this place. While her room at the boarding-house had been stark and impersonal, this one was hers entirely. The furniture was white with gold leaf accents, everything curved and delicate and graceful and com-pletely feminine. The drapes and the coverlet on the bed and the canopy over it were all a pale rose and of some kind of rich material. The wallpaper depicted scenes of young maidens frolicking gaily. In one corner sat a doll's house. Frank walked over to examine it more closely, and he saw it was furnished with remarkable attention to de-tail, even to the curtains on the windows. Everything was all arranged, just so, and the tiny doll family were seated around the dining room table. They even had real china dishes and a maid to serve them. Next to the house stood a chest, and when Frank lifted the lid, he found toys in-side. Some dolls, worn from years of playing, the paint of their faces almost rubbed off and their clothes ragged from use. A top. A life-sized tea set. Everything had a neglected air about it, as if it hadn't been used in some time, but Frank couldn't help noticing the things were still here, near at hand, as if their owner hadn't quite been ready to part with them yet. As if the owner hadn't been ready to leave her childhood just yet.

Frank had been thinking of Alicia VanDamm as a young woman. She was pregnant, after all, so she most certainly had a lover, but now he was struck with how recently she had taken that step into adulthood. So re-cently that her toys were still here in her room, as if she wanted to be able to maintain her ties with the world of childhood while also trying her hand at being an adult.

Frank glanced around again, trying to imagine what kind of a person Alicia VanDamm must have been. Her room spoke of innocence. And purity. Neither of which applied to Alicia VanDamm. Something was out of kilter here, and Frank needed to find out what.

And more importantly, why.

He started his search of the room and conducted it systematically, going through each drawer and cupboard carefully so as not to disturb the contents. Mrs. Hightower would probably know what he'd done, but at least she wouldn't be able to complain he'd left things in a mess. And of course if he didn't leave things in a mess, he could always deny he'd searched the room at all. He reached beneath the mattress and checked under the chair bottoms and behind each piece of furniture. Behind and under every drawer. He even took each of the books off the shelf and shook them out. Examining every possible hiding place. He had no idea what he was looking for, of course. A diary naming her killer would have been just the thing, but naturally, he didn't find one.

Nor did he find anything else. No love letters from the father of her child. No secret messages. Nothing. He'd looked in every possible hiding place, even checking beneath the rugs and tapping on the wall and floor for possible hidden compartments. But if what he failed to find disturbed him, what he did find disturbed him even more: The girl who had lived in this room was still in every way a child. The books on the shelf were mostly lesson books with a few volumes of nursery rhymes and stories. Even the clothes she'd left behind were decidedly juvenile. No scheming seductress had lived here, at least not from any evidence Frank could discover. If he hadn't known about her condition, he might actually have believed Mrs. Hightower's description of Alicia as having been an angel.

But even angels fell, as he remembered from his catechism lessons. Now he'd have to find out how this one had.

Mrs. Hightower had been more than reluctant for the other servants to leave their tasks, but once again Frank was able to intimidate her into accommodating him. He only hoped he wasn't around when she found out VanDamm hadn't given his permission for any of this.

One by one the other servants paraded through the

small back parlor she had given him to use. And one by one they insisted they knew nothing of why Miss Alicia had run away or even how she had accomplished it. Either Mrs. Hightower had instructed them or else they really had no knowledge. Frank was very much afraid it was the latter.

But finally his patience was rewarded. When he'd gone through a half-dozen or so of the people who knew nothing, suddenly, he found a girl who knew everything. And even more than everything. She knew Alicia.

She was a chambermaid, Mrs. Hightower informed him, a pretty girl with bright cinnamon-colored eyes and lots of auburn curls peeking out from beneath her cap. Her name, she told him, was Lizzie.

"Short for Elizabeth, don't you know? But nobody ever calls me that, now me Mum's passed on. She only called it when she was that mad at me, too. I always knowed when she was gonna give me a thrashing, 'cause she'd say, Miss Elizabeth, get yourself in here right now!"

Frank had to bite his lip to keep from grinning in triumph. Instead, he settled back, ready to play his part. "Well, now, Lizzie, I'm trying to find out if anybody knows how Miss Alicia got away from the house the night she left."

For a moment, he thought she was going to be all right, but then her lower lip began to quiver and her eyes flooded with tears, and in the next instant, she was sobbing into her apron. Actually, Frank had been expecting this reaction from someone long before now. He'd been a little disturbed that the other servants had seemed so unmoved by Alicia's death. This probably meant they hadn't been very close to her, but this girl had. Her tears betrayed that closeness. He waited patiently, knowing his patience would be amply rewarded, until she had sniffled her way back to coherence again.

"Oh, I'm that sorry, sir. I didn't mean to cry thataway. Mrs. Hightower would have me hide, but when I think about poor Miss Alicia . . ."

"You knew her well, I guess," Frank ventured.

"I was her maid for two years, her personal lady's maid, but when she comes out here this time, Mrs. Hightower, she tells me, Lizzie, she says, Miss Alicia won't be needing a maid anymore, so we'll make you a chambermaid. A *chambermaid*! I'm a trained lady's maid, I am, and now I have to empty chamber pots! Can you feature it?"

Frank assured her he could not. "Why didn't she need a maid?"

"I'm sure I don't know! Oh, Mrs. Hightower would do for her, help her get dressed and such, but she was the only one ever went near her. None of the rest of us could so much as speak to her, not even me, and I'd been with her for two years!"

Frank had a pretty good idea why the servants were being kept away from Alicia, but he didn't want to share his thoughts with Lizzie.

"Then I guess you wouldn't have any idea how she could've gotten out of the house the night she disappeared."

"Oh, cor, she probably walked right out the front door, don't you know. No reason why she shouldn't, is there?"

"I don't know, is there?" Frank countered, very interested indeed in this theory.

"Not at all. The servants, we all sleep on the third floor, even me since I'm not allowed to do for Miss Alicia anymore. If she wanted to go out, there was nobody to stop her or even to hear her. The front door was locked, but the key's right beside it, so she could just open it and walk out, bold as you please. I mean, there's no reason to hide the key. Who'd think about anybody inside getting out? The locks is to keep people on the outside from getting in, ain't they?"

Frank had to agree that they were. "So none of the servants would have known her plans? Couldn't anybody have helped her get away?"

"Oh, no, sir. It's worth your job to disobey Mrs. Hightower, and none of us even spoke to Miss Alicia since she's been here this time. Oh, except Harvey, of course.''

Frank felt a rush of excitement, but he managed not to betray himself to Lizzie so he wouldn't frighten her. ''Who's Harvey?''

''He's the groom. He'd take her riding every day, or nearly every day. That girl loved to ride, she did. And she loved that horse of hers even more. I never could understand it. She'd always smell like the stable when she got back, and I'd have to pour her a bath and . . .'' Lizzie's voice caught, and she covered her mouth. Her eyes filled with tears again, but she managed to keep her composure this time.

''You must miss her,'' Frank said kindly.

Lizzie lifted her chin and swallowed her tears. ''I been missing her for a while,'' she said, angry now. ''It was so strange, like she was prisoner here . . . except I guess she wasn't really, or else they would've kept her locked up. Then she'd still be here, wouldn't she?''

''Unless they didn't think she had any way of escaping,'' Frank suggested.

''That's true enough,'' Lizzie allowed. ''And Lord knows, she didn't. I mean, who would help her get away? You'd be turned out without a reference.''

''And all the servants are still here, I guess.''

''Oh, yes, every one of us. Nobody here would go against Mr. VanDamm, not even for poor Miss Alicia.''

''Why do you call her poor?''

Lizzie blinked in surprise. ''Because she's dead, ain't she?''

Frank blinked back. ''Well, yes, but is there any other reason?''

''Why should there be? She was rich. Had everything she wanted and more. And such a sweet girl. Never a harsh word for anybody. It was always, Lizzie, if you wouldn't mind, and Lizzie, if you please. Not like she was ordering you around or nothing. Like you was doing her a favor to do for her. A real lady. Not like some I could name.''

Frank could probably name the same one. ''Well, Lizzie, I want to thank you for your time.''

''Did I tell you anything that'll help?'' she asked anxiously. ''I sure want to see whoever killed Miss Alicia get what's coming to him.''

''You helped a lot,'' he said, rewarding her with a smile. ''Now could you tell me where to find Harvey?''

SARAH WAS BONE weary as she made her way down the sidewalk toward her flat. The sun told her the hour was hardly past noon, but she'd been up early delivering a breech baby that hadn't wanted to leave the comfort of his mother's womb. Her arms ached and her legs ached and her head ached and the last thing she wanted was to make small talk, so she groaned inwardly when she saw her neighbor, Mrs. Elsworth, sweeping her front stoop.

Maybe she was just enjoying the delightfully warm day after winter's last gasp had finally given way to true spring, but more likely, she'd seen Sarah approaching and come out on purpose to engage her in conversation. Keeping house for her widowed son wasn't nearly enough to keep her occupied, and she did enjoy hearing about Sarah's work.

''Good morning, Mrs. Elsworth,'' Sarah called as she reached the stoop where the old woman was sweeping.

Mrs. Elsworth looked up in apparent surprise, her wrinkled face breaking into a delighted smile. ''Mrs. Brandt, don't tell me you've been out all night!''

''I certainly have, delivering a fat baby girl who had made up her mind to come into the world backwards.''

''Oh, my, I hope everyone is all right.''

''Right as they can be.'' Only then did Sarah realize that something wasn't quite right with Mrs. Elsworth's sweeping. ''Were you sweeping dirt *into* the house?'' she asked in alarm. Could the old woman be losing her mental faculties?

"Of course I was," she replied without the slightest hesitation. "This is a new broom." She held it up so Sarah could see that for herself. "You've got to sweep something into the house before you sweep anything out with it, or else all your luck will be swept out the door. Surely you knew that."

"Oh, yes, of course," was all Sarah could think to say.

Mrs. Elsworth needed no further encouragement. "Won't you come in and take a bite with me? I'm sure you haven't had breakfast, and I've got some fresh bread and elderberry jam that I put up last year. It's hard to find fresh berries in the city, but Nelson got them in the country for me." Nelson was her son who had his own accounting firm. "You can tell me all about the new baby, and oh, dear, I don't suppose you've seen the papers, but someone sent a bomb to that nice gentleman, Commissioner Roosevelt."

"A *bomb?*" Sarah echoed incredulously. "Are you sure? Did it explode? Was he hurt?"

"Oh, I'm quite sure. It was in the *Times* this morning, but it didn't explode, thank heaven, and no one was hurt. Mr. Roosevelt didn't even receive it. The postman discovered it, I think. I have the paper inside, so you can read it for yourself."

Much as she would like to read the story for herself, it could wait. Right now, Sarah wanted nothing more than to crawl into her bed and sleep the clock around. She was still trying to think of a gracious way to decline the invitation, however, when she saw her salvation coming down the street.

Will Yardley was walking quickly and checking back over his shoulder every few seconds, as if afraid he was being followed.

"I'm afraid I'll have to pass on the elderberry jam, Mrs. Elsworth. It looks like I'm getting a visitor."

Mrs. Elsworth frowned as she stared down the street at the approaching figure. "You don't mean that little guttersnipe, do you? What would a creature like that want with a lady like you?''

''I delivered his wife of a baby girl a few days ago.''

Mrs. Elsworth was instantly all sympathy. ''Oh, my, do you suppose she's taken ill? Childbed fever is a horrible thing. I had a sister who—''

''I remember,'' Sarah said quickly, recalling all too well the story of the sister who had died of it. Mrs. Elsworth had told her about it at least a dozen times. ''I've got to see what Mr. Yardley wants. Good morning to you!''

She hurried to meet Will at her front stoop. He nodded, tipping his cap to her before looking around again. Surely, he didn't think anyone would have followed him to her house. But then, his conscience was probably troubled enough that he was always wary lest one of his past sins catch up with him.

''Are you going out somewheres?'' he asked, not bothering with a greeting.

''Just getting home. Are Dolly and the baby all right?''

He blinked in surprise. ''Sure. Why wouldn't they be? I come because of . . . that other matter.'' He glanced around again, as if he were afraid of eavesdroppers. ''Could we go inside to talk about it? I feel funny talking on the street like this.''

Sarah hid her smile. ''Of course.''

She unlocked the door and led him inside.

He looked around curiously at the room that had once been Tom's office and which now served as hers. She still had some equipment for which she had little use, since she didn't practice the advanced forms of medicine that Tom had, but she was loath to get rid of anything he had once owned. She'd lost too much of him already.

Will's slender hands moved restlessly as he studied the contents of the office, tugging on his earlobe and fingering his chin and massaging his chest, as if he had to keep checking to make sure his physical self was still all there.

''So Dolly and Edith Rose are doing well?'' she asked

as she set down her bag and removed her hat, hanging it on a peg on the wall.

"Just fine," he said, his eyes still taking in the curiosities around him. He seemed especially fascinated by the examining table visible behind a screen in the corner. "She said you was to see her and Rosie yesterday."

Sarah managed not to smile. Dolly had told her he refused to call the baby Edith. "I try to check on the new mothers regularly until they're back on their feet. Dolly said you were out when I called."

"Yeah, I, uh, I had a job."

Sarah could just imagine. She almost said, "In broad daylight?" but managed to restrain herself. Instead she said, "Have you found out where Hamilton Fisher is? Is that why you came?"

Will's restless gaze touched Sarah for a moment, then darted away again. She realized he wasn't quite as interested in her office furnishings as she had thought. Instead, he seemed to be avoiding her gaze. "I don't know where he is, but I found out *who* he is," he said. Oddly, he didn't seem the least bit proud of this admission.

"Who is he?"

Will jammed his wandering hands into his pockets as if trying to confine them. Then he finally turned and faced her, his eyes cold and relentless. "He ain't no cadet, least not that I could find out. He's . . . well, he fancies hisself a *detective*."

"He works for the *police*?" Sarah exclaimed.

"Not likely," Will sneered. "He works private. For some big fancy lawyer uptown what takes care of all the nobs. He hires out and spies on folks and finds out their secrets so the lawyer can get the goods on 'em."

This wasn't making any sense to Sarah. Why would a lawyer's detective be spying on Alicia? "Do you know this lawyer's name? The one he works for, I mean?"

Will nodded once, sharply, and for a second Sarah was afraid that was all the answer she was going to get. Then he said, "Sylvester Mattingly," through gritted teeth, as if speaking the syllables hurt him somehow.

The name sounded vaguely familiar, and Sarah supposed she had probably read it in the newspaper. "What do you know about this Mattingly?"

Will's gaze darted away again, this time to inspect the ceiling, and his lips thinned out to a bloodless line.

"Will?" she prodded.

"I don't know much," he said, as if he were warning her. "I don't deal with his kind, you understand. He's a little above me. But from what I hear, he's a real dangerous man to cross. *Real* dangerous. And they say if you've got enough money, this Mattingly can get you out of any kind of trouble there is."

Any kind? Sarah wondered, remembering the kind of trouble Alicia was in, but she asked, "Even murder?"

Will's gaze was steady and maybe a little frightened. "I wouldn't know that, Mrs. Brandt. You'll have to ask Mr. Mattingly."

6

Frank shouldn't have been surprised to discover that the stables at the VanDamm estate were as neatly kept as the house. He found Harvey mucking out one of the stalls, but the groom wasn't exactly what Frank had been expecting.

The instant Lizzie had mentioned Harvey, Frank had been fairly certain he'd learned the identity of the father of Alicia's child. Up until now, he'd been unable to determine how she could ever have been alone with any man long enough to have conceived that child, and then Lizzie had described the perfect opportunity. Alicia wouldn't have been the first young woman to be seduced by a handsome and charming underling with an eye toward bettering himself, and long horseback rides would have provided the perfect opportunity for such a seduction.

But while he was tall and well built, Harvey wasn't young, and he certainly wasn't handsome or charming, not by anyone's standards. In the dim light of the stable, he appeared to be near forty, and his weathered face showed the effects of a lifetime spent out of doors.

He looked up when he heard Frank outside the door of the stall. Squinting into the shadows, he asked, "What can I do for you, sir?"

"I'm Detective Sergeant Frank Malloy from New York, and if you're Harvey, I'd like to talk to you about Alicia VanDamm."

A spasm of pain twisted his face. Plainly, he felt the girl's loss, although he was too manly to give way to tears as Lizzie had.

"I don't know what I can tell you," he said, leaning his pitchfork against the wall and taking his time making his way out of the stall. He seemed to need that time to gather himself. "I ain't seen her for over a month now, not since she left here."

Frank stepped back to allow him room to come out. Harvey's black hair was damp and curled where it clung to his forehead and neck, and his workshirt showed rings of sweat. His body was sinewy and strong, and Frank tried to see him as a young girl might. No matter how he tried, though, he couldn't picture Harvey as the scheming seducer. Then the groom stepped into a shaft of light that illuminated his face. Frank felt the shock of recognition at the sight of the scar running along his jawline.

Harvey was the man who had pawned Alicia's jewelry.

Now Frank knew that whatever Harvey told him would probably be a lie, a lie designed to protect him and no one else. Armed with that knowledge, Frank grasped his lapels and rocked back on his heels as if every nerve in his body weren't tingling with the awareness that he might very well be confronting Alicia's killer.

"I hear you spent a lot of time with Miss Alicia," Frank ventured.

Harvey nodded. "Yes, sir. She liked to ride more than anything. Loved that little mare of hers. Buttercup's her name. Miss Alicia named her when she was ten. The mare was a birthday present that year."

"She rode every day?"

"Except Sunday. It wasn't proper for her to ride on Sunday."

Frank pretended to consider this. "I see. And was it proper for her to go out alone with you?"

Harvey frowned. "I'm the groom. Somebody had to keep an eye on her, in case anything happened."

"And did something happen?"

"I don't know what you mean."

Frank had a feeling he knew very well. "Weren't you afraid for her to be riding in her condition?"

"What condition was that?" He seemed genuinely puzzled.

Frank studied him for a long moment, waiting for some break that would reveal he was lying. But either he was the best liar Frank had ever encountered, or else he was truly ignorant.

"Alicia was with child."

Harvey's eyes widened with shock for a second before his face flooded with outrage. "You should burn in hell for telling such an ugly lie about that poor, sweet child! Maybe you are the police, but that don't give you the right to speak ill of the dead nor to speak such filth about a girl you didn't even know!"

"You don't think it's possible, then?" Frank asked, as if he really valued Harvey's opinion.

"She weren't no more'n a child herself!"

"She was sixteen," Frank reminded him.

"Just turned! She wasn't even in society yet! A girl like her didn't even know any men!"

"She knew you."

It took Harvey a moment to comprehend, and when he did, his face flushed scarlet.

"God damn you to hell!" He drew back his fist, but Frank had already thrown up his arms in defense before Harvey caught himself. As angry as he was, he hadn't forgotten that Frank was a policeman. Even out here, that meant something.

Harvey dropped his hand, the fury still roiling in his eyes. "She was like a daughter to me! I taught her to ride her first pony, when she was so small her feet wouldn't even reach the stirrups no matter how short I made them. I loved that child, and you think I could hurt her? You better take your filthy mouth and your filthy lies back to New York City with you.''

But Frank still had one ace left to play, one that should dampen Harvey's indignation. ''Don't act so innocent with me, Harvey. I know you stole Alicia's jewelry, and I know where you pawned it. The pawnbroker will identify you.''

The color left his face as rapidly as it had come, and the fury faded from his eyes, leaving only despair. ''How'd you know?'' he asked hoarsely.

''The scar on your jaw. The pawnbroker described you. It isn't often he gets such quality merchandise, so he remembered you very well.''

''I never stole anything,'' he said, trying for belligerence but falling somewhat short. ''She give them to me. Asked could I sell them for her. She needed the money because she was running away. I had to help her, didn't I? I couldn't let her go off alone with no money. What would happen to her?''

Frank glared at him in contempt. ''You say you loved her, and you still helped her run away from her family? What did you think would become of her, a girl alone like that? The money from her jewelry would be gone soon enough, and then how would she live?''

''I thought she'd come to her senses before the money ran out. Or her father would anyway.''

''Her father?''

''He was going to marry her off to some nob. Somebody she hated. She said she'd throw herself in the Sound before she'd do it. She meant it, too. She was young and a girl, but she could be just as bullheaded as her father. I couldn't let her harm herself, could I? So I helped her run away. And I had to make sure she was safe, so I found her a place to live, and I sold the jewelry for her so she'd have money to live. I figured she wouldn't stay long. She'd get scared before too long, and she'd want to come home, but maybe her father would back down first. Maybe he'd be willing to do anything to get her back. That's what I figured, except . . .''

"Except what?" Frank prodded when he hesitated.

Harvey rubbed his work-roughened hands on his pant legs and studied the toes of his worn and muddy boots. When he looked up again, his eyes were full of pain again. "Except we didn't figure out how she was going to get word to him or how she'd know if he'd really changed his mind. She couldn't get in touch with him because he'd find her, and I couldn't tell him I'd helped her get away or that I knew where she was."

"Because you'd lose your job," Frank guessed.

"I'd lose more than that. Mr. VanDamm, he's a hard man. He has no pity in him, and he wouldn't be kind to anybody who crossed him."

Remembering VanDamm, Frank could believe this. Harvey would probably be right to fear for his very life if his employer found out he'd stolen his daughter. At least that's how VanDamm would likely see it.

"You ain't gonna tell him are you?" Harvey asked in sudden alarm, obviously having just realized what he had revealed to a perfect stranger.

"I don't have any reason to. Yet. And unless you killed Alicia—"

"I'd never harm a hair on her head!" Harvey insisted. "And I was here when it happened. You can ask anybody."

"Then you've got no reason to worry. But I'm curious about one thing. How did you get her away?"

"By boat. I hired a fishing boat for the night. Sailed her over and took her to the rooming house I'd found. It was a respectable place. I thought . . ."

His voice broke, and he covered his face with his large hands.

"You thought she'd be safe there," Frank suggested.

Harvey nodded, and his shoulders shook as he wept silently for a few moments. Frank didn't want to watch, but he wasn't quite finished. And a man in the throes of grief might reveal more than was prudent.

When Harvey had regained his composure, he wiped his eyes on his shirtsleeves and gave Frank a look that defied him to disapprove of the display of grief.

Frank was in no position to judge, so he simply said, "Alicia really was with child. She was about six months gone."

Harvey was incredulous. "That just ain't possible!"

"Apparently not. You got any idea who might've been responsible?"

Harvey shook his head, shattered.

"Could that've been why her father wanted her to marry?"

He shook his head again. "I don't know," he said helplessly. "She never said nothing about it to me."

"Who was the man her father wanted her to marry? The one she was running away from?"

"She never said. It was like she couldn't even bear to say his name. And it wasn't my place to ask."

Of course not, although Frank couldn't help thinking how much easier it would have been if he had. He'd have to go back and talk to the housekeeper again. She'd know. Or maybe Lizzie would. Frank didn't think Lizzie missed much, although she hadn't known about Alicia's pregnancy. Frank would have bet money on it. Mrs. Hightower knew, though. That's why she'd kept the other servants away from Alicia, so they wouldn't find out. She wouldn't have been able to keep that secret forever, though.

"Detective?"

Frank looked up, startled out of his reverie.

"Do you know . . . are they going to bury her here?" His voice sounded small with grief, and Frank couldn't help thinking how differently her family had responded to the news of her death. He'd seen much more true mourning from the hired help than from any of her so-called loved ones.

"I don't know where they're going to bury her," Frank said.

Just one more thing he didn't know, added to a very long list.

SARAH WAS SAMPLING the pot of stew she'd had simmering all afternoon when she heard the doorbell jangle. With a sigh of exasperation, she replaced the heavy lid on the big pot and carefully slid it to a cooler place on her coal stove. She wasn't a very accomplished cook. Her early training had assumed she would have servants to handle those duties, and since Tom's death, she hadn't often been inspired to prepare anything fancier than the odd chop or steak. And it seemed that every time she did accomplish some culinary feat, as she just had with the stew, someone would decide to give birth before she had a chance to eat it.

Wiping her hands on her apron, she made her way resignedly out of her living quarters into the office area. She could see a man's silhouette on the window. Ordinarily, she would have asked who it was, but she realized instantly that she already knew and opened the door to Detective Sergeant Frank Malloy.

He looked so unhappy to be there, she couldn't help but smile. "Good evening, Detective," she said cheerfully.

He didn't smile back. "I got your message."

Although it had taken all her fortitude, Sarah had forced herself to return to Police Headquarters to inform Malloy of what she had learned about Hamilton Fisher. This time, when he wasn't available, she had declined the desk sergeant's sly invitation to wait—one visit to the interrogation rooms was enough—and simply left word that she had some important information for Malloy.

"I'm sure you'll understand why I didn't wait for you this time," she said, still smiling because he still looked so annoyed.

"Don't think for one minute that I came here because

you sent for me, Mrs. Brandt. The main reason I'm here
is to find out who exactly it was told you to investigate
this case yourself?'' He looked as if he expected her to
feel some shame for having done so. Sarah believed this
was unreasonable of him.

"I'm only trying to help," she said.

He was unimpressed. "I don't need any help. Especially yours."

"Have you found out who Ham Fisher is yet?" she
challenged.

The color came to his face, and Sarah couldn't be sure
if it was anger or embarrassment. She rather thought it
was anger.

"Mrs. Brandt," he said very distinctly, as if he were
holding his temper with great difficulty, "a girl was murdered. Whoever killed her wouldn't hesitate to kill another
woman if he thought she was going to get him caught.
Have you thought about that while you've been running
around asking questions?"

Actually, she hadn't, but she didn't want Malloy to
think he'd frightened her. "I'm just gathering information. *Secondhand* information. The killer will never even
know I was the one asking about him."

He seemed unimpressed by this argument, too. "You're
sure about this, are you? I guess you midwife for a lot of
killers, which is how you know so much about them."

Now Sarah was getting angry, too. "I'm not stupid, and
I'm not going to be foolish, either, Mr. Malloy. I'm not
going to try to *find* the killer myself. I'm just trying to
help *you* find him."

For a second she was sure he was going to insist once
again that he didn't need her help, but apparently, he
thought better of it. "I guess if you're set on getting yourself killed, I shouldn't complain. This time the killer
might leave some clues that would make him easier to
find."

Sarah refused to rise to his bait. "Rest assured that I'm
not quite *that* anxious to help," she assured him sweetly.

She heard the door to the Elsworth house next door open, and she knew she'd been foolish to allow this conversation to go on so long right here on her doorstep. Certainly, it would have attracted Mrs. Elsworth's attention, and if Sarah didn't take action, it would be attracting more than her attention in another moment.

"Maybe we should discuss this inside," she suggested, looking meaningfully at the figure in black who had appeared on the next porch.

Mrs. Elsworth waved. "Nice evening, isn't it?" she called. "Such a change after the snow the other day."

Sarah agreed and returned the wave. "Should I introduce you?" she asked Malloy in a whisper. "Or should we go inside?"

He didn't appear too eager to accept the invitation, but he was just as reluctant as she to continue this conversation in front of eavesdroppers. She stepped aside to allow him to enter.

"That's Mrs. Elsworth," she explained, closing the door. "Nothing is ever too insignificant to escape her attention."

Malloy grunted his reply and stepped into her office.

He wasn't as fascinated by her equipment as Will Yardley had been. He took it in with one swift glance before turning his attention back to her. "All right. What do you know about Ham Fisher?" he asked, as if he didn't expect very much at all.

"Apparently, I was wrong about him being a cadet, or at least that's not his main occupation," she said. "My, uh, informant tells me that he works as a private detective for an attorney named Sylvester Mattingly."

Malloy couldn't hide his surprise, although Sarah suspected he wanted to. "Mattingly? Who told you this?"

"I wouldn't want to put you in danger by revealing my source," Sarah said, delighted at the opportunity to prick him a little.

Malloy regarded her for a long moment, his dark eyes equally outraged and admiring. He might hate her sass, but he enjoyed her spirit. Sarah decided to show him a little more of it.

"I don't often deliver babies for killers, but I do occasionally encounter people who are, shall we say, a little less than honest. Everyone has babies, Mr. Malloy, the just and the unjust alike."

He ignored this. "If Fisher was a detective, why would he have been following Alicia VanDamm?"

"Probably he was trying to find her for her family."

Malloy shook his head. "Then why didn't they know where she was? He lived in the house almost a week. If he'd just been sent to trace her, as soon as he located her, they would've swarmed down and dragged her home. And he wouldn't've had any reason to move into the house at all."

Sarah hated to admit it, but he was right. "Could he have been trying to find her for someone else?"

He weighed this for a long moment, and Sarah was somewhat gratified to realize he was at least giving her theory the courtesy of his consideration. "Then we have to ask the same question: Why didn't he just tell *that* person where she was? Why move into the house and watch her for days?"

"Maybe the person trying to find her was afraid of shocking her, considering her condition. Maybe she would've been too upset—or even frightened—if they'd forced her to return home, and she might have lost the baby."

"But wouldn't that be the best thing that could happen? She was much too far along for even a marriage to explain her condition. There'd be a scandal no matter what, and from what you told me, these people hate scandal."

Sarah sighed in dismay. "You're right. I guess I'm no good at this. You're the detective, not me!"

He raised his eyebrows at her. "Isn't that what I've been trying to tell you?"

Sarah had to admit he'd won that round, although she didn't say it aloud.

"I guess you were getting your supper," he said dismissively, probably smelling the stew. "If that's all you had to tell me, I'll let you get to it."

He might be finished with her, but she wasn't finished with him, not by a long shot. "Have you questioned the VanDamms's servants yet?"

"I can't imagine that's any of your business, Mrs. Brandt," he replied dismissively, turning to go.

"Maybe not, but I do want to know all about it. Could I bribe you with supper in exchange for your information?"

He raised his eyebrows in feigned surprise. "Is that how you found out about Fisher?" he countered.

"I never reveal my interrogation techniques, Detective. So, do we have a deal?"

Malloy shook his head again. "Thanks anyway, but I'm afraid I'm not very hungry," he said, but at that very instant, his stomach growled rather determinedly.

Sarah grinned. "Although my medical training is limited to nursing skills, I'm fairly sure that indicates that you are a liar, Detective. And allow me to add that I'm a very good cook. If you stay, I'll even make you a deal: If you tell me what you found out in Mamoraneck, I'll promise not to bother you again."

"I guess it would be rude to call you a liar in return," Frank said, thinking she was probably the most interesting woman he'd met in years. Which was why he would be insane to accept this invitation. Allowing Sarah Brandt to become more involved in this murder investigation could be dangerous, and not just because it might get her killed. Frank couldn't afford any entanglements, and Sarah Brandt was just the kind of woman who caused them.

"Since when are you concerned about being rude? Please, don't disillusion me by becoming polite so late in our acquaintance, Detective. You can wash up in the sink. Right this way."

Frank opened his mouth to show her just how impolite he could be, but his stomach growled again, and he remembered he hadn't eaten since morning. And something did smell awfully good. Well, what could it hurt? He'd eat her food, give her a few unimportant tidbits of information and be on his way. And then he'd never have to see her again.

The middle room of her flat was the kitchen. The light from the front window barely reached here, so a gas jet on the wall provided most of the illumination. He could see she'd spent some time making the room comfortable. A table and chairs sat on one side, and the stove, sink and icebox took up the other. A picture of a country scene hung on the wall above the table, and a flowered skirt decorated the front of the sink. There was even a bouquet of spring flowers on the table, the kind sold for pennies by ragged, homeless little girls in the street. He could just see Sarah Brandt handing one of them a nickel and telling her to keep the change.

She began to set the table while he washed his hands. At home, he would have removed his jacket and rolled up his sleeves, but he didn't want to be that informal with Sarah Brandt, so he just pushed his sleeves back as far as he could and was very careful not to get them wet in the spray of water from the pump. Only after he was finished did he realize he hadn't bothered to remove his hat. She must think him a barbarian, although why he should care what she thought of him, he had no idea.

He pulled off his derby and hung it on the ear of the chair she indicated he should use and sat down. He was thinking this was all a terrible mistake in the instant before she set a steaming bowl of stew in front of him. Then he decided that perhaps it wasn't quite as big a mistake as all that.

"What did you find out from the VanDamms's servants?" she asked, setting a plate of bread down on the table. It was bakery bread, but Frank had lost his taste for homemade, hardly ever being home to eat any.

"I found out that when she was sent to the house there, the servants weren't allowed to speak to her. Nobody was, in fact. The housekeeper kept her pretty much a prisoner in her room.''

"That's understandable, considering her condition, although I don't imagine they could've kept it a secret for long. But surely her maid told you something.''

"Even her maid wasn't allowed to speak to her. Only the housekeeper.''

Mrs. Brandt was in the process of taking a seat opposite his, and she stopped halfway down in her chair to consider this for a moment. "How strange,'' she said, sinking down into the chair at last.

"The maid thought so. But Alicia did go out riding every day. With a groom,'' he added, wondering if she would jump to the same conclusion he had.

"A groom?'' A crease formed between her eyes as she considered this information.

"Yes,'' he remarked casually. "He seems to be the only man she was ever alone with outside of her own family.''

"He's young? A boy her own age?'' From her expression, she thought he'd solved the mystery.

But Frank shook his head, raising a spoonful of stew to his mouth. It was hot, but he blew on it and tasted. Not as good as his mother's, but the company was better. Which wasn't saying much, but at least it was something. "No, he's older than me, I'd guess. Probably near forty. But he's a nice looking fellow. And he's known her all her life. She'd be suggestible. If he wanted to take advantage of her, she wouldn't know—''

"No,'' she said decisively. "The groom isn't the father of her baby.''

Frank swallowed down the automatic prickle of annoyance at her certainty, even though he was inclined to agree. "Why not?'' he challenged.

"Because it wouldn't take long for her family to figure out. And he wouldn't still be there if it was true. He'd be ... I don't know, gone. Perhaps even dead. I'm not sure how men like Cornelius VanDamm deal with servants who seduce their daughters, but I don't imagine they show any mercy.''

"How would he find out, though? If the girl didn't tell him . . .''

"She would have told him. He'd browbeat her until she did, and believe me, a girl like Alicia wouldn't be able to hold out long against a man like her father. And he'd suspect the groom first off, if he is indeed the only man she's ever alone with. I guarantee that Mr. Van-Damm knew who the father of the baby was. And if it was a servant, that servant will have vanished.''

"It's not a servant, then. Lizzie—that's her maid—told me they're all still working there.''

"Well, then, who did this Lizzie think it was?'' she asked, her fine eyes lighting with interest.

Frank chose not to notice. "She didn't even know about . . . about the girl's secret. The groom didn't seem to, either.''

He took a renewed interest in his supper, feeling suddenly awkward to be once again discussing such a delicate subject, this time over dinner, as if it was the most natural thing in the world, which it wasn't, not to Frank.

She must not have shared his discomfort, however. "Did you find out how she got away from the house without being caught?''

"The groom helped her. Hired a fishing boat. He sold her jewelry for her and found her the room at the Higgins's house.''

Her lips pursed as she considered this information. "Mr. VanDamm certainly doesn't know all this or the groom wouldn't still be there.''

"He doesn't.''

"Are you going to tell him?''

He wasn't sure if she disapproved or not, but he didn't really care. "Not unless it serves my purpose.'' It was the only answer he could give, and he was oddly gratified by her apparent approval.

"So we still don't know who the father of her child

was,'' she mused, and Frank felt his hackles rising again.

"Mrs. Brandt, there is no *we* in this investigation. I'm the detective. You're, not.'' He'd almost said she was nothing, but he'd thought better of it just in time. He figured Sarah Brandt would take offense, and besides, she wasn't really nothing, no matter how much he might wish it.

"I did find out who Hamilton Fisher is,'' she reminded him.

He had to give her that. "You'd just better hope he doesn't come looking for you some dark night.''

She seemed amused at the thought. "So if the groom isn't the father of her child—and I think we can be rather certain of that—then who was?''

Frank thought he had already reminded her this wasn't her business, but obviously, she didn't care. She just kept right on, not even waiting for Frank to respond.

"Mina—her sister—insisted that Alicia didn't have any gentlemen friends. She hadn't even entered society yet, so that would eliminate possible suitors.''

Frank merely grunted as he continued to devour his stew.

"What is it?'' she demanded.

He looked up in surprise and swallowed a mouthful of meat and potatoes. "What is what?''

"What you aren't telling me. I said Alicia didn't have any suitors, and you disagreed.''

"I did not!''

She gave him a pitying look. "You know something you haven't told me. Don't try to deny it.''

"You shouldn't be too surprised at that,'' he warned her. "There's no reason for me to tell you anything at all.''

She obviously couldn't be insulted. "Alicia *did* have a suitor, didn't she? Who was he?''

Frank was beginning to wonder if Sarah Brandt might be a witch. Very deliberately, he took another piece of bread from the plate, tore off a bite and popped it in his mouth. Chewing slowly, he regarded her, marveling at the way she met his stare levelly, not even blinking, when hardened criminals usually flinched. Well, what the hell, maybe she could help him make sense of this.

"Harvey, that's the groom, he said she ran away because her father wanted her to marry somebody she hated."

"Good heavens! She was barely sixteen!"

"And six months gone with child," he reminded her. "Naturally, he'd want to marry her off to *somebody*."

"But that man wasn't necessarily the father, was he?"

Frank shrugged. "There's only a couple people can tell us that, and the one most likely to is dead."

"And the rest will probably lie."

Frank stared at her again. Really, she had missed her calling. Of course, the police didn't employ female detectives, but if they did, Sarah Brandt would have been pretty good. He saw she was thinking, and he knew that could be dangerous.

"It's still none of your business, Mrs. Brandt," he reminded her. "No matter how much you want to see the killer caught, it's my job to catch him, not yours."

"But I could—"

"*No.*" He gave her the glare that stopped felons in their tracks, but she merely frowned.

"Do you think Cornelius VanDamm is going to tell *you* anything? Or that Mina will? Or Mrs. VanDamm?"

"Do you think they'll tell you either?" he countered.

"I could find out," she insisted.

"No," he said again. "Stay out of it." He sighed wearily. "I thought you said if I told you what I know, you'd promise not to interfere anymore."

"I said I'd promise not to bother you anymore. I don't think it would be a bother if I found out who Alicia's father wanted her to marry."

"It will bother me if you don't stop meddling in my investigation."

"I found out who Hamilton Fisher is," she reminded

him again. "I told you to question the servants to find out more about her."

"And you might've put yourself in danger in the meantime. You've done enough. Let the police do their job now, Mrs. Brandt."

Her face hardened with a bitterness that shocked him, and anger flared in her blue-gray eyes. "I'm fully aware of how the police do their job, Detective Sergeant Malloy, so you'll forgive me if I'm less than confident in your ability to solve this case."

"What are you talking about?" he demanded, angry himself.

"I'm talking about a murder that happened three years ago and still isn't solved."

"Was this someone you knew?" he asked skeptically.

"My husband."

For a full minute, Frank could only stare. He'd known she was a widow, of course, but he'd never troubled himself to wonder what had become of the late Mr. Brandt. "How did it happen?"

"Tom was coming home late one night from a case. I didn't think it odd when I woke up the next morning and he wasn't here. He was frequently gone all night. Then the police came and told me he'd been found dead in an alley. His money was gone, and his skull was . . ." her voice caught, but she swallowed down whatever emotions threatened to choke her and forced herself to go on. "His skull was fractured."

"It's almost impossible to solve a case like that," Frank said, feeling oddly defensive. "A robbery at night, with no witnesses. No connection between the killer and the victim. No clues or evidence."

"They could have *tried*," she countered, plainly not interested in reason or logic. "People like that don't keep secrets. They brag to their friends. Someone knew who killed Tom. A few well-placed bribes, and someone would have—"

"Why didn't you offer a bribe, then? You offered one

to me quick enough,'' he recalled with bitterness of his own.

"I didn't know the rules back then, and I was too grief-stricken to learn them at the time. I thought the police would find the killer because it was the right thing to do. I know better now, and I intend to see that this killer doesn't get away."

"Even if it means using yourself as bait?" he asked baldly, but if he'd hoped to shock her, he failed.

"If that's what it takes, Mr. Malloy. If that's what it takes."

7

SARAH HAD NEVER CARED FOR BEING ORDERED around. Her father had pretty much ruined her for it before she was out of the nursery, and after Maggie's death, she'd determined never to do anything a man ordered her to do if it went against her better judgement. Of course, Detective Malloy might be right about her inquiries putting her in danger. Even her better judgment had to bow to common sense, but she wasn't going to be foolish, no matter what he might think. And certainly, a visit to the VanDamms couldn't possibly put her in any danger at all.

The windows of the VanDamm town house were draped in black, and a black mourning wreath hung on the door. Alicia's funeral had been private, probably to avoid the kind of speculation that would only deepen the scandal of her death, and the family was most likely in seclusion for the same reason. Busybodies would be anxious to learn the least tidbit of information, and Cornelius and Mina would be shrewd enough to avoid giving them a chance to gather that tidbit. Still, Sarah had reason to believe she might gain admittance when no one else would.

She lifted the heavy brass knocker and let it fall. The resounding clunk seemed to echo in the cavernous house, and before long the door opened slightly, enough so she could see Alfred's familiar face through the crack.

"Miss Decker," he said in surprise and quickly caught himself. "I mean Mrs. . . . Mrs. Brandt, is it?"

"Yes, Alfred, and thank you for remembering. I don't mean to intrude, and I know the family is in mourning, but I was wondering if Miss Mina is receiving visitors. And if she isn't, if she would receive me anyway."

Alfred frowned uncertainly, and Sarah realized how very uncharacteristic this was for him. Alfred had been a butler his entire life, and he knew the rules of etiquette better than any seasoned society hostess. On the other hand, those rules didn't necessarily cover the present situation, since well-mannered people were never supposed to be murdered. The very idea was unthinkable. So unthinkable, in fact, that even Alfred was beginning to doubt the rules by which he had lived his entire life.

Certainly, a family in private mourning, as the Van-Damms were, would not be receiving visitors so soon after the funeral. And most certainly, a woman of Sarah's current social standing wouldn't ordinarily be received at all, unless she had business here and entered through the service door. But nothing was ordinary about the situation of Alicia VanDamm's death, which meant that all the conventional rules no longer applied. Or they still might. And Alfred, whose position required him to be certain about everything, was no longer certain about anything at all. And, Sarah realized, he must also be dealing with his own grief. He'd known Alicia since the day she was born, and he most certainly would be feeling her loss. Now that she noticed, he seemed to have aged considerably since her last visit mere days ago. Suddenly, he was an old man whose entire world had been shaken to its foundation.

"I'm not certain if Miss Mina is receiving or not," he told her. "Or if she would make an exception for you, Mrs. Brandt. Would you like to come in for a moment while I inquire?"

Sarah was most happy to wait. Alfred left her sitting on an upholstered bench in the front hallway while he made his way into the nether reaches of the house to find Mina VanDamm and obtain her instructions.

The house was unnaturally still, as if even the clocks had stopped ticking in deference to the family's grief. Abovestairs, the servants would be speaking in hushed tones, and the family would be closeted in their chambers. Sarah found it difficult to imagine that Mina was spending her time truly mourning her sister, although she would put on a good act for anyone who happened to call, as she had done for Sarah the other day. Mrs. VanDamm would undoubtedly be prostrate and probably heavily sedated. Her doctor wouldn't need much convincing to prescribe an opiate to calm her, and many women of her class took them freely on far less provocation than the loss of a child. Finally, Sarah considered Mr. VanDamm. He'd looked haggard when she was here before, and she could easily imagine him mourning Alicia. Not, perhaps, with the obvious emotion his wife would display, but in his own way. The way her father had mourned Maggie, knowing his actions had caused her to die in such a horrible manner while still believing he had been right in those actions. How men like that could live with themselves, Sarah had no idea.

After a long time, Sarah heard Alfred's shuffling steps returning. He emerged from a door at the end of the hallway, his expression properly somber but his eyes improperly bleak.

"I'm sorry, Mrs. Brandt, but Miss Mina is unable to receive visitors today. She said she was certain you'd understand."

Sarah understood perfectly, but she wasn't sure exactly why she wasn't being admitted. Perhaps Mina truly wasn't feeling up to visitors or perhaps she simply hadn't bothered to dress and do her hair today so she wasn't presentable. Or perhaps—and this was the reason Sarah feared most—she had decided Sarah wasn't worthy of her attentions. If that was the case, then Sarah wouldn't be able to obtain any more information from the family.

Concealing her disappointment, she thanked Alfred. He was escorting her to the front door when they heard the door to one of the other rooms open, and a gentleman emerged. He was slightly past middle years, wearing a suit that fit so well, it could only have been handcrafted to fit him. His thick hair was silver and painstakingly arranged. He nodded politely at Sarah, although she saw the question in his eyes. He wondered what someone like her was doing here, especially at this time.

"Mr. Mattingly," Alfred greeted him, and every nerve in Sarah's body jolted to attention. "I'll get your hat in just a moment," he promised, opening the front door to show Sarah out.

Was it possible? Could this be the attorney for whom Hamilton Fisher had worked? And what was his connection to the VanDamm family? Could he have been asked to hire Fisher to find Alicia for them? Although this was a most logical explanation, she couldn't help remembering Malloy's skepticism when she'd suggested that very thing. If the VanDamms had hired Mattingly to find Alicia, why hadn't Fisher simply informed them of her whereabouts when he located her? Why had Fisher moved into the house where she was living and tried to strike up an acquaintance with her instead? But if Mattingly was acquainted with the family, and he was obviously an intimate friend if he'd been admitted when the family was in seclusion, then why would he have sent someone to find Alicia without their knowledge and then not told them?

Alfred made no move to introduce Sarah to Mattingly. A butler would never presume to introduce visitors to each other, and even if he had, an introduction between Sarah and Mattingly would have been in questionable taste, considering their different social classes. Not for the first time, Sarah silently cursed the rigid rules that governed society. In a different time or place, she might have simply introduced herself and made some inquiries of Mr. Mattingly that would give her the information she so desperately sought. Which was probably what Malloy would do if he were here now.

As Alfred ushered her out the door, she bit back a smile at the thought of how she would enjoy the privileges of being a police detective for even one day. Malloy would be interested to know that Mattingly was at least acquainted with the VanDamm family. But what was their relationship? Was he simply a close family friend or was he VanDamm's attorney? And would even Malloy be able to find out? He wouldn't know how to question these people or how to win their confidence. They'd see him as an Irish thug—or worse—and might even refuse to talk with him entirely.

Did the police have the power to force someone like Mattingly to answer their questions if he didn't choose to? Somehow, Sarah doubted it, although she found the thought of the distinguished attorney being slapped around in the filthy interrogation room she'd seen extremely interesting. She thought that perhaps Detective Sergeant Frank Malloy might, too.

Sarah lingered on the sidewalk in front of the Van-Damm's house for a while, walking slowly so Mr. Mattingly might catch up with her when he made his exit. Then she might venture to strike up a conversation with him, if she could think of something sensible to say. But in the next moment a carriage pulled up at the Van-Damm's curb, and Mr. Mattingly went straight down the VanDamm's front steps and climbed into it.

Too bad his carriage hadn't been waiting there when she came out. She might have been able to get some information from his driver or his footman. Servants were an invaluable source of information about their employers, as Malloy had learned. But there was an equally reliable source that Sarah had not yet tapped. One from which she had cut herself off years earlier out of anger and bitterness.

When she thought about it now, however, she found her anger and bitterness had faded considerably. Perhaps the time had finally come to reestablish those ties. She had been thinking she should for a while now, but she hadn't had a reason. Or rather, she hadn't had an excuse. She'd needed such an excuse to salvage her pride, and now she had the perfect one.

SARAH HADN'T BEEN to the house since Tom's funeral, and even then it had been strange to her. Although three long years had passed since her last visit, she remembered the way well. It wasn't far from the VanDamms's home, just around the corner on Fifty-Seventh Street and a few blocks east, which she walked with determined strides.

The noise from Fifth Avenue faded behind her as she went. There were no tracks or horsecars on Fifty-Seventh Street, nothing to disturb the elegance and serenity of the neighborhood. The house was even more imposing than she had remembered, one of a seemingly endless row of Italianate brownstone town houses that gleamed in the warm sunlight. The neighbors were such luminaries as the Auchinclosses, the Sloanes, the Rogers, and even the Roosevelts.

Malloy would probably make fun of her for even knowing such things.

But as Sarah reached for the perfectly polished brass knocker, she forgot all about Malloy. Anxiety suddenly twisted her stomach, but she refused to acknowledge it. She had nothing to fear, she told herself. She was a grown woman who had her own life, and nothing and no one could change that, certainly nothing and no one in this house, not unless she allowed it herself. And since she had no intention of doing so, she was safe from any attack on her independence.

Besides, she was certain not to encounter the one person she least desired to see here today because he was miles away.

A maid she didn't know answered her knock, and the girl stared at her in surprise. Sarah didn't look like the usual visitor to this house.

"I'm Sarah Brandt," she said, "and I'd like to see my mother, if she's at home."

As he looked at the plush surroundings, Frank figured he'd probably made a big mistake by coming here. The offices of Mattingly and Springer were plainly designed to appeal to people of a completely different social class. Folks like Frank probably came and went by the service entrance, if they came and went at all. From the way the clerk had looked at him when he'd walked through the hand-carved oak door, he guessed it was the latter.

"May I help you?" the clerk asked. Frank noticed he didn't add "sir." The fellow was young, not more than twenty-two or -three, and extremely thin. The bones of his face seemed to be straining to get through his tight, pale flesh. That alone would have made him unpleasant to look at, but his expression was pinched, too, like he smelled something bad. Maybe he did. Frank hadn't changed his shirt in a day or two.

"I'm here to see Sylvester Mattingly," Frank said. No "Mr." Mattingly. No "please." No "if he's in." Frank could be rude, too.

"Is this pertaining to a case Mr. Mattingly is handling?" the boy sniffed. Plainly, he doubted this very much.

"It's pertaining to the death of Miss Alicia Van-Damm."

Frank would have bet the boy's face was already as white as it could get, but he would've been wrong. His eyes even seemed to bulge out a little. Funny how the name VanDamm could get a reaction. Or maybe it was the fact of Alicia's death.

Whatever it was, it had rattled the skinny clerk. He started fiddling nervously with his paper sleeve protectors, and he ducked his head so that his green eyeshade shielded his face. "Who . . . ? May I tell Mr. Mattingly who is calling?" he stammered, no longer quite so sure of himself.

"Tell him Detective Sergeant Frank Malloy of the New York City Police."

At this, the boy's head came up again, and this time his eyes were definitely bulging. "Please, have a seat," he offered in a choked whisper before fairly running from the room.

He closed the inner door behind him, leaving Frank alone in the reception room. The place felt closed in, even though the room was large and had a high ceiling. Probably, the illusion came from the depth of the carpets, the thickness of the maroon velvet drapes, and the ornately carved plaster ceiling. Everything seemed heavy, from the oak of the doors to the oak of the clerk's desk. Probably designed to absorb sound, so that every conversation held here would remain in strictest confidence. Frank figured the people who needed such a high-priced lawyer talked about a lot of things that needed to remain confidential.

Frank seated himself in one of the overstuffed chairs provided for visitors. Across from him hung a portrait of an elderly man who'd had lifelong bowel problems, if his expression was any indication. Frank noticed the elaborate chandelier hadn't been wired for electricity, as if such a thing would be considered vulgar in this bastion of conservatism. All he could say was, Sarah Brandt better be right about Mattingly knowing where to find that Fisher fellow.

After a few moments, the clerk returned. "Mr. Mattingly is expecting a client very shortly, but he can spare you a few minutes. If you will follow me."

Frank was sorry he hadn't been there to see Mattingly's face when the clerk had announced him. He wondered if he'd been as shocked as the clerk. If so, he'd had enough time to recover, Frank noted when he stepped into Mattingly's office.

This room was just as plush as the outer room, although the colors were darker and duller, browns and tans this time. Mattingly sat behind a desk that seemed a mile wide and a half a mile deep. He didn't seem pleased to see Frank, and he didn't get up to greet him.

Frank couldn't judge Mattingly's height since the desk would have dwarfed even a large man, but he seemed insignificant sitting there in the high-backed chair. His hair was thick and white and expertly barbered. His coat was tailor-made and filled out his narrow shoulders with artful padding. His face sagged with age, and his eyes glittered like glass beneath heavy lids. He might be very good at concealing his emotions, but those eyes gave him away this time. Frank's visit had made him furious.

Mattingly waited until the clerk had closed the door firmly, if silently, behind him before he said, "Detective Sergeant Malloy," as if getting a feel for the words in his mouth. They seemed to have an unpleasant flavor. "I'm used to dealing with the police, but never with anyone below the rank of captain."

Just as Frank has suspected. Mattingly wouldn't waste his bribe money on a lowly detective. "This time it looks like you're stuck with me. I'm the one investigating the death of Alicia VanDamm."

"A dreadful business, to be sure," he said, although his tone betrayed no hint of grief or even regret. "But I can't imagine why you've come *here*. How do you suppose I can aid your investigation?"

He hadn't asked Frank to sit down—a deliberate omission, Frank was sure—but Frank ostentatiously seated himself in one of the chairs facing the desk. They were leather and remarkably comfortable. He waited for Mattingly's frown of annoyance before saying, "I'm looking for Hamilton Fisher. My sources say he works for you."

Frank had been hoping for fear, or at least surprise, but he got only more anger. Mattingly's thin lips whitened and his dark eyes narrowed. "I've never heard of this man. I'm afraid your sources are mistaken. If that is what you came for, you wasted your time and mine. Now if you will excuse me, Mr. Malloy, I'm expecting a client momentarily."

Frank didn't move. "That's funny, because my sources said that Fisher works for you as a sort of private detective. I guess even a high-priced lawyer like yourself needs to do some snooping every now and then. A fellow like this Fisher could come in real handy."

"I told you, Detective Sergeant, I never—"

"Sure, whatever you say, but I just think it's kind of funny that somebody who people say works for you was living in the same boardinghouse as Miss VanDamm and that he disappeared the same night she got herself killed. Now if I was of a suspicious nature, I might think this Fisher had something to do with her death or at least that he knows something the police might find interesting."

Mattingly was used to disguising his true feelings, although a fury such as he was experiencing at the moment was impossible to completely conceal. He had the sense not to succumb to it, however, much to Frank's disappointment. He took some time to gather himself, folding his knobby-fingered hands carefully on the desk in front of him. He studied the liver spots of the backs of those hands for a long moment, as if seeking some guidance there. When he looked up, he was in complete control of himself.

"Detective Sergeant, I have already told you, I am not acquainted with the gentleman you are seeking. I must ask you again—"

"Did you know Alicia VanDamm?"

For an instant, Mattingly almost lost his patience. "I know her entire family. Everyone knows the Van-Damms."

Probably, he meant, "Everyone who is anyone knows the VanDamms." Frank wouldn't qualify, of course.

"Do you know the VanDamms socially or professionally?"

"I can't believe that is any of your business," Mattingly said with the confidence of one powerful enough that he needn't fear the police.

"And I can't believe you don't want to help me find

out who killed Alicia VanDamm. The girl was strangled, Mr. Mattingly, and I'm trying to find and punish the brute who did it, and here you are, treating me like I'm the third cop to come in here asking you to buy tickets to the policeman's ball.''

Frank got the impression that Mattingly wanted to wrap those long, bony fingers around his neck and choke him the way somebody had choked Alicia VanDamm. He only got that impression from his sixth sense, however, since Mattingly was doing his very best not to betray any emotion whatever. Finally, however, he allowed himself a bit more impatience.

''Really, Detective Sergeant, I think you are overstating the case. If I am short with you, it's because you are wasting my time as well as your own, as I have already pointed out. You come in here asking me about a man I never heard of and accusing me of . . . well, accusing me of heaven knows what, and then you accuse me of withholding information that I do not have. I believe I have every reason to be annoyed with you, particularly when I have already asked you to leave. Don't think I won't mention this to your superiors.''

Oh, yes, Frank thought, *please be sure to tell Commissioner Roosevelt just exactly how annoyed you are with me.* Aloud, he said, ''Thanks for your help, Mr. Mattingly. I'll be sure to mention your assistance to Mr. VanDamm.''

''Do that,'' he countered, calling Frank's bluff beautifully. ''And don't be surprised if he has already heard about it from me.''

THE MAID BLINKED at Sarah in surprise. ''Your mother?'' she echoed in confusion. Perhaps she thought Sarah was daughter to one of the servants.

''Mrs. Decker is my mother,'' she explained with a small smile.

For a moment, she was afraid the girl was going to close the door in her face in retaliation for telling such a bold-faced lie, but apparently she thought better of that impulse.

"I . . . I'll have to see if she's at home," she said finally, and after another moment of thought, she invited Sarah inside to wait.

Although she had worn her best dress for the visit to the VanDamm's today, Sarah knew she still did not meet the standards society had set for being fashionably attired. These days her clothing tended toward the practical rather than the stylish, and she might even, if she allowed herself to admit it, be a bit shabby in the bargain. If she was going to start moving in the more exalted social circles, as she had been these past few days, she would have to start paying some attention to her wardrobe again.

The girl returned almost immediately, and now her eyes were wide in her small face, and her manner had changed from hesitant to ingratiating. "I'm sorry I didn't recognize you, Miss Decker, but I'm new, and I didn't know. Mrs. Decker asks will you wait in the morning room until she comes down?"

Sarah released the breath she hadn't realized she'd been holding as relief flooded through her. Although she hadn't really expected to be turned away, the possibility had been there all the same. Her parents had been just as angry as she when she'd stormed out of their life after Tom's death. But apparently, the years had mellowed them, too. Or at least the years had mellowed her mother.

Sarah was only too glad to wait. This wasn't her mother's usual afternoon "at home," the time when she formally received visitors, so she wouldn't be dressed properly. She would also never allow Sarah to see her for the first time in three years looking less than her best, so a delay was inevitable.

The morning room was the room her mother used for her private pursuits, writing letters, reading, managing the household. More simply furnished than the formal rooms where visitors were usually received, it had a comfortable, homey feel to it. Plainly, her mother wanted their first visit in three years to be unhampered by the rigid social conventions that ruled the rest of their lives.

The room smelled faintly of her mother's perfume, the light floral scent she had used as long as Sarah could remember, and the aroma brought back bittersweet memories of happier times.

How could she have allowed so many years to pass without seeing her own mother? The argument that had separated them had seemed so very important at the time, but now, recalling the loving woman who had raised her, Sarah could only feel regret that she had been so stubborn. In punishing her parents, she had also punished herself by depriving herself of the comfort only a mother could give.

Restless with her memories, Sarah strolled around the room, examining everything. She recognized some of the pieces from the house on Washington Square where she had grown up. The desk was the same one her mother had always used. Sarah could remember darting between its graceful, curving legs as a child, trying to capture her mother's attention.

On the desktop was a half-written note in her mother's careful hand, thanking someone for a dinner party. The table in front of the window was new, but Sarah recognized the vase on it. Her mother had bought it at a market in Egypt on one of her trips abroad. A glass-fronted curio cabinet held other treasures, some of which Sarah remembered and others that were new. She was still studying them, remembering the stories behind them, when the door opened and her mother rushed into the room.

''Sarah!'' she cried, coming toward her with hands outstretched. Sarah took them in her own and was surprised at how cold they were. As if her mother had sustained a shock, which of course she had. And was she trembling? Perhaps just a little, or maybe it was Sarah's own nerves making her think so.

For a moment, she allowed herself to feel the pure joy of seeing her mother again. Inhaling her mother's unique scent and kissing her still-smooth cheeks, Sarah basked in the absolute love she saw radiating from her mother's eyes. As she pulled away, those eyes devoured her, taking in every detail of her appearance in an instant.

"You look . . . well," she said, but the words held a question. Plainly, she assumed only some tragedy would have brought her home.

"I'm very well, thank you. In fact, I've never been better."

Her mother looked doubtful. And worried. "Are you sure? Your hands . . . Whatever have you been doing with them, Sarah? They're like shoe leather!"

Sarah looked down self-consciously at where her mother still gripped her fingers. "I've been working, Mother. I have to earn my keep, you know."

"No, you don't," her mother chided, and Sarah saw all the old retributions darkening her eyes.

For a second, Sarah thought perhaps she'd made a mistake in coming. What made her think anything would have changed in this house no matter how much time had passed? But then her mother shook herself, as if consciously shrugging off the old patterns that had alienated them for so long, and she made herself smile brightly, the perfect hostess again.

"Well, never mind about that. Come and sit down, and tell me what you've been doing and what brought you here on such a fine day. They say it's like summertime out there today. Can you believe it? After we had snow just a week ago?"

Sarah allowed her mother to lead her to the settee by the window that overlooked the garden. Outside, the ground and the trees were just beginning to green with new life in the sudden fine weather, giving Sarah hope that perhaps she could begin a new life as well.

"I came to see how you were," she said when they were seated.

Her mother wasn't fooled by the polite lie. "You just woke up this morning after three years and wondered how

I was," she scoffed, but there was no anger in her tone, only sadness.

"No, I didn't," she admitted. "Something happened, something terrible, and it made me realize how short life is and how we shouldn't waste a moment of it nursing old grudges."

Her mother closed her eyes for a moment, as if sending up a silent prayer of thanks, and when she opened them again, the shadows were gone. "Oh, Sarah, how many times I've longed to hear you say that. But what terrible thing happened? You said you were well—"

"I'm perfectly fine and disgustingly healthy." She patted her mother's hand reassuringly. "What happened doesn't concern me at all, except that I know the people involved. So do you. The VanDamms."

"Oh, my, yes. Poor, sweet Alicia. She was so young and always seemed so healthy. I guess you never know. They said it was a fever that took her, and so quickly. By the time they even thought to send for a doctor, she was gone."

Sarah had wondered what story they were giving out. This one was as good as any, she supposed. Many people died of unexplained fevers every day. "Alicia didn't die of a fever, Mother. She was murdered."

"*Murdered?*" she echoed incredulously. "That's impossible! Whoever would have murdered her? And *why*, for heaven's sake?"

As briefly as she could, Sarah explained that Alicia had run away from home and had been living in a boarding-house where she was found dead. Plainly, her mother couldn't believe such a thing could happen.

"How could she get away? She was only a child! How would she know where to go or even how to get a room?"

"I believe someone must have helped her," Sarah said, deciding not to reveal everything she knew. Her mother had been known to gossip, and Sarah didn't want to be the cause of the groom Harvey getting fired. "The police think she must have had a lover. Perhaps he helped her get away.''

"That's nonsense," her mother insisted. "Alicia was just a child. She wouldn't even know any young men.''

"She knew at least one," Sarah said. "She was expecting a baby.''

If her mother had been shocked before, she was stunned now. Speechless, she could only stare at Sarah for a long moment. Finally, she asked, "You're sure? There could be no mistake?''

"No mistake. She was already six months along.''

Her mother considered this information, weighing it with the facts Sarah had already told her. "Of course, that would explain why they sent her to the country. So she could have the baby secretly.''

Then they both remembered a girl who had been sent to France for the very same reason, a girl who had escaped to die as well. But neither of them was ready to speak of Maggie, not when their reconciliation was so new. They looked away, not wanting to meet each other's eyes while those memories were still in their minds.

"What I don't understand," Sarah said determinedly, hoping to steer them both away from their painful memories, "is why wouldn't they have just arranged a marriage for her with the baby's father?''

"Oh, my, any number of reasons. If he was unsuitable . . .'' Her voice trailed off as they once again remembered Maggie and her unsuitable match. "Or perhaps he was already married," she added after an awkward moment.

This was something Sarah hadn't considered. But she couldn't believe that Alicia could have been discreet enough to be impregnated without stirring at least a whiff of scandal.

"Surely, someone would know if that were the case. Have you heard anything about her? Anything at all that might explain what happened? Perhaps she was engaged, or her parents were arranging a marriage for her," she added, recalling the groom's reason for helping Alicia run away.

Her mother considered again, and Sarah waited patiently. Women like her mother, intelligent, talented women who had no socially acceptable outlet for their energies, filled their idle hours by visiting and learning as much about their neighbors as they could. In less elegant circles, this would have been called gossiping, but no one in her mother's social circle would have used so vulgar a word to describe their activities. Still, that was what they did, day after day and year after year. No word or deed was too insignificant to escape their attentions, and they spent their entire lives analyzing one another's behavior. This was why Sarah was certain that if Alicia VanDamm had become pregnant, which she most certainly had, someone would know something about it.

"There was one thing," her mother said at last, "but it was so fantastic, I didn't credit it. And I don't think anyone else did, either."

"What was it?" Sarah asked, unable to disguise her eagerness.

"You understand that I don't believe in gossiping about my neighbors," she said primly, and Sarah forced herself not to smile.

"Of course not, but any information you have might help us find out who killed her."

"*Us?*" her mother echoed in surprise. "Sarah, just how does all this concern *you,* and who else would it involve?"

Sarah could have bitten her tongue. Good thing Malloy hadn't heard her slip. She was getting a little tired of his lectures about how she really wasn't investigating this case. "I was able to help the police in their investigation. Because I knew Alicia," she added at her mother's frown of disapproval.

"The police?" she sniffed. "Really, dear, you shouldn't become involved with the police. You know the kind of men who are drawn to that profession. They're hardly the sort of people with whom you should associate.''

Her mother would probably faint if she saw some of the people with whom Sarah associated quite intimately every day of her life, but she decided not to mention that.

''Surely, Mother, you know that the Roosevelt's son, Theodore, is a police commissioner now. He's done a lot to reform the police force.''

''Yes, and I know someone sent him a bomb in the mail the other day, too. Can you imagine such a thing? So much for his efforts at reform!''

Sarah decided to take another tack. ''In any case, the detective who is working on Alicia's case is quite . . . respectable, I'm sure,'' she tried lamely, trying not to choke on all the lies. Roosevelt's reforms hadn't changed very much about the department yet, except to make people angry at not being able to go to a saloon on Sunday, and even worse was knowing Malloy wouldn't exactly be flattered by her description of him. ''And I just want to know for my own satisfaction who killed Alicia. I can't stand the thought of the person who snuffed out her life walking around a free man while she lies cold in the ground.''

The thought seemed to disturb her mother as well, although it could simply have been the ugliness of the image that upset her. Whatever it was, it provided the incentive Sarah needed.

''As I said, I hardly credit this story about Alicia, but if you think it might help . . .''

''I'm sure anything would help,'' Sarah said.

Her mother frowned again, uncertain this time. ''There was a rumor—and mind you, it was only a rumor; I never heard it from anyone who actually knew it to be true— that Cornelius *was* trying to arrange a marriage for Alicia.''

''Whom did they want her to marry?'' Sarah asked, trying not to sound too eager.

''That's the strange part. You see, Alicia was quite pretty and would have had many suitors as soon as she was out. There would be no reason to arrange something ahead of time, as one would with a daughter less . . . desirable.''

She didn't have to explain to Sarah, who had been quite eligible herself at one time, although she had chosen another destiny. Sarah nodded encouragingly.

"Which was why no one could believe that Cornelius would waste such a prize on . . . on Sylvester Mattingly.''

8

NOW IT WAS SARAH'S TURN TO BE STUNNED. SYL-
vester Mattingly! A vision of the man she had seen on
the VanDamm's doorstep such a short time ago flickered
before her mind's eye. Then she tried to picture that elderly gentleman with dewy, young Alicia VanDamm, but
even her usually vivid imagination rebelled at such a blas-
phemy.

"Good heavens," she murmured.

"Exactly," her mother said. "I take it you are acquainted with Mr. Mattingly."

"I've . . . seen him."

"He's old enough to be Alicia's grandfather," her
mother said, confirming Sarah's impression. "No one
could believe her family was seriously considering a marriage between them, which is why no one *did* believe it.
Someone must have started the rumor as some sort of
joke. At least that's what we decided. And when there
was no engagement announced, we were sure of it."

Sarah's mind was reeling. She could hardly think what
to ask next. "Was there . . . ? Did anyone know Alicia
had disappeared?"

"I hadn't heard anything, and I doubt anyone else had,
either. She wasn't out yet, so she would hardly be missed

from society. Many families send their young daughters away for months at a time, to school and such. No one would even notice her absence. Oh, Sarah, this business with Alicia is all so horrible,'' she said, taking Sarah's hand in hers. ''But I don't care how awful the tragedy was if it brought you back to us. Does that make me evil?''

Sarah smiled and squeezed her mother's hand. ''I don't think so. Bringing us back together again might be the one good thing to come from Alicia's death.''

Her mother stared at her for a long moment, giving Sarah the opportunity to notice subtle changes that she'd been too preoccupied to observe before. Her mother had always been plump, as women of her class were expected to be, but she seemed thinner now, as if time had chiseled off the outer layer of softness. Her eyes were still blue but not as bright as Sarah remembered, and the gold of her hair was now mixed with a generous amount of silver. While she had been blessed with good skin and had taken great pains all of her life to preserve her complexion, time had scratched her a bit. The creases from her nose to her mouth were deeper than Sarah remembered, and the firm line of her jaw had blurred. Sarah couldn't help wondering how much of this was just the normal ravages of time and how much of it might have been caused by the loss of both her daughters. At least Sarah still had it within her power to give one of them back to her.

''I haven't even asked how *you* are,'' Sarah said. ''You look very well.''

''I look older,'' she corrected primly. ''How could I not? But you're right, I'm well. Your father will be so sorry he missed you. He's in Albany, you know.''

Sarah did know. She'd read it in the *Times*. He was addressing the legislature about something or other, which was why Sarah hadn't felt the slightest qualm about coming here today, knowing she wouldn't have to see him just yet. ''How is he?''

Her mother gave her a glance, as if trying to judge the

sincerity of her inquiry. "He's not as well as I am, I'm afraid."

Sarah felt a pang, although she wasn't sure if it was concern or simply guilt for not being quite as concerned as she should have been. "Is something wrong? Has he been ill?"

"It's his stomach. He . . . Well, I think he worries too much. You know how he takes everything to heart."

There had been a time when Sarah was sure her father didn't even *have* a heart, but she wouldn't mention that now. "Has he seen a doctor? What do they say?"

Her mother shrugged one shoulder helplessly. "You know how they are. Sometimes I don't think doctors know anything at all."

Sarah could have agreed. She'd seen far too many childbirths botched by supposedly expert physicians. On the other hand, she knew how caring her husband had been. "Medicine isn't an exact science. There's so much we don't know about the human body. But most doctors are competent," she pointed out.

Her mother was instantly contrite. "I didn't mean . . . Oh, my dear, I hope I haven't stirred any painful memories for you."

"Don't be silly. And Mother, we'll drive each other to distraction if we keep imagining we've given offense about things that happened in the past. We have to put all of that behind us now and go on."

"Of course," she agreed eagerly. "It's just . . . I'm not sure what to say to you anymore. You seem so . . . so different."

"I *am* different. I'm older, too, and I have my own life. But I'm still your daughter. And I'm not fragile or bitter." She hoped that was true, at least. "Don't worry about offending me. You never used to worry about that before," she reminded her gently.

Her mother managed a small smile at that. "I didn't, did I? But I never really intended to offend you. I was only concerned with your well-being, Sarah. I still don't think it's proper for a woman to live alone and to . . . well, to do the things you do.''

"Women have been delivering babies since the beginning of time, Mother.''

"But not women of your class, Sarah. You were intended for better things.''

"For visiting my neighbors and attending parties and teas and ordering servants around?'' she scoffed.

Sarah saw at once she'd gone too far. Her mother's face seemed to crumble beneath the weight of Sarah's contempt.

"Oh, Mother, I'm sorry!'' she said quickly. "I didn't come here to quarrel. I came here to make up with you.''

"I was hoping that was true. When Milly told me you were here, I hardly knew what to think. Or what to expect. Sarah, what *can* I expect? Are you going to vanish from my life again, or will I see you regularly now? Should I tell your father you were here? Will you come to dinner next week?''

"Of course you can tell Father I was here,'' Sarah said with a bravado she didn't exactly feel. The thought of facing him again, after the harsh words they had exchanged at their last meeting, made her own stomach slightly sick. "And of course I'll see you regularly now. I'd love to come to dinner, too, but I can't make plans very far in advance, I'm afraid. I never know when I'll be needed since babies don't keep regular hours, but perhaps I could come by for tea one afternoon.'' There, that would guarantee a brief visit if things didn't go well.

"That would be wonderful!'' Sarah felt another pang at the longing she saw in her mother's eyes. "I'll be sure your father is here, if you'll send word ahead.''

Sarah made no promises. She would have to wait a day or two to see how truly brave she was. Walking through the city alone at night was nothing compared to facing her father's wrath again. Would he still be angry or would he have mellowed with the years? Somehow, Sarah could not imagine her father mellowing in a millennium.

They chatted for a while about people Sarah had known, her mother bringing her up to date on their lives and activities. She told Sarah about a trip to Paris her parents had taken and about some parties she had recently attended. Sarah listened politely and asked questions, recognizing her mother's need to keep her there as long as possible. Perhaps she realized Sarah's ambivalence about returning and was afraid to let her go. Whatever the reason, Sarah let her babble on for another hour before making her excuses.

Outside, the weather was even warmer than it had been earlier. They really were having an early spring. Sarah began to regret having worn such a heavy dress. She walked the few blocks to the Sixth Avenue elevated train station, trying not to exert herself too much in the heat, and gratefully took shelter on the shade of the covered staircase that led up to the platform.

As she climbed the stairs, she recalled what her mother had told her about Alicia and Sylvester Mattingly. Many people in the VanDamms's social set would see nothing unusual in her father arranging a marriage for her, and while they might be shocked by his selection of a groom and the vast age difference between the couple, few would condemn such a choice outright. In many ways it would make a certain perverse sense to them. If Alicia's father wanted to be certain she would be protected and financially secure, an older husband was the logical choice.

Or perhaps Mr. Mattingly had done VanDamm some favor or performed him some service for which Alicia was to be the reward. While this would give the matter a more cold-blooded, businesslike flavor, few would have condemned this motivation, either. Men had been paying debts and sealing bargains with their daughters for centuries. Just because the VanDamm house had electric lights and a telephone didn't mean they had accepted *every* trapping of progress.

Sarah wondered what sort of debt would require the mythical virgin sacrifice, but then, Alicia hadn't been a virgin. As Sarah stood on the platform watching the next train rumbling along the elevated track toward the station, she considered the possibility that perhaps Cornelius VanDamm wasn't the debtor at all. Perhaps Mattingly had been the one who owed VanDamm a favor. And perhaps he had been prevailed upon to settle it by taking Alicia as his wife. Already pregnant, she would be soiled goods to be sure, and providing a name and respectability for her child would be enough to provide payment in full for just about any kind of debt. Still, her youth and beauty would provide more than ample compensation to Mattingly for having claimed her child as his own. And even if people doubted he had fathered that child, no one would ever admit it to his face.

The train stopped, and the passengers filed out. The cars weren't terribly crowded at this time of day, so Sarah was able to find a seat in the first car she entered. There were still empty seats a few moments later when the train started again, and Sarah was glad she had gotten away from her mother when she did. In another hour, the platforms would be packed with workers returning to their homes in other parts of the city, and the conductors wouldn't allow the trains to leave the station until they were so jammed that not another human body could be squeezed on board. The accidental contact one made with strangers under such circumstances was disconcerting enough, but far too many men took advantage of the situation to initiate more than accidental and far from proper contact. Sarah had made retaliatory use of her hat pin on more than one occasion under such circumstances, and she was grateful for the opportunity on this trip to simply sit and ponder the facts she had learned today.

She would have to contact Malloy again, although she should probably wait a day or two. Although he'd been fairly civil when he left her flat the other night, she didn't want to try his patience too much. When she considered how well their last meeting had gone, she thought perhaps she should have tried feeding him much sooner. With a small smile, she even considered the advisability of carrying something edible with her at all times, just in case she encountered him. Barring that, she should at least have something substantive to tell him before tracking him down again. The news about a rumored marriage between Alicia and Mattingly hardly qualified unless she could verify it.

Or unless she could think of a reason why it might have caused Alicia's death. That, she realized as she watched buildings and apartments speed by the train's window close enough for her to reach out and touch if she'd wished to risk losing an arm, might take a little more thought.

FRANK KNEW SOMETHING was wrong the minute he stepped into the room. The detectives all had desks in one large room in Police Headquarters, and this afternoon, everyone who happened to be here was nonchalantly ignoring Frank. Too nonchalantly. They were merely pretending not to notice him and really watching him like hawks and waiting expectantly for something. Frank could feel it in the air like a vapor. What they could be waiting for, Frank couldn't imagine until he reached his own desk and saw the envelope. The ivory vellum envelope addressed to him in a decidedly feminine hand.

Damn, no wonder they were watching him.

"Is it a love letter, Frank?" a falsetto voice inquired from across the room. Frank didn't even glance up.

"O'Shaughnessy said she's a real peach. A blonde," someone else reported.

"A *blonde*!" The phrase echoed through the room as the rest of them repeated it incredulously.

"She's an informant," Frank said to the room at large, but of course they didn't want to believe something so innocent.

"I never had a stool pigeon send me a love letter," Harry Kelly said.

"You never had *anybody* send you a love letter," Bill Broghan hooted.

"And you couldn't read it even if they did," Frank said, still staring at the envelope. He didn't have to turn it over to see who it was from, and he certainly hadn't needed to hear her description. Only one person in the world would be sending him a note like this. He was very much afraid he was going to have to strangle Sarah Brandt. His only regret would be that he would never make Captain.

But it might be worth it.

"Ain't you gonna read it, Frank?" someone coaxed.

"Read it out loud," Bill suggested. "Don't be stingy."

"I can't read it out loud," Frank said. "It would take me too long to explain all the big words to you."

"Or all the dirty words," Harry said slyly.

Frank gave him a look. "I thought you already knew all the dirty words."

"He's got you there, Harry," Bill hooted.

"I thought you swore off women, Frank," Harry said. "Where'd this blonde bit of fluff come from?"

"I told you, she's an informant." *She's also a pain in the backside*, he added silently, fingering the envelope. The paper was quality, just like Sarah Brandt. Just like Alicia VanDamm. What the hell was he doing involved with any of them? He knew how to handle crooks and killers and con men. He didn't know how to handle ladies, dead or alive. And he had no intention of handling Sarah Brandt at all.

With a resigned sigh, he picked up the envelope and broke the seal. He could feel the eyes of all the other detectives watching him intently, waiting for some reaction. Frank was going to do his best to disappoint them.

"Dear Mr. Malloy," her note began. He should read them that part, if they were expecting a love letter. "I have learned some very interesting information about Sylvester Mattingly's relationship with Alicia. It seems that rumors were circulating among the VanDamms's acquain-

tances that Mr. VanDamm was arranging a marriage between Alicia and Mattingly. I have a theory that might
explain Alicia's circumstances which I would rather not
put in writing. If you will call upon me at your earliest
convenience, I will be happy to explain it to you.'' It was
signed, ''In haste, Sarah Brandt.''

''That son of a bitch,'' Frank muttered, recalling in
great detail his conversation with Sylvester Mattingly. No
wonder he hadn't wanted to cooperate with Frank's investigation. He was the one Alicia had been running away
from all along! And when he thought about Mattingly so
much as touching that poor girl . . .

''Bad news, Frank?'' Bill asked with phony concern.

''She throwing you over for another fellow?'' Harry
smirked.

''Yeah, that's right,'' Frank agreed, wishing he would
be that lucky. Unfortunately, he was afraid Sarah Brandt's
intense interest in him would continue as long as he was
investigating Alicia VanDamm's murder. And as for Mrs.
Brandt and her theories, he would have bet a year's salary
that she'd have one, and an equal amount that it wouldn't
do him any good. So far, this case had been one blind
alley after another, all thanks to Sarah Brandt and her
useless information.

He was still debating the advisability of meeting with
Mrs. Brandt again—could he be civil to her if he did?
And would it be a complete waste of his time?—when
one of the officers from downstairs came into the room.
Frank hardly noticed until he realized the man was com-
ing right up to him.

''Malloy?''

Frank nodded curtly.

''Got a message.'' The fellow looked sort of smug,
knowing the effect this message would have. ''Superintendent Conlin wants to see you in his office right away.''

Once again a murmur went through the room as the
other detectives reacted to the summons. This couldn't be
good news. Conlin didn't interfere with individual detec-

tives. In fact, he didn't concern himself with their work at all, letting Chief of Detectives Steers have a free hand with them, so this wasn't any kind of routine consultation. This was something serious and probably dangerous, too. Dangerous for Frank, that is. If he did or said the wrong thing, he could forget about making Captain. He could even forget about working for the police department anymore.

And why was he so sure that Sarah Brandt's interference was somehow to blame for this summons?

Chief Conlin's office was on the second floor, with all the other important offices. Roosevelt himself kept one here, complete with his girl secretary, the only female ever to work in such a capacity in the history of the New York City Police. Frank hoped Sarah Brandt didn't find out about the girl secretary. Next thing he knew, she'd be Roosevelt's right-hand man. Or woman.

Conlin kept a male secretary, as was proper, and the fellow showed him into the inner sanctum immediately. Frank wasn't sure if he should be apprehensive or not, so he settled for wary. The office was comfortably furnished, but nothing like Sylvester Mattingly's. Conlin sat behind his desk in a large chair. He was a man of middle years, of medium height and slight build with light blue eyes and a sallow complexion. He might have been considered nondescript, except for the power he wielded in his new position.

"Sit down . . . Mallory, is it?"

"Malloy," Frank corrected him. He took the offered chair. It wasn't as comfortable as the one in Mattingly's office, either.

"I understand you're working on the murder of Miss Alicia VanDamm," Conlin said, leaning back and stroking his mustache thoughtfully.

"That's right." Frank waited, not a bit surprised. This was the only case he had that might have caused anyone concern.

"An ugly business. A young girl like that, cut down in

her prime.'' He shook his head sadly, his face expressing his profound distress as such an event.

Frank was impressed. He'd heard that the new superintendent had been trained in public speaking by his brother who was an actor, and Conlin certainly exhibited the grace and style of a professional actor. Those skills would stand him in good stead in his current position, but Frank wasn't fooled by this phony concern for Alicia VanDamm. Conlin would only be concerned with how the investigation of her case affected one person: himself.

Frank nodded once, to let him know he agreed so far. Every instinct was rebelling, however, warning him something bad was going to happen. Something really bad. Wariness gave way to dread.

"Do you know the VanDamm family?''

"I've met them. During the investigation.''

The chief frowned, looking down at the polished surface of his desktop as if weighing his words carefully. Just the way an actor would play a man of power. "Then perhaps you can understand their concerns, which are different from what many people would consider standard in this situation.''

"I'd guess their main concern would be finding out who killed their daughter,'' Frank tried.

"Most people would,'' the chief agreed, folding his hands on his desk and leaning forward to give Frank the impression he was confiding in him. "Most people want revenge, Malloy. They call it justice, but revenge is what they really want. It won't bring their loved one back, but it gives them some measure of comfort.''

Frank knew this was true, but he also knew the superintendent hadn't yet made his point, although he was becoming more certain by the moment he knew what that point would be. He continued to wait, anger forming an acidic ball in his stomach.

"The VanDamms aren't like most people, however. They are much more intelligent than most people, and they understand that revenge won't bring their daughter

back. They also know that bringing her killer to justice
might compound the damage that has already been done
by blackening their daughter's good name and reputation.''

Not to mention their own, Frank thought, but of course
he didn't say it aloud. He'd never make Captain by talking
back to the superintendent. In fact, he'd be back to pounding a beat, if he wasn't careful.

"Because the VanDamms might well have to endure
even more distress if you continue your investigation,
Malloy, I'm taking you off this case. I think your chances
of actually finding the killer are very slim, and since even
doing so wouldn't accomplish anything constructive,
there's no point in proceeding.''

"It would get a killer off the streets," Frank couldn't
resist pointing out. The hot ball of anger had become mol-
ten fury, and he had to close his hands into fists to keep
from slapping them down on the superintendent's shiny
desk in frustration.

"Hundreds of killers walk our streets every day, Malloy. We can't catch them all. And we won't be trying to
catch this one.'' Steer's voice was hard, leaving no room
for negotiation. "Do you understand?''

Frank understood completely. Someone important didn't
want the case solved, and because of Sarah Brandt's note,
he understood even more than the superintendent. "I already have some feelers out. What if I accidentally find the
killer?''

The chief's gaze was razor sharp when it met Frank's.
"You won't.''

It WAS THE hottest day of the year so far, and Frank's
mood was just as hot as he made his way through Greenwich Village. He didn't even think of knocking when he
reached the front door of the office. He simply pushed it
open and marched in. Still furious, he needed a second to
realize that Mrs. Brandt was not alone. Another woman
was sitting with her, an elderly lady.

Was she a patient? No, the two of them appeared to be only talking, thank God, and they both looked up in surprise.

"Well, now, looks like somebody put his hat on backward this morning," the old woman said with some amusement.

"Mr. Malloy," Mrs. Brandt said in that cultured voice of hers, as if he hadn't just made a complete fool of himself. "I wasn't expecting you."

The old woman was looking him over as if judging his suitability for being there. "You look like you've been rushing, sir," she observed wryly. "A man your size should be more careful in this heat. You could bring on apoplexy."

If he hadn't been so furious, he might have simply fled. Ordinarily, he didn't relish being a source of amusement for elderly females, but he needed to speak to Sarah Brandt, and at this point, he was even willing to apologize, if that was what it took.

"I didn't know you had company," he managed to say in a fairly civil tone. "I'll wait outside."

"Oh, don't mind me," the old woman said, rising from her chair. "You must have something very important to talk to Sarah about. I'll just be on my way, Mr. . . . ." She let her voice trail off expectantly.

"Mrs. Elsworth, this is Detective Sergeant Malloy of the New York City Police," Mrs. Brandt said, rising to her feet as well. "Mr. Malloy, this is my neighbor, Mrs. Elsworth."

The old lady was still looking him over very carefully, obviously feeling he needed to pass inspection before she'd leave him alone with Sarah Brandt.

"I dropped a knife this morning," she said, as if that should mean something. When no one responded, she continued, "That's how I knew I'd be getting a visitor soon. Although I guess you're really Sarah's visitor, aren't you? So perhaps I'd best be on my way. So nice to have made your acquaintance, Detective Sergeant."

Frank didn't return the compliment, although he did hold the door open for her, if only to hurry her on her way. No one spoke until the old woman was gone.

"Mr. Malloy," Mrs. Brandt said again, but this time she wasn't surprised. This time she was eager, if only to learn why Frank had come barging into her office. "What is it? Have you found out something?"

"You could say that, but I doubt it's what you think."

Now she was intrigued. "Please, sit down," she said, offering him the chair in which the old woman had been sitting a moment ago.

Frank didn't much like the idea of sitting in a chair reserved for her patients, and he didn't feel much like sitting anyway. He wouldn't be here that long anyway.

"They've taken me off the case," he announced baldly.

"*What?* Who did it? The VanDamms? Surely, they don't have the authority—"

"It was probably them behind it, but the order came from the Superintendent. Directly. I'm not to do any more investigation. The VanDamms don't care who killed their daughter, and they don't want her memory tarnished by me finding him."

"That's preposterous!"

Her outrage made him realize that he'd sought her out as much to share his own fury as to inform her of the circumstances that had caused it. "I thought so, but my opinion didn't count for much." Frank wanted to pace, but space in the small office was at a premium. He could only manage a few steps in any direction before encountering something too substantial to push out of the way.

"But surely . . . I mean . . . Oh, dear . . ." she stammered, bringing Frank up short. For the first time he really looked at her. She seemed stricken.

"What is it?"

"I . . . I learned something about Alicia and . . . and Sylvester Mattingly. Did you get my note?"

"Yeah, I got it. In fact, I'm pretty sure Mattingly is

why I was taken off the case. I went to see him yesterday, at his office.''

"Yesterday? That was even before I knew about him and Alicia. Why did you . . . ? Oh, to ask him about Hamilton Fisher,'' she recalled. ''Why, he might have hired Fisher to find Alicia for himself and not for the family at all! What did he say when you questioned him?''

"Nothing. He's a lawyer. They don't tell the police anything, as a general rule, and especially not if it would hurt them. Who told you about this marriage business? Any chance it isn't true?''

''I told you, it was a rumor, but my . . . my mother told me about it. She didn't really believe it, but everyone had heard it. Everyone in her social circle, that is,'' she clarified when he frowned at her.

Things were starting to fall into place. ''All right, this is what happened: The girl found out her father was going to marry her off to an old geezer—somebody she hated, according to Harvey the groom, who knew her pretty well—so she runs away and hides, hoping her father will change his mind. No wonder Mattingly didn't tell me anything. Not many men would want a story like that going around.''

''Maybe it's even worse than that,'' she said, surprising him.

''What could be worse?''

''Have you forgotten Alicia was with child? Who was the father of that child?''

Frank hadn't forgotten. Well, maybe just for a second. ''Probably the groom, Harvey. It has to be. Nobody else ever got near her.''

''What about her fiancé?''

''*Mattingly?*'' Frank was incredulous. ''Why would he . . . ?''

''To force her to marry him,'' she said. ''It wouldn't be the first time a reluctant woman has been persuaded to marry a man she wouldn't otherwise choose. He ruins her and makes her believe no other man will ever have her.

And if she conceives a child, she has no choice but to accept him.''

"But she *did* conceive a child," Malloy said, forgetting in the heat of the moment to be embarrassed by the subject. "And her family knew it. If that's what happened, why didn't she marry Mattingly?''

"Perhaps she kept it a secret until it was too late. By the time she ran away, she was too far along to pretend the child was conceived in wedlock, so her family had sent her to the country until after it was born. They could dispose of the child and still marry her to Mattingly. She'd be even more compliant, knowing the price she'd already paid.''

"That's crazy," Frank protested. "Why would they be that eager for her to marry that old son of a . . ." He caught himself just in time, although he doubted Sarah Brandt would be too shocked to hear him swear.

"I suspect it's some kind of a debt. A debt of honor, perhaps, that would be even more binding than a financial debt. Or it might even be some type of blackmail. If Mattingly handles Mr. VanDamm's business affairs, he would know things that might better be kept secret. Powerful men have been using their daughters to settle business arrangements for centuries, Mr. Malloy.''

Frank pushed his hat back on his head and took a few more paces, wishing he had some room to really walk. He needed to walk to figure this out. None of it was making any sense, at least to him.

"But it's useless to think about it now," she said after a moment.

He looked up in surprise, pausing in mid-stride. "Why?''

She looked just as surprised. "Because you've been taken off the case. I guess this means that no one else will be investigating it, either.''

"No one in the department," he said, watching her closely to see if she would get the implication.

Another woman would have looked away, but Sarah

Brandt met his gaze steadily, her blue-gray eyes dark with questions. She did not disappoint him. "Who else would be investigating it, then?"

"Maybe somebody who has a personal interest in finding Alicia VanDamm's killer. Somebody who wants to see justice done and who maybe wants a little revenge, too. Somebody who knew her when she was a kid."

Her eyes grew wide with surprise. "I'm not a detective!"

Frank couldn't hide his disgust. "You've been working as hard on this case as I have," he reminded her. "Finding out a lot of information, too." He was amazed to realize that admitting this caused him no discomfort at all.

And she wasn't as difficult to convince as he had thought. In fact, she seemed pleased. "Do you really think . . . ? I mean, what could I do?"

That was the question, of course. Frank scratched his head, then settled his hat more firmly. "You could keep asking questions, just like you have been. You could go back to the VanDamms and find out what they're saying. Tell them how distressed you are that the police aren't looking for Alicia's killer anymore. You could even go to some of the abortionists and see if they'll tell you anything they wouldn't tell me."

She was staring at him now. Not merely listening intently to what he was saying but openly staring, as if she'd suddenly noticed something about him she'd never seen before. Somehow resisting the urge to make sure he was all buttoned up properly, he glared at her. "What's the matter?"

She smiled like a cat with its head in the cream pitcher, setting Frank's teeth on edge. "I just realized that you must want to see Alicia's murder solved as much as I do."

"Is that so hard to believe?" Frank hated the tone of defensiveness he heard in his own voice.

"I already told you, I know how the police work, Mr. Malloy. They aren't interested in solving crimes unless there's something in it for them. I'm not accusing you of anything,'' she said quickly, when he would have protested. ''I'm just stating a fact. I even understand it. Police officers aren't paid very handsomely, so naturally, ambitious men will always be eager to improve their lot. Didn't you say something about making Captain?''

What did she know about it? Frank wished he could afford the luxury of simple ambition. His motivations for gaining advancement were far more ordinary. She didn't need to know that, though.

''That's right,'' he said. ''I want to be a captain, and I'm improving my chances by not investigating this case anymore.''

''Yet you still want to see it solved. May I ask you why?''

Frank didn't have to tell her a thing, he knew, but if he didn't, she might not want to do what he was asking. And he very much wanted her to, although he didn't allow himself to consider his real motives too closely. ''Probably for the same reason you do, Mrs. Brandt. As far as I can tell, Alicia VanDamm was a nice girl who deserved a chance in life. She never got that chance, and I want to find out why. I'd also like to see the person who killed her get punished, especially if it's any of the people I've met so far.''

His answer seemed to please her. ''I'd like to see them *all* punished,'' she admitted. ''I think when we find her killer, we'll discover that more than one person was involved in her death, even if it was just because their selfishness put her in danger in the first place. But suppose I do find out who killed her or at least find some information that would help. What good will it do if the police won't arrest the killer?''

''I've been thinking about this, and I guess there's only one thing you *can* do. You can take your story to Commissioner Roosevelt.''

''Roosevelt? Why?''

''Because he's determined to clean up the department.

He'd love a scandal like this, and he'd love forcing the superintendent to investigate the murder of a poor, innocent girl, especially if he didn't want to. The press would love it, too."

"The newspapers?" Plainly, this did not please her. "Why would we have to involve them?"

"Because Roosevelt loves publicity. Why do you think he travels around the city at night with a newspaper reporter?" he asked, referring to Roosevelt's habit of prowling in the darkness accompanied by Jacob Riis, checking to make sure policemen were at their posts. "Not only is he trying to find cops neglecting their duty, he wants to have his own personal reporter with him to put the story in the paper. Alicia's story would rouse public opinion like nothing else he's done so far, so the police couldn't ignore Roosevelt, even if they wanted to. They'd have to take some action, and Roosevelt would look like some kind of champion."

"And justice will be done."

Frank only wished he believed in justice. Then he remembered what Conlin had said, and he knew what he really wanted was revenge. "Alicia's killer will be punished," he corrected her.

She nodded, understanding his unspoken message. "Alicia will still be dead, so there can be no true justice. But at least there can be some punishment."

Frank fervently hoped so. He could think of so many people who deserved it. "Then you'll do it?"

She looked surprised that he would even ask. "Of course I will. I just . . . I'm not sure I know where to start."

"You've already started, Mrs. Brandt. You just have to keep on."

9

SARAH READILY ADMITTED SHE WAS FLATTERED BY
Frank Malloy's request that she investigate Alicia's murder. She would never admit it to *him*, of course, but she
was, nonetheless. She was almost as flattered as she was
outraged by Malloy's news that his superiors had taken
him off the case. She could understand if he wasn't doing
a good job or if they were merely assigning such an important case to someone with more seniority or some such
thing. But to simply tell him the case was closed without
any intention of ever finding Alicia's killer was more than
she could bear. What choice did she have but to accept
the challenge of solving Alicia's murder herself?

She hadn't mentioned to Malloy how she had fanta-
sized about being a detective. She also hadn't mentioned
how she had once questioned his dedication to finding
Alicia's killer. Whatever she might have thought of him
before, he had vindicated himself by his request. And she
wasn't even counting the fact that he had entrusted a
''mere'' female with the task, but if she had, it would
have counted heavily in his favor. If she wasn't careful,
she might start to think well of Malloy. Or at least not
quite so badly.

But all of that could wait for another day when she had

the time and energy to think about such things at her leisure. In the meantime she had a murderer to catch. She and Malloy had discussed possible courses of action, and the one that seemed most logical to Sarah was a return to the Higgins house where it had all started.

Today was going to be even hotter than yesterday, and the newspaper was starting to talk about a heat wave. If this was only April, what would July be like? In spite of the building heat, she found Mrs. Higgins in the kitchen preparing the noon meal for her lodgers. She would've preferred finding the new mother still in bed, but a quick examination of mother and child showed they were doing fine.

"I see you've got all your rooms rented," Sarah remarked as she sat at the kitchen table, cradling the baby, while his mother worked at the stove.

"Yes, but for how long?" Mrs. Higgins asked plaintively. "Good lodgers is so hard to find, and the ones we've got now don't fit that description. I'd reckon they'll be gone before the month is out, owing rent into the bargain."

"Then you'll find some better lodgers," Sarah said reasonably. "Of course, when the police catch the man who killed Miss VanDamm, you'd have a much easier time renting your rooms."

"That's certain," Mrs. Higgins agreed, lifting a spoonful of soup to her mouth to taste. Apparently she was satisfied. She laid the spoon down on its rest and heaved the heavy cover back onto the cast iron soup pot with a clang, holding the handle with a corner of her apron. "But how will they ever catch him now? Nobody's been around in a week. I don't think they're even looking anymore."

How true, Sarah thought, but she said, "I'm sure they'll find the killer soon. Is there some reason the police should have come back? Have you heard anything or has someone remembered something?"

Mrs. Higgins shook her head and turned a ball of dough out of the crockery bowl in which she had mixed it and began to knead it with practiced strokes. "Not that I know of. It's just . . . the children are still so upset. They have nightmares. They think the killer is coming back to get them."

Sarah felt an instant empathy with them. How many times had she dreamed she was Maggie, bleeding to death on a tenement floor? And she had been nearly grown when that happened. Their little imaginations must be running wild.

"I'd be happy to talk to them, if you think it would help. I know you've reassured them, but sometimes they don't believe their parents. If an outsider—another grownup—tells them they don't need to be afraid, they might believe it."

Mrs. Higgins's lined face brightened instantly. "Oh, would you, Mrs. Brandt? They all think the world of you. Mary Grace says she's going to bring ladies babies when she grows up, just like Mrs. Brandt does."

Sarah smiled, absurdly gratified by the compliment. "I'd be happy to speak to them." From the sounds she could hear through the open kitchen doorway, she was sure she'd find most of them playing in the tiny yard behind the house. Probably, they'd been sent outside to escape the heat. "I'll just take little Harry out for some air," she offered, shifting the baby to her shoulder as she rose from the chair.

The Higgins children were racing around out in the yard, along with several of the neighbor's children, engaged in some game only they could understand. Drawn by the novelty of a visitor, they came to her immediately, circling around like shy fireflies. She called each of them by name and tousled a few heads before seating herself on the steps. The smaller ones claimed the seats nearest to her, snuggling up and preening, basking in the undivided attention of a stranger. Little Harry gurgled contentedly, squinting in the bright morning sunlight where he lay on Sarah's lap.

They chatted for a while, Sarah inquiring politely into

their activities before bringing up the subject of bad dreams and bad men who came to get little children in the night. She hoped she wasn't lying when she assured them the bad man who had hurt Alicia was gone and wouldn't be back. At least she could be fairly certain he wouldn't be back to the Higgins house. After a few minutes, the novelty of her presence wore off, and the younger children wandered away, back to their games. Sally and Mary Grace claimed the seats vacated by the little ones and asked what they perceived to be more grown-up questions, until Sally, too, grew bored. She took her doll back to the makeshift playhouse her father had built out of wood scraps in a corner of the yard, leaving Mary Grace alone with Sarah.

Sarah smiled at Mary Grace as she bounced Harry gently in her lap, but the girl didn't smile back. She wished Mary Grace didn't look so old for her years. Sarah could almost believe she carried the weight of the world on her slender shoulders.

"That black bag you carry, is that what you bring the babies in?" Mary Grace asked suddenly.

Sarah bit back a smile, knowing if she showed amusement, she would damage Mary Grace's fragile pride. "Is that what your mother says?"

"She says it's none of my business, and I'll understand when I'm older."

She wouldn't *ever* understand it if no one ever explained it to her, Sarah thought. "What do you think?"

Mary Grace frowned thoughtfully and pulled on one of her pigtails. "I think the baby was in my mother's stomach."

"What makes you think so?"

"Because her stomach was big when we went to bed that night, and in the morning it was small again, and Harry was born."

"You're very smart to figure that out, Mary Grace," Sarah said, a little relieved that Mary Grace was so perceptive and Sarah wouldn't have to risk telling her something her mother would be angry to hear about.

"What I *can't* figure out is how Harry got *out* of her stomach," Mary Grace said, her small face pinched in frustration.

Sarah wasn't about to explain this to a girl of ten years. The actual mechanics of birth were still hard for Sarah to accept, even after all her years of experience. Explaining to a young girl how a baby could pass through an opening she probably didn't yet know existed wasn't something she was about to attempt on this spring morning.

"That's what the midwife does," she said by way of compromise. "I help the baby come out. Like your mother says, it's something you'll understand when you're older, but you don't have to worry about it right now. It will be a long time before you have to think about babies." At least she hoped so, remembering how very young Alicia VanDamm had been.

Sarah expected Mary Grace to wander off, too, now that their conversation was over, but she sat where she was, pretending to play with Harry, letting him grab her fingers with his tiny hands. Sarah sensed the girl had another question she wanted to ask and was just trying to work up the courage. She just hoped it was one she could answer honestly without incurring Mrs. Higgins's wrath.

Finally, she said, without looking up, "There was two of them."

"Two of who?" Sarah asked.

"In Alice's room that night." She glanced up to see if she'd shocked Sarah. She had, of course, but Sarah managed to register only surprise. She didn't want to frighten Mary Grace into silence.

"You saw the men who went to Alicia's—um, Alice's room?" she asked.

"Wasn't men. It was a man and a woman."

A thousand questions swirled in Sarah's mind, but she resisted the urge to throw all of them at the girl at once. If she was too eager or overanxious, Mary Grace might feel she was doing something wrong, and Sarah would learn nothing more. "Was it someone you knew? Ham Fisher, maybe?"

Mary Grace shook her head. "He was there, but it wasn't him. He let them in, I think. They come to the back door, and somebody let them in. Then Mr. Fisher goes out. He was carrying the bag he brought with him when he come. I guess it was his clothes, 'cause Mama said all his things was gone the next morning."

"The man and woman, what did they look like?"

"I don't know. It was dark," she said simply.

Of course it was. "But you recognized Ham Fisher," Sarah reminded her, shifting Harry and bouncing him a little when he started to fuss.

"I knowed the way he walks."

"Could you tell anything about the man and woman? Were they tall or short? Was there anything unusual or familiar about them?"

"Tall *and* short. He was tall and straight up and down. She was short and round, like a ball. She walked slow. She had a stick in her hand, a cane, I think it was, like she was crippled or something. He had to help her up the steps."

"Why didn't you tell anybody this before, Mary Grace?" Sarah asked.

The girl smoothed the fabric of her skirt. As the oldest child, she never had to wear hand-me-downs, so the quality was still good. "Nobody asked me," she said simply.

Sarah would enjoy telling Malloy that he'd missed a good bet by not questioning the children. She wondered that they didn't teach detectives how important that could be. "But I didn't ask you either," she pointed out.

Mary Grace flashed her a look. Her eyes were still shadowed. "I thought if I told the policeman . . . You won't tell my Mama, will you?"

"Why not?"

"Because I was supposed to be asleep. I like to sit up late, when everybody's asleep and everything's real quiet, but Mama yells at me. She says I need my rest. I think she just gets mad because I don't wake up when she calls me in the morning.''

Sarah could believe this. She could also imagine how a girl like Mary Grace might treasure a few minutes of solitude in a house so full of people. But she couldn't spend too much time worrying about Mary Grace's sleeping habits. She had a job to do, one Malloy would probably do much better since he was trained to do it. But Malloy wasn't here, and Sarah would have to manage somehow on her own. What would Malloy ask if he were here? What else would be important to know?

"Did you . . . did you hear anything that night? Any noise from Alice's room or people talking in there?''

"Her room's too far away, and I fell asleep. For a while, anyways.''

"What woke you up?''

"I guess it was the back door opening. My bed's right by the window. I saw the man leaving.''

"The man and woman, you mean.''

"No, just the man. And he was hurrying, like something was chasing him, only nothing was.''

"But you didn't see the woman?''

"No, she never come out, not that I saw. You won't tell my Mama, will you?'' she asked anxiously.

"No, I won't tell her a thing. But I'm glad you told me. This might help the police catch whoever hurt Alice.''

"I want you to catch him,'' Mary Grace said earnestly. "I dream he's coming back for me. I dream he's coming right through the window to get me, and when I wake up, I'm shaking.''

"Oh, dear,'' Sarah exclaimed, sliding her free arm around the girl's slender body and pulling her close. "You don't have to be afraid. He doesn't know you saw him, so he wouldn't have any reason to come back for you, and besides, he's going to stay as far away from this house as he can.''

"Do you think so?'' she asked doubtfully.

"I *know* so," Sarah replied, holding her close. She just wished Mary Grace looked a little more convinced.

Even though Sarah had wanted to go see Malloy at once, she headed home instead. After all, she couldn't go to him with every single clue. The people at Headquarters would get suspicious, and if they figured out that Malloy had put her on the case, he might be in terrible trouble. Besides, he'd said he'd check in with her every few days to see if she'd learned anything, so she would just have to wait until he showed up at her office again. It wasn't as if she'd discovered the killer's name or anything. She just knew that a man and a woman had gone into Alicia's room that night. The woman might have been an abortionist, and if she was, the description might identify her to Malloy, who had interviewed a goodly selection of them. But who was the man? She wished she knew more than that he was tall and straight. She supposed Mary Grace had meant he wasn't fat, but that could describe half the men in New York. It most certainly described Mr. VanDamm, Sylvester Mattingly, and probably even the groom, Harvey.

But if the woman was the abortionist, and they could find her, she could identify the man for them. If she would, that is. Sarah had little reason to hope the woman would betray someone who had probably paid her for her silence and who was already a murderer. Unless, perhaps, she feared for her life if she *didn't* betray him. Well, Malloy had much more experience at this than she did. He'd know what to do next.

Sarah was in her kitchen, braving the heat to bake some cookies for the Higgins children as a reward for Mary Grace's information, when someone rang her bell. She opened her door to find one of the dirty, shoeless boys known as street Arabs who made their precarious living any way they could.

"Mrs. Yardley, she says to come quick. Her baby's real

sick,'' he told her anxiously, hopping from one bare foot to the other in his urgency to be off again.

Remembering young Dolly and the babies she had already lost, Sarah hurried. On her way out, she captured one of the freshly baked cookies for the boy, who gobbled it up without a word of thanks. The afternoon heat was oppressive, and Sarah took her parasol along with her bag.

Although Sarah was technically a midwife, she was also a trained nurse and was often called upon to treat illnesses as well as childbirth. New mothers always seemed to think of her first if their babies became ill.

"What's wrong with the baby, do you know?" she asked the boy, who had to slow down so he wouldn't outpace her. He wouldn't get paid until she appeared, so he was sticking close to her.

"I don't know nothing. I was just to fetch you is all."

Sarah quickened her pace, even though she could already feel the sweat forming beneath her clothes. Maybe she should consider a bicycle, so at times like this she could move more quickly through the city streets. They were all the rage, and even the police used bicycles now. They were one of Commissioner Roosevelt's innovations, and just the other day she'd seen an article in the *Times* that the bicycle force was being expanded. Every now and then she saw a story about a "wheel man" stopping a runaway horse and wagon from the seat of his cycle, even though that hardly seemed possible. Somehow she couldn't imagine herself on one of the comic contraptions, however. Perhaps if she were younger and not so worried about her dignity.

At last she reached the tenement building on First Avenue where the Yardleys lived. Will Yardley stood on the front stoop, apparently watching for her. He shouted something when he saw her and the boy approaching and hurried to meet her. He even took her bag, carrying it the last few paces and up the stairs. Sarah could hear the baby's cries even out on the street. At least she was still alive and fairly strong, if the volume of her wailing was any indication.

"I told Dolly to send for a doctor, but she wouldn't have none of it," he was saying. "She only wanted you. Said you was the one kept this one from dying when it was born, and you'd keep her alive now."

Sarah was gratified to see that he seemed genuinely distressed by his daughter's illness. Perhaps he'd finally reconciled himself to the child after all. She would have asked him what was wrong with the baby, but by then they were on the stoop, and it was only a step into the Yardley's flat.

Sarah found Dolly walking the floor with the screaming baby over her shoulder. Her face was pale, her hair a mess, and she looked near exhaustion. "Oh, thank heaven you're here, Missus," she said. "My girl is that sick, she is."

"What seems to be the trouble?" Sarah asked, taking the squalling infant from her mother's arms.

"She's been up all night long, crying, and I can't figure out what's the matter!" They had to shout to be heard over Rosy's cries.

"Will she nurse?"

"Yes, but that just seems to make it worse. When she's done, she just starts screaming again."

"Has she been sick at all?"

"Not at all except for the crying!" Dolly said, on the verge of tears herself.

Sarah laid the baby on the kitchen table and checked her for rash and fever. She seemed warm, but considering the weather and the fact that she'd been held against her mother's body for a while, that was only to be expected. Or perhaps she had a low fever. Sarah listened to the baby's heart and lungs with her stethoscope and, to her great relief, found nothing wrong there. Having eliminated every serious possibility, she knew the answer.

"She has the colic," Sarah said.

"The colic? What's that?"

"It's a bad stomachache. See the way she pulls her legs up when she cries? That's because her stomach hurts."

"But how could she have a stomachache? She don't eat nothin' 'cept my milk. Do you think I'm poisonin' her?" she asked in horror.

"Oh, no, of course not. The colic is something some newborns get. Nobody knows why, and unfortunately, nobody really knows how to cure it. Usually, it lasts for six months—"

"*Six months?*"

"—and then the baby just grows out of it, and it stops. That's why they call it the six months colic."

Dolly looked stricken. "You mean she's gonna cry like this for six months? I'll have to go to Bellevue!" she cried, naming the local insane asylum. "And Will's gonna go right along with me!"

"I didn't say we couldn't help her," Sarah assured her. "I'll show you some tricks that will make her more comfortable and help you all keep your sanity."

Sarah showed Dolly how to carry the baby over her arm, which seemed to soothe her instantly. Meanwhile, she warmed some rags to lay on the baby's stomach. Within an hour, the exhausted child was sleeping peacefully.

When Dolly had laid her in the bed, she sank down in a chair and gave Sarah a desperate look. "You don't have to tell me no lies just to make it easier, Mrs. Brandt. Just tell me straight out, is she gonna die? Don't be afraid to say the truth. I don't wanna—"

"No, of course she isn't going to die. Not from colic. I told you, lots of babies get it. They just cry a lot, and then one day you wake up and it's over, and your baby will be happy and healthy."

Dolly's large eyes filled with tears. "You're sure?"

"I'm positive."

Dolly grabbed Sarah's hand and pressed it to her lips in a gesture both touching and humbling. "Oh, Missus, thank you for coming. I don't know what I—''

"Now don't give me more credit than I deserve. Rosie isn't even really sick,'' Sarah demurred, gently extricating her hand. "And now I think I'd better start taking care of my other patient. You need some rest, too, Dolly, but first let me fix you something to eat. Then I want you to sleep until the baby wakes up. That's an order.''

Within a few minutes, Dolly was fed and tucked into bed with her child, both of them sound asleep. Sarah found Will Yardley, still perched on the front stoop. He was nursing a glass of something that looked suspiciously like beer, and he looked as frazzled and exhausted as Dolly had.

"Is she gonna live?'' he asked Sarah.

Sarah knew it wasn't a silly question. Babies died of seemingly minor ailments every day in the tenements. At least this time she could give him hope. "She's got the colic. It's nothing but a stomachache.'' Sarah explained it again, trying to use terms Will could understand.

"And she won't die of it?''

"Not of the colic.'' That much she could promise. As for whatever else came along, well, that was in God's hands. "I'll be back again tomorrow to see how they're doing, but right now, they both just need to get some sleep.''

"Could a doctor do anything more?''

"No,'' Sarah said quite honestly. There were no magic potions to cure the mysterious maladies that plagued mankind, no matter what the claims of patent medicines might be. At least Rosie's ailment could be cured by time.

Will nodded, accepting her word. His young face looked haggard, and for the first time she realized how young he was. He couldn't be more than twenty-five, if that, but his face showed every year of his life, and his eyes gleamed with a wisdom hard-earned. She thought of the boy who had come to fetch her today, and wondered if Will was the kind of man he would grow into, if indeed he lived long enough to grow up. Few did.

Will ran a grubby hand over his weary face. "I don't know what I'll do with Dolly if anything happens to that kid. I thought she took it hard when she lost them other ones, but this one . . . she sets store by this one, Mrs. Brandt."

From the red rims of Will's eyes, Sarah suspected he did, too, but she wouldn't challenge his manhood by asking him to admit it. "I'll take good care of both of them, Will."

"I'll pay you for this time," Will offered, perhaps afraid she might not give him good service if it was a trade, like before. Or perhaps he was simply afraid of being neglected if she thought he couldn't afford her fee.

Sarah wasn't so well-off that she could afford to turn down a fee, but when she recalled the bargain she had made with Will the last time, she wondered if he might not be of use to her again. "You won't have to pay me anything at all if you can find out some more information about that man I asked you about before."

"That Fisher swell?"

"That's the one."

Will frowned suspiciously. "I heard it won't be very good for my health if I go messing around with that Mattingly fellow he works for."

"You won't have to."

Will was still suspicious. "Then what do you want to know?"

Sarah thought it over and decided she might as well go for broke. "I'd like to know where to find him."

Will's frown deepened. "Why would you wanna know that? You ain't going after him yourself, are you?"

"Oh, no, I wouldn't think of it," she said, then wondered if that were true. If she knew where Ham Fisher was—the man who had perhaps admitted Alicia's killer to the Higgins house—would she be patient enough to wait for Malloy? That was a question she couldn't answer until she knew. "I just need to know where he is, Will. And when I do, a friend of mine wants to talk to him. A male friend,'' she added, in case he was still worried.

Will was still worried. "I owe you, Mrs. Brandt, so I'll do what I can, but I can't make no promises. It's a big city, and there's a thousand places a fellow like that can hide if he don't want to be found.''

Sarah smiled at Will Yardley. "I know you'll do your best, Will.''

IT WAS THE end of a very long, very hot day when Frank climbed the stairs to his flat. The smell of cooking cabbage hung heavily in the stifling air of the littered stairwell, along with other, even less savory aromas. Too many people living too close together. He could hear the sounds of the McMullins arguing, her screeching and him booming in response. The words were indistinguishable, but Frank knew he wouldn't understand the fight even if he could understand the words. There'd be some crashing of pots and pans and then silence for a long time afterward. That's how it always went. Nothing much changed in this building, even when he was gone for days at a time, which he mostly was.

When he reached the door to his flat on the second floor, he tried the knob before hunting for his key. As he'd suspected, it turned under his hand. How many times had he told his mother to keep the door locked? Maybe she *wanted* somebody to break in and murder her.

She'd probably reason that at least he'd have to pay attention to her then, if for no other reason than to investigate the crime.

She was in the front room in front of the open window to catch what breeze there was when he walked in, rocking and sewing by the light of the gas jet. She looked up from her mending when the door opened. Her expression was all phony surprise.

"Well, now, sir, and what might you be wanting? If you're selling something, I'm just a poor old woman with no money to spend on fripperies, mind you, so you might as well be on your way.''

"Ma," he said in warning, but it didn't faze her.

"And if you've come here for no good, let me warn you, I've got a son who's a police detective, and he'll hunt you down like a dog. I hear he's pretty good at his job, although I wouldn't know for myself, since I hardly ever get to see him."

"Enough, Ma." Frank stepped into the room and closed the door behind him. "I'm not in the mood."

"*Frances?*" she cried in feigned surprise. "Is it you? I swear, it's been so long, I've forgot what you look like."

He could have argued that he'd been here just last Thursday, but of course, that was five days ago now, and she'd hardly consider that a recent visit. Technically, he lived here, but he spent far more time in the police dormitory and elsewhere. His mother was part of the reason why, if only part.

"Do you have anything to eat?" he asked, hanging his hat on a peg by the door and shrugging out of his suit coat. At least he didn't have to stand on formality here. It was one of the few advantages of coming home.

"Of course I have something to eat. My son, the big fancy police detective, he brings me money every week. I go to Mass every morning to thank the Blessed Virgin that I have such a generous son."

Briefly, Frank considered performing that murder he had been thinking about earlier himself. Unfortunately, he needed the old woman too much. "Would it be too much trouble for you to fix me something?" he asked instead, managing to keep his voice even, mainly because he was too tired for an argument. "I haven't eaten since morning."

As he'd suspected, her motherly instincts overcame her need to make him feel guilty. Something about a hungry child, no matter what his age, was a temptation no woman could resist. She laid her mending aside and rose instantly. "You get washed up. It'll only take a minute. I've got a stew I just made today, your favorite. I put carrots in it, just the way you like."

Frank washed up at the kitchen sink and dried his hands and face on an immaculate towel. Everything in the apartment was immaculate, in fact. The floors were spotless, the furniture polished and shining, even the windows shone. Frank almost felt like he was contaminating the place by his presence. Another reason to stay away.

As if he needed one.

Sitting down at the scrubbed table, Frank remembered the meal he'd eaten with Sarah Brandt. Although her cooking wasn't up to his mother's standards, she'd been a lot better company. Or maybe that was just because they'd only been talking about his work. Frank always felt comfortable when he was talking about his work. His mother, of course, never wanted to hear about what he did. What he did frightened her, and besides, she had her own world. And her own concerns. Frank was sometimes one of them.

She worked in silence, heating the stew. The rich aroma made his stomach clench painfully, and he tried to remember why he hadn't stopped for lunch today. A stool pigeon had kept him busy most of the afternoon, a little weasel of a man who claimed to know who had robbed that big warehouse on the docks. If Frank could solve that case, he'd be able to add a reward of several hundred dollars to his savings. A promotion to Captain cost $14,000, or at least it used to, before Roosevelt and his reformers took over. But the reformers wouldn't last. Someday soon things would be just the way they used to be, and Frank would need that $14,000. He still had a long way to go.

His mother set the plate down in front of him, and he looked at her—really looked at her—for the first time since he'd come in. She was tired. And when had her hair gotten so gray? She was a small woman, shorter than average, and over the years her once-trim figure had broadened in the beam, but she was still a long way from fat. Frank could remember her working long days over a washtub to bring in extra money when he and his sisters had been young. He wondered vaguely how a woman so small had managed such hard physical labor, something he'd never even considered before. She hadn't seemed small then, since he'd been a child himself, and he hadn't thought of those days in years, not since he'd gotten work and been able to ease her load somewhat.

Frank shoveled in a spoonful of stew and chewed gratefully. "This is good, Ma," he said, startling her. But his mother wasn't one for compliments, and neither was he. She was instantly suspicious, and went on the attack.

"He's asleep, and thank you for asking," she said tartly, taking a seat opposite him so she could glare.

Frank allowed himself another bite of stew. "I figured. It's late."

"Is that why you waited until now to come? So he'd be asleep, and you wouldn't have to see him?"

"I waited until late because that's when I was finished with my work," Frank said. He tried not to sound defensive, but the stew suddenly tasted like sawdust in his mouth. He broke off a piece of bread, dipped it in the gravy, and stuffed it in his mouth defiantly. "You know I work long hours. You know I can't get home very often."

"You got home easy enough when Kathleen was alive," she reminded him.

"I was a patrolman then. I worked my shift and went home." The shifts had been twenty-four hours long, too, so he really hadn't been home a lot, even in those days. But his mother wasn't going to be bothered by facts when she had a point to make.

"He asks for you. I don't know what to tell him."

He really wanted to kill her then, for telling such an awful, hurtful lie. "He doesn't talk, Ma. He *can't* talk."

"He talks. He don't talk plain, like you and me, but I understand what he wants. I show him your picture, the one of you and Kathleen when you got married, and I tell him, 'That's your Da.' And he asks for you. He knows who you are, even though he don't see you more than once in a blue moon.''

''I've got my job to do, don't I?'' he asked, hating the guilt he felt clawing inside of him. Hating her and himself and everybody in the world.

''You've got more than one job, Frances Xavier Malloy.''

''Only one that puts food on the table and a roof over your head. Over *his* head. Or would you rather live on the streets?''

His feeble attempt to make her feel guilty in return failed miserably. She was the master at it. ''Finish your supper,'' she told him, as if he was a boy again. ''Then you can go in and see him.''

What a rare treat, he thought bitterly. By now the delicious meal was a leaden lump in his stomach, and whatever appetite he'd had vanished. ''I'll see him now,'' he said resignedly, throwing down his spoon and pushing his chair back with a scrape.

''Now, Frances, finish your supper,'' she tried, but he was gone to do his penance, opening the door to the bedroom.

The room was dark and silent except for the rasp of breathing. His mother's bed took up one corner and the crib the other. The light from the gas jet in the kitchen spilled in, enough for him to see when his eyes had made the adjustment. Every instinct told him to flee. Every instinct rebelled against putting himself through this. It never got any easier. If anything, after three years, it was harder than ever to look upon the face of disaster, but still he forced his footsteps across the few feet of floor to the side of the crib.

The crib was large, larger than a regular baby's crib. A carpenter had built it for him special. A necessary expense that had come out of his captain's fund. Not that he begrudged the money, but still, every dollar that came out would mean he'd need that much longer to gather enough money. Time he didn't have to waste.

Frank wrapped his fingers around the side railing of the bed and looked down. The face lay in shadows, but Frank could see it well enough. He knew it by heart, after all. The beautiful face. Kathleen's face shrunk down to child size. Kathleen's beautiful blue eyes, closed now in sleep, thank God, so he didn't have to see them and feel the pain he still felt every time he looked into them and saw only emptiness.

His son and heir. The blanket covered his twisted legs, the legs that would never walk, and the night had closed the empty eyes so Frank wouldn't have to see that no matter what his mother said, his own child didn't recognize him and probably never would and would most certainly never call him by name.

They'd told him the grief for Kathleen would dim with the passing of time, but he still felt it fiercely each time he saw his son, the legacy of her awful, needless death. The pain in his heart was like a gaping hole, a bottomless pit he could never fill, no matter how hard he tried. He'd been holding on for three years, now, and if he ever let go, he might fall into that pit and lose himself forever.

How many times had he been tempted to do just that? Only one thing had stopped him. His son. Kathleen's son. The boy who would grow tall but who would never grow up, who would need someone to look after him for his entire life. Frank was that someone, and so he had to make Captain, to make sure his son would never want for anything as long as he lived.

Without consciously deciding to, Frank reached down and stroked the red-gold curls that his mother refused to cut. They felt like silk beneath his rough fingers, and the boy stirred slightly in his sleep.

That was when Frank understood about Alicia Van-Damm. She'd been just as helpless as his boy, in her own way, helpless and afraid and no one had taken care of her. That was wrong. Frank knew it in the depths of what little soul he still possessed. He wouldn't be able to right that wrong. He wouldn't be able to help Alicia VanDamm.

She was long past such help now, but at least he could avenge her death. A blow for justice in an unjust world. Usually, Frank didn't feel he could afford the luxury of justice, but just this once, and just because he had Sarah Brandt to help him, he was going to indulge himself.

He only hoped Sarah Brandt was up to the task.

10

SARAH FELT A BIT STRANGE IN HER NEW OUTFIT, probably because it had been so long since she'd had one. As much as she hated indulging herself in new clothes when she had no place to wear them, she'd felt her current situation justified the purchase of something more presentable than her usually serviceable, if unstylish, attire. If she was going to be calling on the elite members of the city's society, she shouldn't have to risk being ordered to use the servant's entrance.

And of course, when she'd seen the Macy's advertisement on the front page of the *Times*, she hadn't been able to resist the price. Only twenty-four dollars, when it would usually cost thirty. She could always wear the suit to church, she told herself. The hussar blue serge reefer suit—with silk lining throughout—wasn't so very grand that she would look out of place among ordinary folk, but it was presentable enough that she wouldn't have to suffer raised eyebrows from a butler or a maid when she sought admittance to her own family's home.

She really should be going to visit her mother. And she would. Very soon. As soon as this business was settled, she told herself. Now that she'd settled things with her mother, she had no more excuse not to go. Except, of course, that she wasn't ready to see her father just yet. And she did have to take care of this business about Alicia. The instant Alicia's murder was solved and her killer brought to justice, however, she'd have time to think about herself and take care of family business.

Until then, she had a job to do.

The *Times* said that the temperature yesterday had been eighty-four degrees, a record high for that date, but today was cooler, thank heavens. Still warm for April, but only pleasantly so. A lovely day for a stroll in the nicer neighborhoods of the city. The house on Marble Row was still draped in black crepe, and when Alfred answered her knock, he didn't seem the least surprised to see her.

"Mrs. Brandt, won't you come in? I'll see if Miss Mina is home," he said, which gave her hope. At least he hadn't been ordered to turn her away at the door.

This time Sarah had come during regular visiting hours, too, taking the chance that the VanDamms wouldn't be receiving much company yet and she wouldn't have to share Mina with other curious acquaintances. Assuming, of course, she was going to be admitted at all. The memory of being refused admittance the last time was still nagging at her when Alfred returned and told her Miss Mina would receive her in the front parlor.

Sarah needed a minute to collect herself and conceal her immense relief. It wouldn't do to go in to Mina looking joyous with triumph when she was supposedly paying a condolence call. When she was sure her expression was suitably somber, she allowed Alfred to escort her into the parlor.

Mina was ensconced on a sofa at the far end of the room, her back to the heavily draped window. Her black crepe gown was obviously new and in the height of fashion, its mutton-chop sleeves positively enormous. Certainly, she would have missed the jewelry that her mourning forbade, but she managed to look quite elegant all the same.

She extended a limp hand to Sarah, who was glad to

see she was alone. Extracting information from her would
be difficult enough without competing with other visitors
for her attention.

"How are you, Mina?" Sarah asked with as much concern as she could muster, taking the hand Mina offered
in both of her own.

"As well as I can be under the circumstances, I suppose," she allowed with a dramatic sigh. "Please, sit
down, and tell me what's going on in the world. I haven't
been out of doors since poor Alicia's funeral."

Sarah was fairly certain Mina wasn't interested in hearing about the controversy over the enforcement of the
Raines Law, which decreed that saloons should be closed
on Sunday or about the dry goods store that had burned
down the other day. Rather, she'd want to know the latest
gossip from the society she couldn't enjoy because of her
mourning. Unfortunately, Sarah knew no more of it than
Mina did.

"I'm afraid I'm rather dull and don't have any news to
share. But tell me, have the police learned anything
new?" Sarah asked, having decided to play innocent. "Do
they have any idea yet who killed poor Alicia?"

Sarah thought she caught a glimpse of annoyance in
Mina's eyes before she lowered them to touch her handkerchief to her nose ever so delicately. "I'm sure I don't
know. Father is the one they speak to. I couldn't bear to
speak of it in any case. But I'll tell you the truth, I doubt
they'll ever find her killer. You know how incompetent
the police are. It's a wonder it's even safe for a woman
to walk the streets anymore."

"I know you were able to recover Alicia's jewelry,"
Sarah reminded her. "Has your father offered a reward
for her killer, too?"

Mina looked at her as if she'd just spit on the floor.
"Most certainly not! How could you put a price on someone's life?"

How indeed, particularly when finding Alicia's jewelry
seemed more important to them than avenging her death.

Sarah decided not to explain to Mina the ways of the world where police efficiency was concerned. She'd be wasting her time, particularly since she knew the Van-Damms had already ordered the police to cease the investigation, so Mina would have no interest in the subject. She decided to try a different approach.

"I can't help thinking that if they could just locate that young man, the one who was living in the boardinghouse and who disappeared the night she died, they might learn something. He must have some information. Since he ran away, he might have seen something that night. Perhaps he even knows who her killer is."

"Most likely he *is* her killer, so it seems doubtful he'll ever show his face again. Even if the police were trying to find him, he's probably a hundred miles away by now. He'd certainly be a fool if he wasn't."

"But if he would just come back, we could at least be sure. I know the police believe he knows something. I wouldn't mind asking him some questions myself."

Mina seemed intrigued. "And exactly what would you ask Alicia's killer if you had the opportunity?"

Sarah pretended to consider. "Oh, for instance, I'd ask him why he was so interested in Alicia."

"Really, Sarah, don't you already know the answer to that? Alicia was lovely and young and female," Mina said, not bothering to hide her animosity. "That explains why any man would be interested in her."

"And I'd want to know if he saw someone come into the house that night. The doors would have been locked, so how did the killer get in? Perhaps this Fisher fellow was the one who opened the door. And we also know an abortionist came to see Alicia that night. If we could—"

"An *abortionist*? What on earth are you talking about?"

"An abortionist is a person who . . . who helps women get rid of babies they don't want," Sarah explained, recalling she hadn't known such people existed, either, when she'd lived in Mina's world.

Mina seemed shocked. Her face had paled. "What makes you think a person like this visited Alicia that night?"

"The police found one of her instruments in Alicia's room. I'm sure if we could find this woman, she could at least tell us who hired her and—"

"Really, Sarah, this is ridiculous. You already told me that Alicia was with child, and now you want me to believe someone came to her room that night and got rid of the baby for her. Which is it?"

"Both. If someone did come to perform an abortion on Alicia, I'm sure they refused when they saw how far along she was. Performing the procedure at that time would have been much too dangerous. The woman would have refused and left the house. But the person who hired her could have remained behind with Alicia, and if he did, he must be Alicia's killer. Maybe he was Alicia's lover, the father of her child. If so, he might have reason to want her dead. If we just knew who he was—"

"I tell you, Alicia had no lover. The very thought is preposterous. If that's who the police are looking for, no wonder they can't find anything."

"I'm afraid Alicia most certainly did have a lover. She was with child," Sarah reminded her.

Mina's face was stark white now, but from what emotion, Sarah couldn't be sure. Certainly, she was shocked and embarrassed and outraged and probably angry, too. Sarah was sure no one had ever talked to her about such things before in her entire life. But then, her sister had never been murdered before, either.

"No one in authority has told me such a thing about Alicia's condition," Mina said, as if she could negate the fact by the force of her denial.

"Then I'm telling you, and the police detective in charge of the case told me himself. Your sister must have known at least one man. Was there someone who befriended her? Someone who could have had the opportunity to seduce her? A family friend, perhaps? Someone you'd never suspect.''

Sarah knew she was foolish to expect Mina to implicate Sylvester Mattingly outright, but she couldn't help trying to tempt her.

Mina leaned her head back against the cushions and pressed her handkerchief to her mouth for a long moment, as if forcibly controlling her emotions. When she had collected herself, she said, ''This is all so horrible.'' Then her gaze touched Sarah, and Sarah saw the cunning in her pale eyes. ''But I wonder at you, Sarah. Why do you care so much about all this, and how do you know so much about the case?''

''I've been very concerned from the beginning,'' Sarah explained. ''Since I saw Alicia the night before she died, I feel connected somehow. And one of the police detectives has been very kind in answering my questions and keeping me informed about what's happening.''

Mina sniffed in derision. ''Are you consorting with a *policeman*? Really, Sarah, you have no more judgment in men than your sister did.''

Anger flooded Sarah, nearly choking her, but she somehow managed to bite back the sharp retort she so desperately wanted to make. She settled for, ''I sometimes think I'm the only one who cares if Alicia's killer is found.''

For a second, Sarah thought perhaps Mina was going to agree with her. But then she said, ''I'm really very tired, Sarah. This has been a terrible strain on all of us. I know you'll excuse me if I cut our visit short.''

Effectively dismissed, Sarah had no choice but to leave. She rose and took a moment to put her gloves on, hoping that Mina would feel compelled to say something into the silence. But she disappointed Sarah by simply waiting until she was finished. Then she summoned a maid to see her out.

Out on the sidewalk, Sarah savored the sounds of busy Fifth Avenue. Briefly, she considered taking a hansom cab back to Greenwich Village. She needed some time to digest her visit with Mina and to figure out if she had learned anything at all. But the fare would be exorbitant, and she could be just as alone with her thoughts on the El.

Feeling slightly out of place in her new gown among the working people on the train, Sarah watched the buildings speeding by, absently noting the advertising signs plastered on nearly every exposed surface of those buildings. "Castoria" and "Ivory Soap, It Floats," and "Sozodont Toothpaste" and "Buffalo Lithia Water" were all being touted as the cure for whatever ailed a body, from female complaints to bad breath.

By the time the train reached Fortieth Street, Sarah had decided that Mina had told her nothing useful. What she really needed was to see Malloy for a consultation. She needed his guidance and his perspective and most of all, his experience to help her decide what to do next. After a while, even the murmur of the wheels on the tracks seemed to hum his name. Malloy, Malloy, Malloy. *Come soon, Malloy. I've run out of things to do.*

Malloy didn't come until the following evening. Sarah had long since finished her supper and was reading one of Tom's medical journals when she heard his knock. Recognizing his silhouette through the curtain, she felt a surge of anticipation she hadn't felt since she'd lost Tom. For all the satisfaction her work gave her, Sarah realized her life had lacked a certain amount of excitement in recent years. In fact, except for the occasional difficult birth, it had lacked any excitement at all. But Detective Sergeant Malloy had changed all that by asking her to help him solve Alicia's murder. She might never actually like him—he represented too many things of which she disapproved for that to ever happen—but she must always be grateful to him for giving her a purpose outside herself for the first time in far too long.

"Malloy," she greeted him warmly. "Come in. I've been busy, and I have a lot to tell you."

He looked bone weary, and his shirt was limp and wrinkled, as if he'd worn it for more than one day in the recent heat. He did, at least, remove his hat this time. Sarah took it and hung it on the coat tree by the door.

"Have you eaten?" she found herself asking. Why she should care, she had no idea, but he looked as if he needed someone to look after him. Sarah's long dormant feminine instincts demanded she do so.

"I'm fine," he said, a little gruffly, she thought. "Don't go to any trouble for me."

"Come into the kitchen and sit down anyway. I've got some coffee left from supper. You look like you could use some."

She thought he smiled a little at that, although she couldn't be sure. It might simply have been a grimace. But he followed her into the kitchen, and he drank the coffee she poured for him.

"What have you found out?" he asked when he'd finished half the cup in one swallow.

"Well, let's see. Where should I begin?" she mused, taking a seat opposite him and picking up her own cup. "I went back to the Higgins house, and this time I talked to the children."

"The *children*?"

"Yes, you probably thought they were asleep when Alicia was killed, but Mary Grace wasn't. She's the oldest girl. Her bed is right by the window, and she was awake that night. She saw a man and a woman come into the house."

"When was this?" Suddenly, Malloy didn't look quite so tired anymore.

"Mary Grace didn't know the time, but it must have been late, after everyone else was in bed. The man was tall and thin, and the woman was short and round and walked with a cane. The man had to help her up the stairs, Mary Grace said."

"Did she recognize either of them?"

"She said she didn't. It was dark, of course, but she recognized Hamilton Fisher when he came out later. She said she could tell it was him by the way he walked, and he was carrying his bag with him. If she'd known the man and woman, I think she would have recognized them, too.''

''She saw Fisher leave then?''

''Yes, she thought he was the one who let the man and woman into the house, although she didn't see him do it. She must be right, too, since nothing else makes sense. And shortly afterward, he left. He was carrying a satchel, so Mary Grace thought he was leaving for good, which of course he was.''

''But she didn't think she knew the man and woman.''

''No, but I believe we can assume the woman was the abortionist. The man brought her, and . . .''

''And he tried to get her to perform the abortion, but Alicia wouldn't allow it.''

''Or more likely, the abortionist wouldn't do it when she found out how far along Alicia was. She wouldn't want to take a chance of Alicia dying, and a procedure so late in the pregnancy would be very dangerous.''

''So she didn't do it, and then what?'' Malloy was thinking out loud, trying to come up with a scenario that made sense. ''She stood there while the man killed Alicia?''

''No, Mary Grace said she saw the man leaving later, alone. She said he was running as if someone was chasing him, although no one was. I think the woman, the abortionist, must have left when she found out she had nothing to do there. The man stayed with Alicia. Perhaps they quarreled, or perhaps he'd simply intended to kill her all along if he couldn't get her to agree to the abortion. In any event, however he came to do it, he strangled her. Then he must have become frightened by what he'd done, so he ran away.''

''I hate to admit it, Mrs. Brandt, but your theory makes a lot of sense,'' he said with just the trace of a smile. ''Now all we need to know is who he was.''

"Or at least who *she* was, since she could certainly identify him for us."

"Oh, I already know who *she* is," Malloy said with infuriating confidence as he drained his cup.

"You do? How?"

"I questioned all the abortionists in town, remember? Only one of them is short and fat and walks with a cane. The Russian woman, Petrovka."

"Emma Petrovka, of course!" Sarah cried. "I should have guessed it myself. I know her slightly. Our paths have crossed once or twice."

Sarah had thought Mrs. Petrovka an awful woman, but not for any reason other than her profession. She seemed competent and well-mannered, and many women were grateful for her services, as Sarah knew only too well. Perhaps Alicia would have been if given the choice in time.

"Will you question her again?" Sarah asked. "Can you make her tell you who the man was?"

This time Malloy did smile. It was a funny, crooked little thing that looked oddly out of place on his broad face. "I'm not allowed to question anybody, Mrs. Brandt. I'm off the case, remember?"

Oh, dear, she'd forgotten. But then she recalled who was really investigating this case. "But *I'm* not off the case, am I? I could question Mrs. Petrovka!"

"Are you sure you want to? This isn't like interrogating the Higgins children. You're getting pretty close to the killer."

"Mrs. Petrovka isn't the killer," Sarah scoffed.

"No, but she most likely knows who is. If she tells you anything, not necessarily who he is but anything at all that could lead you to him, you'd be in danger."

"How would the killer know?"

Malloy frowned. "She might tell him. He might already be bribing her for her silence, so she'd feel a sense of loyalty or at least obligation to tell him. Or maybe she doesn't even know Alicia was killed that night she visited her. Then you both would be in danger.''

"I'm not afraid. I'll go see her in the daylight.''

"Do you think people don't get killed in the daylight?'' he asked, obviously horrified at her hopeless naivete.

"I think I'll be safe from a crippled old woman,'' she said, amused by his dismay. Could Malloy really be concerned for her safety?

Before he could reply, another visitor knocked on Sarah's door.

"Who's that?'' Malloy asked, on his feet in an instant.

"I guess I won't know until I open the door,'' Sarah allowed.

"It's kind of late for visitors.'' He was frowning like a disapproving father.

Sarah decided not to point out that *he* was there, and surely, he also counted as a visitor since he didn't live there. "I'm a midwife, Malloy. I get visitors at all hours of the day *and* night. This is actually early compared to some.''

He followed her into the front room, maintaining a discreet distance so he would be out of sight of whoever was at the door but still close enough to hear what was said. Trying to be amused rather than annoyed by his presumption, Sarah asked who was there.

"It's Will Yardley, Mrs. Brandt.''

Sarah threw the door open. "Is it the baby? Is she sick again?''

Will looked surprised and very young in the shadows. "Oh, no, she's doing just fine. That tea you told Dolly to make did the trick. It's that other thing. I got the information you wanted.'' He glanced over his shoulder, as if checking to be sure no one was following him, and Sarah decided this was simply a habit.

"Come in and tell me what you learned,'' she said, stepping back so he could enter. She closed the door behind him so he would feel safer.

When he judged it was secure and they could not be

overheard, he said, "The fellow you was looking for, Fisher?"

"Yes, did you find him?" she asked eagerly.

"Not him exactly, but a friend of mine what knows him, he seen him down in the Bowery."

"The *Bowery*?" Sarah echoed in surprise. She would have expected Sylvester Mattingly's employee to have a better address than the city's lowest slum.

"Yeah, he's been living in a flophouse down there. Place they call the Brass Lantern."

A flophouse? This was the lowest of accommodations, only one step above sleeping on the street. For a nickel, a man could "flop" on the floor, for a few cents more he could have a hammock, and if he really wanted luxury, a dime would buy a cot for the night. Men slept shoulder to shoulder in the most appalling conditions, and only the lowest of the low could be found there. This made no sense at all. What would Ham Fisher, a man who fancied himself a private detective, be doing in a place like that?

"Are you sure it's him?" Malloy demanded, stepping out of the shadows.

Will started and swore an oath. "What's a copper doin' here, Mrs. Brandt? You didn't tell me about no coppers bein' mixed up in this."

He would have bolted, but Sarah grabbed his sleeve and held on tight. "Mr. Malloy is a friend of mine, Will. He's just visiting."

"The hell you say. You telling me he ain't no copper?"

Sarah wondered how he could tell Malloy's occupation simply by looking at him, but she supposed that was a skill Will would have developed early in life. "He's trying to solve a murder."

"This Fisher killed somebody?" Will asked, even more alarmed.

"No, but he might know who did. It was a young girl, Will, only sixteen. Not much younger than Dolly."

"This ain't none of my business. I gotta go."

"Maybe you'd like to answer Mrs. Brandt's questions

down at Police Headquarters,'' Malloy said in a voice she'd never heard before. It frightened even her.

The color drained from Will's face, and she had to hold him with both hands.

"Stop it!'' she ordered Malloy. "You're frightening him!''

"That's the best way to deal with the likes of him,'' Malloy insisted.

"Not in *my* house,'' Sarah insisted right back. "Will, he isn't taking you anywhere, not after you came here and did me a favor. I want to thank you for that. This Brass Lantern, where is it located?''

"I know where it is,'' Malloy said. "You can let him go, if that's all he knows.''

She glared at Malloy, although it didn't seem to faze him, then turned to Will with a smile. "Thank you for coming, Will. And tell Dolly I'll check on her and the baby in a day or two.''

"You didn't tell me about no coppers,'' he repeated plaintively, giving Malloy one last desperate look before bolting for the door.

When he was gone, Sarah turned to Malloy in disgust. "Is that how you treat all your informants? It's a wonder you ever solve any crimes at all!''

"I lack your charm, Mrs. Brandt. I have to use the tools I've got.''

"Well, remind me never to commit a murder in New York. I would hate to see your 'tools' firsthand.''

Sarah brushed past him and returned to the kitchen where she refilled her cup. When she saw he had followed her back, she filled his, too. He took that as an invitation to sit again, which he did. Sarah wanted to be angry with him, but she had to admit, she wasn't. Not really. He was only doing his job, or what would have been his job if someone hadn't taken him off the case. Since she was trying to do the same thing, she shouldn't fault him for using different methods than she would have chosen.

"Now, tell me where this Brass Lantern is so I can find

Ham Fisher," she said, taking the seat opposite him.

He smiled again, that odd little grin that looked as if he seldom used it. Obviously, she had startled it out of him. "You're not going to the Brass Lantern."

"Then who will?"

"I'll go. Nobody will question what I'm doing there," he added when she would have protested. "I can always say I'm working on another case. I find a lot of suspects at places like the Brass Lantern."

"I can imagine."

He sipped his coffee, watching her over the rim of his cup with what looked like admiration, but perhaps she was mistaken. Maybe he was just laughing at her again.

"Then I'll find Mrs. Petrovka and see if she'll tell me who took her to see Alicia that night, and you'll go to the Brass Lantern to talk to Fisher. One of us is bound to find out who the killer is, and then what will we do?"

Malloy took another sip of his coffee. "Then we go see Roosevelt."

Sarah had no trouble finding Emma Petrovka's address. The woman advertised openly in the newspapers, even though her profession was patently illegal. No one ever prosecuted abortionists. There was too much real crime in the city for the police to have time to bother with such trifles, especially when no one was likely to pay a reward for apprehending them. Unless Petrovka killed too many patients, and even then no one would care unless one of them was someone of importance.

Sarah was going over a speech in her head when she left her house that morning, trying to figure out what to say that would sound like a plausible reason for having sought out an abortionist. Mrs. Elsworth's cheery greeting interrupted her thoughts. The woman was sweeping her immaculate porch. If she came out to sweep every time someone she wanted to talk to walked down the street— and Sarah was fairly certain she did—it must get swept a dozen times a day.

"Looks like it's going to be another warm one, today, Mrs. Brandt. Off to deliver a baby this morning, are you?" she asked.

"No, I've got an appointment," Sarah said. It wasn't quite a lie. She had an appointment even if Mrs. Petrovka didn't.

"Be careful then. I baked some bread this morning, and the top of the loaf split. I've been worried sick ever since. You know what that means, don't you? There's going to be a funeral soon."

"It won't be mine," Sarah assured her, wondering with amusement if anything ever happened to Mrs. Elsworth that didn't have some sinister interpretation. "But I'll be careful."

"See that you are. And watch out for those infernal bicyclists. Did you see the story in the *Times* this morning? Some fellow ran his cycle into a wagon and very nearly killed himself and everyone else involved!"

Sarah promised again to be careful and managed to escape without hearing about any other superstitions.

By the time she reached Gramercy Park, she had settled on an excuse for her visit to Mrs. Petrovka. She would say she was consulting her because one of her patients had requested the services of someone like Petrovka, but Sarah wasn't certain the procedure could still be performed so late in the pregnancy. This, she thought, would be a natural opening for mentioning Alicia's case. Not that she expected Petrovka to bring it up, but Sarah certainly intended to.

Petrovka's house was small but meticulously kept. The steps were swept clean, and the windows sparkled. Behind them, Sarah could see lace curtains, and the door fittings were solid brass. Emma Petrovka had made a very comfortable life for herself out of the misfortunes of others.

Steeling herself for a confrontation with a woman she despised, Sarah lifted the knocker and let it fall. She waited a reasonable time before knocking again, louder and more insistently this time. Apparently, no one was home. Disappointed, Sarah had decided she would have to come back later, but as she was turning away she noticed something about the front curtain she hadn't seen before. One edge was pulled away from the window, as if someone was peering out, except when she looked more closely, no one was there. The curtain seemed to be caught at an odd angle on a piece of furniture. Curious now, Sarah leaned over the porch railing for a better view, and what she saw made her gasp.

Galvanized now, she tried the door, something she would never have dreamed of doing before, and to her surprise, it opened under her hand. Later she would realize she should have been afraid, but at the moment, all she could think of was trying to help.

The door opened into a center hallway. Stairs went up to the second floor and the parlor opened off to the right. The pocket doors stood open, and now Sarah could see clearly what she had only glimpsed through the window. Emma Petrovka lay sprawled on the parlor floor, and for all her intentions of coming to the woman's aid, Sarah saw instantly that her help was no longer needed.

FRANK COULDN'T BELIEVE this. He gazed down at the mound of Emma Petrovka's body and frowned. The bruises on her throat were just like those on Alicia VanDamm's. Which only meant that they'd both been strangled in the same way, not necessarily that they'd been strangled by the same person.

Frank could imagine that the woman hadn't had a friend in the world, but he also couldn't imagine anyone hating her enough to kill her in such a personal way. Except, of course, Alicia's killer. If Petrovka really had known who the killer was, it was only natural he'd want her dead, and he could want her dead so badly, he might have surrendered to the impulse to murder a second time. What Frank couldn't figure out was why he'd waited until now to get rid of her. Obviously, it wasn't because he knew Sarah and Frank knew about her, because no one had known that but the two of them.

He found Sarah Brandt sitting in the dining room. She was alone at the large mahogany table, her hands folded primly, her expression grim.

He was a little annoyed at her for asking for him by name. Actually, she'd insisted that the officers send for him, making such a fuss that the whole department would probably be talking about it. They would want to know why she'd insisted that he come instead of another detective, but he supposed he could explain it away. Nobody but them needed to know Petrovka's death was connected to the VanDamm killing, so they could just say she asked for him because she knew him from the other case. Or maybe Frank could make them believe she was sweet on him. At least it would give them something else to talk about.

"You still think it's safe to go looking for a killer in the daylight?" he asked her softly so none of the other officers would overhear.

She gave him a mutinous look. "You don't know she was killed in the daytime," she whispered back.

"Seems likely. Unless abortionists are used to getting cases in the middle of the night, too. It looks like she opened the door to whoever it was willingly, so most likely it wasn't the middle of the night. And if she opened the door to him, she must not have thought she had any reason to be afraid."

"So she wasn't afraid of Alicia's killer, which makes it likely she didn't even know Alicia had been murdered." She frowned. "If only I'd come yesterday. Maybe . . ."

"Maybe you'd be dead, too. And you didn't know about her yesterday."

"How long has she been dead? Do you have any proof she died this morning?"

"In this heat, the body would've spoiled if she'd been dead longer than a few hours. And she's still stiff. After death, the body—"

"I know about *rigor mortis*," she said impatiently. "It sets in after an hour or two and lasts for seven to ten hours and then the body grows limber again."

"Do you feel up to going through her things?" he asked. "Maybe we can find something."

She looked up in surprise. "What would we be looking for?"

He reached into his pocket and pulled out the curette they had found in Alicia's room. "To see if she's missing this."

Her eyes lighted with instant comprehension. "Of course! Why didn't I think of that?"

She was on her feet instantly. "Her examining room is in the back. That's the most logical place to start."

The killer hadn't disturbed anything in the house, probably because he knew there would be no evidence here linking him to Petrovka, or even to Alicia's murder so long as Petrovka was dead and couldn't identify him. The examining room was spotlessly clean and in perfect order. Mrs. Brandt began a systematic search, going through each drawer and cabinet as thoroughly as he would have himself. Frank couldn't help but think how she'd changed since the day he'd forced her to look through Alicia's things. She'd been so hesitant then, but now . . . He'd make a detective of her yet.

"What's so funny, Malloy?" she wanted to know when she looked up and caught him staring.

"Nothing's funny," he said sobering instantly. "A woman has been murdered."

She wasn't fooled. "Am I doing this wrong?"

Perversely, he wanted to tell her she was, but he couldn't lie. "Not at all. Couldn't do it better myself."

"Then why don't you help?" she snapped. "Start on that side of the room."

"What am I looking for?"

"The instruments will probably be rolled up in a soft cloth and tied."

Malloy was the one who found them. They were just

as she had said, in a drawer. The cloth was black, and when he untied the string holding it, it rolled out to reveal a set of instruments similar to the one he'd found in Alicia VanDamm's room the morning after her death. The sizes were graduated, and each instrument was in its own individual pocket. One of the pockets was empty.

"Did you find it?" she asked, hurrying over to see.

He handed her the curette from his pocket. "Is this the one missing?"

She examined the curettes in the set, pulling them out and holding them to the light, then comparing them with the one they'd found. "Yes," she decided. "It matches the others, and it's the size that's missing. This proves Emma Petrovka must have been the one in Alicia's room that night."

"For all the good that does us," he said.

She sighed, a sad sound. Frank had forgotten how forlorn a woman's sigh could be. "I don't suppose you've found Mr. Fisher yet, have you?"

"He wasn't in when I called this morning," he said, "but that's not unusual. Nobody stays around a flophouse during the day. I'll check back late tonight."

"He's the last one alive who knows who went to Alicia's room that night. What happens if you don't find him?"

He could see from the look in her eyes that she already knew the answer, but he said it anyway. "Then we might never find out who killed Alicia VanDamm."

II

FRANK FOUND THE BRASS LANTERN A LOT NOISIER this evening than it had been earlier in the day. Nightfall had brought the lodgers back to claim their beds or their share of the floor space that was offered, to anyone who could pay, for a few pennies. The "beds" were lengths of dirty, sagging canvas strung between rows of rough-hewn boards. Less than a foot of space separated each hammock, and a man could reach up and touch the bunk above him. Privacy was in short supply in a place like this. No wonder Will Yardley's friend had no trouble spotting Hamilton Fisher.

The proprietor stood at the door, collecting nickels and pennies and cuffing those who thought to sneak in without paying back out into the street. He frowned when he saw Frank and grew instantly defensive.

"I keep an orderly house here, I do," he insisted belligerently. "There's no call to come barging in here. I pay my protection money."

"I'm not here to bother you. I'm looking for somebody," Frank said, tossing him a silver dollar. "Tall fellow with buck teeth. Might be calling himself Hamilton Fisher."

"I don't care what anybody calls hisself," the man replied. He smelled of garlic and sweat. "Do you think I keep a register? This ain't the Plaza Hotel, now is it?"

"I said he's got buck teeth. Seen anybody like that?" Frank said, not even tempted to give the fellow any more money. Frank liked his informants to be more cooperative than this, so he wasn't going to encourage bad behavior by reaching into his pocket again, and if this fellow didn't get more friendly, Frank was going to have to get rough.

The man waited, jutting out his greasy beard and hooking his thumbs in his suspenders. But Frank could wait, too, and he did, glaring his policeman's glare, which had been perfected after years of practice. As he had anticipated, he won the staring match.

"Might be somebody by that description inside," the man allowed.

Frank acknowledged the cooperation with a nod and stepped into the building. Most of the bunks were occupied. The men laid down fully clothed because any article of clothing left unattended would be claimed by someone else before the night was over. A group of men were playing cards for matches in a corner, and someone on a top bunk was snoring like a foghorn blasting its way down the Hudson River.

Frank walked up the aisle, glancing at each man in turn. Fisher had been clean shaven when Sarah Brandt saw him last, but he might have let his grooming lapse since he was living harder now. The teeth would be his only certain distinguishing characteristic.

Most of the men recognized his profession immediately and watched his progress warily. People of this class, which was almost the lowest in the city, would fear the police and rightly so. Most of them were felons of some sort or another and could be assumed to have committed a crime of some magnitude within the last twenty-four hours. Even if they hadn't, they might be picked up and charged with something, then beaten into confessing to it. Frank believed such police behavior was simple laziness, but these men needn't know this. Better if they were afraid of him.

Someone kicked the foghorn snorer, jarring loose a snort and a string of profanity from him and raucous laughter from everyone else. Frank moved on. The room smelled of sleep and filth and the stink of too many people in too small a space. It was, Frank had long since determined, the aroma of despair. The bare brick walls, the unfinished ceiling, the scarred muddy floors. Not one element designed for comfort in the whole place, because, of course, comfort could not be bought for a nickel.

Too many men were lying in shadow, safe from Frank's probing gaze, but before long, a weasel of a man sidled up to him, baring his rotting teeth in an ingratiating smile. "Who might you be looking for, governor?" he asked "Maybe I could be of help. Roscoe's my name, and I always play straight with coppers because they play straight with me."

Frank took a moment to look the fellow over from the crown of his greasy hair to the soles of his broken shoes. His suit was too big, probably because it had once belonged to someone else, someone who may not have parted with it willingly. Stolen or not, it was showing green in spots where the fabric was so worn that even the color had come off.

Since this Roscoe was clearly not the man he was looking for, Frank figured it was safe to ask for a little help. "I'm looking for a young man, tall and blond with buck teeth. Might have only been around a week or so. His name is Ham Fisher, although he probably isn't using it right now."

Roscoe scratched his head, almost dislodging his shapeless hat in the process. "Don't know if I recollect such a fellow here, governor. My memory ain't what it used to be . . ." His voice trailed off expectantly.

Frank reached into his pocket and pulled out a dime. This was enough to buy Roscoe an all-night drunk on stale beer. His rheumy eyes lit up, and he grabbed for the coin, but Frank held it out of his reach.

"How's your memory doing, Roscoe?" Frank asked. "Is it improving at all?"

"Oh, my, yes, it's improving quite considerable," he allowed. "In fact, I think I seen the very fellow you're looking for right down at the end of this row." He pointed vaguely and reached for the coin again.

Frank tucked it inside his closed fist. "Maybe you'll show me exactly which bed," Frank suggested.

Roscoe licked his lips, probably already tasting his first beer. "Sure, governor, I'd be pleased to show you. Right this way."

Frank followed the little tramp, earning glares from all the men they passed. Frank cowed each of them in turn, taking pride in making one after the other drop his gaze, until at last they reached the bunk Roscoe had indicated.

"That's him," he said, pointing to a shadowy figure curled on his side and balanced precariously with his hat pulled over his face. Roscoe reached again for the dime, but Frank wasn't going to pay until he was sure he'd gotten his money's worth.

"*Fisher!*" he bellowed, and the figure on the bed jerked awake, jarring loose his hat and in the next minute dumping himself unceremoniously onto the floor. Howls of laughter rose up around them, and Frank tossed Roscoe his dime.

Fisher looked around desperately, until he finally noticed Frank. He needed only another moment to discern the danger he was in, and he was on his feet in a minute and out from between the bunks, ready to bolt.

Frank was one second quicker, however, and he grabbed the boy in a choke hold with one arm, twisting his arm behind his back with his other one. "I'd like to ask you a few questions, Mr. Fisher," Frank said, half-walking, half-dragging him along the aisle back toward the door.

"I don't know nothing," he gasped, trying to struggle

but failing. Frank had him too far off balance and in too much pain.

"You're being too modest, Mr. Fisher. I'll bet you know lots of things. How do you know I'm not going to be asking you something you *do* know? But then," he added as he dragged Fisher out into the street, "maybe you know perfectly well what I'm here to find out and that's why you're so set on running."

An alley yawned nearby, and Frank hustled him into it, slamming him up against the brick wall and bracing him there with a forearm against his throat. "Now, then, let's set a few rules. First of all, don't lie to me, or I'll have to show you what I know about giving the third degree."

Fisher made a gurgling sound that might have been a protest, but Frank didn't really care if it was or not.

"First question: Why were you following Alicia VanDamm?"

Fisher shook his head violently in denial, but Frank merely increased the pressure on Fisher's throat slightly, until his eyes started bulging in his head. Judging that he'd gone far enough, he released the pressure enough for Fisher to draw a desperate breath.

"We can go down to Police Headquarters if you'd rather," Frank suggested. "We've got rooms there where we can question our prisoners in comfort. Our comfort, you understand, not yours. And I've got a cell I can lock you in until I remember to come back to get you. That might be a few days. I'm pretty busy, so you'd do better to answer me now and save yourself some time in the hole. What do you say?"

He could see Fisher was thinking it over, weighing his options. Plainly, he was afraid to cooperate with Frank, but he was also afraid to refuse. Frank decided that whatever he feared Mattingly would do, Frank's threat had the advantage of being the most immediate. That surely gave him an advantage.

He tried another question, an easier one this time. "Who hired you to follow Alicia VanDamm?"

Whatever loyalty he'd had, evaporated. "Sylvester Mattingly," he gasped.

This wasn't news, but at least he'd gotten the boy to tell the truth.

"Why did he want to find the girl?"

"I don't know. It ain't my place to ask. I just do like I'm told."

This was also probably true. "All right, then, if you were supposed to find her, why didn't you just tell Mattingly where she was? Why did you move into the boardinghouse with her for a week?"

His eyes rolled as he looked around desperately for some escape, but he found none.

"It's late, and I'm tired, Mr. Fisher," Frank said. "If you make me exert myself, I'm going to be in a very bad mood."

"She had something," he reluctantly admitted.

"Something you were supposed to steal? Her jewelry, maybe?" Would the VanDamms have hired someone just to get the jewels back and the hell with their daughter?

"I never stole nothing! Not no jewelry, anyways," he added quickly when Frank started to press on his throat again.

"What then?"

"A . . . a book."

This made no sense. "What book?"

"It was a diary, they told me. She wrote in it all the time. I was to find it and make sure I brought it back before they went to fetch her."

Frank recognized the irony of this. Hadn't he hoped to find just such a book when he'd searched Alicia's room last week?

"And did you find it?" he asked.

Fisher rolled his eyes again. Even in the shadows of the alley, Frank could see his fear. And smell it, too. Fisher reeked of it. "I don't know," he tried, but Frank was having none of it. He leaned in, bearing down with his forearm again until Fisher was writhing.

After a few moments, Frank released him. "I'm only going to ask you once more, Mr. Fisher," he said while the boy gasped for breath. "Did you find the diary?"

"I found it, but . . ."

"But what?" Frank demanded.

"He said it was the wrong one."

"Who said?"

"Mr. Mattingly. He said it wasn't the right book. He said there was another one, and that was the one he wanted, but she hardly ever left her room, so I never had much time to look for it. I didn't find another one, though, even though I tried. It just wasn't there."

This made no sense to Frank. "The girl kept *two* diaries?"

"The one he wanted was the old one. The one she'd had for years. What I found was just from when she'd left home. The old one wasn't in her room."

"So you killed her and ran away," Frank guessed.

"*No!*" he cried, his body fairly trembling with fear. "I never touched her! She was alive when I left the house!"

"You're pretty sure of that, which probably means you killed her."

"No, no, I swear! I saw her let somebody into her room, and then I got my stuff and left. She was alive then."

"Who did you let into the house that night? If what you say is true, maybe he was the one who killed her."

Fisher was quaking now, like a man possessed. Surely, he knew that betraying Mattingly wasn't the smartest thing he'd ever done. "It wasn't just a man. He had a woman with him, too."

"And you know who they are, don't you?"

"I don't! I swear!"

"Stop swearing and tell me the truth. Who was the man?"

"I don't know. Some swell. I never saw him before. Mattingly sent me word he'd be coming that night, and I should let him in. That's all I know!"

"What did he look like?"

"I told you, a swell. Expensive clothes. Skinny little mustache."

"Blond or dark?"

"Blond. Talked through his nose, like they all do. Walked like he had a stick up his ass."

"How old was he?"

"How should I know? Maybe your age. I don't know for sure. He didn't really let me get a good look at him, and I sure as hell didn't care."

"What about the woman? Did she call him by name?"

"She called him 'sir.' That's all. That's all I know. Now let me go!"

Frank was pretty sure he knew more. "Just one more thing, Fisher. What are you doing in the Brass Lantern?"

Frank caught a glimpse of the sass that must have been the boy's stock and trade. "I was trying to get some sleep when you rousted me out."

Frank gave him a slap. Just a friendly one, nothing serious, just to remind the boy who was in charge and that he knew Fisher was responsible for Alicia VanDamm being dead. "You know what I mean. Mattingly must pay you well enough so you don't have to sleep in a flophouse. And look at you." He took in the boy's dirty clothes and week's growth of beard with a disdainful glance. "A swell like Mattingly would demand a little more flash from his hired help."

"I . . . I don't work for him no more," he insisted.

"And why not? He fire you after Miss VanDamm turned up dead?"

"No, I . . ."

"You what?" Frank demanded, raising his hand to strike the boy again. But he didn't have to.

"I quit!"

"Why?"

"I . . . They didn't say they was gonna kill her! She was a nice girl. They didn't have no call to kill her!"

Frank didn't quite believe the boy's sense of honor had

been so badly offended. "And you figured they'd try to pin it on you, didn't you? That's why you ran. That's why you're living here instead of at your flat."

The boy was trembling again. "I didn't touch her, not ever. They went into her room, and I left. Mattingly told me to get out when they came, so I did. When I heard she was dead . . . I mean, that's why you're here, ain't it? Because they said I killed her? They're trying to pin it on me, ain't they?"

It would've been a good idea, Frank thought. In fact, he could have done so himself, just to get the case solved. A boy like this would be an easy target, with no friends to help him. Mattingly certainly wouldn't, not if he'd framed the boy for the murder. But Frank had a witness who'd seen Fisher leaving the house before Alicia was killed. Or at least when her mysterious visitors were still with her.

"Well?" Fisher asked, his voice reedy with terror.

"I just wanted some information," he told the boy, releasing him at last.

His legs threatened to buckle, but pride kept him on his feet. Clutching the wall for support, he glared at Frank, or tried to. It was more of a cringe. "You ain't taking me down to the station house?" he asked, afraid to trust his good fortune.

"I know you didn't kill the girl, so you can quit running. The police aren't looking for you. But is somebody else?"

Fear flickered across the boy's face again. "I couldn't say."

"But if you could, you'd say that you think Mattingly and maybe the fellow you let into the house that night are trying to find you so they can say you killed her."

"Even a fool could see that's the best thing to do," he admitted. "Nobody'd believe me over them, not for a minute."

"I think you can forget about it, then. It only took me a few days to find you, and I wasn't trying very hard.

Mattingly knows how to find somebody in this town. If he wanted to frame you, you'd be in the Tombs by now," he said, naming the prison building used by the city. They were going to tear the place down, but Frank figured that no matter how modern the new prison was, it would always be called "The Tombs."

"Maybe it ain't Mattingly I got to be worried about," he said quietly. "Nor the Tombs, neither."

"What do you mean?"

The boy swallowed, trying to get some moisture back into his mouth, and his gaze darted up and down the alley, as if trying to judge who might be the bigger threat, Malloy or some unseen pursuer. "I mean, I know who the swell was who come to her room that night."

"Who was it? Mattingly?" Frank demanded, resisting the urge to grab the boy again and shake the truth out of him.

But the boy shook his head. "Wasn't him. It was . . ." He looked around again, making sure they were alone. "Well, I heard Miss VanDamm call him 'Papa.' "

A FOOL'S ERRAND. That's what Sarah was on. She didn't even know why she was going back to the VanDamm's house, but she was getting too restless sitting at home, waiting to hear back from Malloy. She had to do something.

She was hardly down her front steps, however, when someone called a warning.

"Stop, dear, don't go any farther!" Mrs. Elsworth cried, hurrying down her own porch steps. Apparently, she'd been watching out her front window for something to happen in the neighborhood that would require her attention. "You dropped your glove!"

Sarah looked to see it lying near the top step, and started back for it.

"Don't pick it up!" Mrs. Elsworth shrieked in terror, causing Sarah to nearly stumble on the steps. "Bad luck, you know!" she explained when Sarah gaped at her.

Sarah swallowed down her exasperation. "Am I supposed to let it lie there?" she asked, trying not to sound sarcastic.

"Of course not!" Mrs. Elsworth said, her eyes wide at such a ridiculous notion. "I'll pick it up for you. And that's *good* fortune for you today, to have someone else pick up your glove."

Amazingly spry for her age, she brushed past Sarah and flitted up the steps, snatching the glove, then handing it back to Sarah with a flourish. "There!"

"Well, thank you," Sarah said, trying to appear suitably grateful.

"Are you off to help a baby into the world?" she asked, plainly delighted to have been of service.

"No, I have an . . . an appointment," she said, although it wasn't any truer than it had been the last time she'd said it.

"Nothing serious, I hope." Her face crinkled in concern.

"Oh, no, it's just a visit with an old friend." This was stretching the truth a bit, but Mrs. Elsworth didn't need to know everything, however much she might wish to.

"With that gentleman who called on you the other day?" she asked coyly.

"I told you, that was a police detective, and he wasn't calling on me. He's working on a case, and I was able to give him some information."

"Of course, dear, whatever you say." Mrs. Elsworth smiled knowingly. "But I'd wager he *would* be calling on you if you'd give him the slightest encouragement."

Sarah was hard pressed not to laugh out loud at such a ridiculous notion. "I assure you that Detective Sergeant Malloy barely tolerates me, Mrs. Elsworth, and the feeling is mutual. Once his case is solved, we'll most likely never set eyes on one another again."

"Oh, my, young people can be so blind," she clucked, shaking her head in dismay. "He does seem like a very nice man, Sarah, even if he is a policeman. You mustn't dismiss him too lightly. You never know where your destiny might lie.''

Sarah thought Malloy had seemed rude and obnoxious that day he'd met Mrs. Elsworth, and she was sure Malloy wasn't any part of her destiny, but she wasn't going to argue the point standing on the sidewalk. ''I'll give the matter some thought,'' she lied to escape further blandishments.

''I should hope so,'' Mrs. Elsworth said. ''Now I'd best let you be on your way. Watch the weather, though, dear. There's a storm brewing, and you don't want to be caught out in it.''

Sarah glanced at the cloudless sky in surprise. The day was unseasonably warm again, and the air was still. ''It doesn't look like rain,'' she pointed out.

''I know, but I tried to light a candle this morning, and the blessed thing just wouldn't catch. That means a storm's coming, sure as sunrise. Maybe you should take an umbrella, but . . . oh, dear, it's bad luck to go back once you've started out,'' she mused. ''Oh, I know, I could lend you mine!''

She would have darted off to fetch it, but Sarah stopped her. ''I'll only be gone a short while,'' she assured the old woman with a meaningful glance at the clear sky. ''That storm must still be a long way off.''

''Just take care that you're home before it starts,'' Mrs. Elsworth warned. ''It's going to be a bad one.''

Sarah was still shaking her head when she reached the corner.

But as she paused on the VanDamm doorstep nearly an hour later, she couldn't help giving the sky one last look. Still no hint of impending doom. Mrs. Elsworth's candlewick must have just gotten wet.

As usual, Alfred answered the VanDamm's door. His eyes were still sad, and he now moved as if he carried the weight of the world with him.

''I'm sorry, Mrs. Brandt, but Miss Mina isn't at home today,'' he told her before she even asked.

Sarah wanted to curse with frustration, but she knew that would shock Alfred so much he'd probably never admit her again. Instead, she chose to simply bend one of the rules of decorum instead of smashing it entirely. "Is Miss Mina really away from home, or is she just not receiving *me*?"

Alfred was visibly shocked at such a breach of etiquette. No one in the VanDamm's social circle would dream of making such an inquiry and certainly not of a servant. If one were being snubbed, one would eventually surmise it and just stop calling. Sarah didn't have the time or the patience for any more fruitless trips uptown if she had been banned from the VanDamm home, however, so she had to ask.

"I'm sure I don't know to what you might be referring, Mrs. Brandt," he informed her stiffly.

Sarah resisted the urge to shake him. "Can you just tell me if she's really away from home?"

He stared at her for a long moment, as if trying to decide if she were demented or not. Or perhaps he was determining whether she was worthy of this information. Finally, he said, "She's visiting friends in the country."

Hiding her relief, Sarah was about to thank him and be on her way, when she remembered that another female lived in this house, one upon whom she might also pay a call, or at least try. "Is Mrs. VanDamm at home, by any chance?"

Now Alfred really was shocked. "Mrs. VanDamm is an invalid, and she doesn't receive callers."

That probably meant she only received a few of her nearest and dearest friends, and probably her doctors, too. Sarah did not fit into those categories, but she was also beyond caring if she shocked Alfred any further. "Would you ask her if she would receive me? Give her my card, and . . . does she know I saw Alicia the night before she died?"

Alfred's face seemed frozen in shock. "I'm sure I

couldn't say what Mrs. VanDamm does and does not know.''

"If she doesn't, then please inform her. Tell her I'd like to talk to her about how Alicia looked that night.''

She thrust her card at Alfred, the one that announced her as a midwife, after folding down the corner to announce she was paying her respects. He took it as gingerly as if she were handing him a live snake.

"I feel I must inform you again, Mrs. VanDamm does not receive visitors,'' he reminded her almost desperately.

"I'll wait in my usual place,'' she said, undeterred.

Alfred was gone for quite a while, so long in fact that Sarah began to fear something might have happened to him. Could he have gotten lost or fallen ill? But surely, Alfred knew his way around the house, and she would have heard some disturbance if he had been found prone someplace. So she tried to believe the wait was good news. A simple refusal would have been given instantly, and she would have been sent on her way. The delay indicated that at least her visit was being considered.

At last Alfred reappeared, looking even more disturbed than he had before. "Mrs. VanDamm will receive you in her rooms,'' he said, unable to hide his amazement. "Bridget will show you.''

The maid had come halfway down the steps and was looking at Sarah as if she were a rare specimen in a zoo.

"Thank you,'' she said to Alfred, then hesitated when he looked as if he wanted to say something more.

"Mrs. VanDamm hasn't been well for . . . for some time,'' he said, each word sounding as if it were being dragged from his throat. Most likely it was, since he was breaking every unwritten rule of discretion by speaking of this at all. "She's . . . Miss Alicia's death was a shock to her.''

Sarah nodded, understanding the implied warning, although she wasn't quite certain what the warning was for. She supposed she would find out soon enough.

She followed the maid up the stairs and down the hallway to the proper door. Bridget knocked and slipped inside for a moment. Sarah heard her say, "Mrs. Brandt is here, ma'am," and some murmured consent. Then Bridget admitted her.

The room was dim and stuffy, the cheerful sunlight of this April morning held at bay by heavy velvet draperies drawn tightly over every window. In contrast, the furniture was light and elegant, if a bit ornate for Sarah's taste. To her amazement, the bed was an enormous canopy sitting on a platform and surrounded by what Sarah could only call a fence, albeit a low and merely decorative one.

Reminding herself she wasn't here to critique the decor, she looked around and found Mrs. VanDamm reclining on a fainting couch by the fireplace, much as Mina had been the first time she'd called on her. Mrs. VanDamm looked much more natural in this position, however, probably because she'd had a lot more practice at playing the invalid. She wore a ruffled and flowered dressing gown, and her legs were draped with a crocheted coverlet in spite of the heat. The table beside her held an assortment of bottles and jars, and the room was redolent of the competing odors of camphor and lavender.

"Sarah Decker?" Mrs. VanDamm asked, her voice at once feeble and intense. She looked remarkably unchanged since the last time Sarah had seen her years earlier. The lines of her face had deepened a bit, but her skin was still flawless and smooth, probably because she hadn't seen the light of day in all those years. Her hair had silvered gracefully, and it was artfully arranged. This was probably what had caused the delay in Sarah being summoned to her.

"Yes, Mrs. VanDamm," Sarah said, going to the couch where she lay. She smiled her professional smile and took the slender hand the older woman offered. "Except I'm Sarah Brandt now."

"Oh, yes, I remember that you married. But something dreadful happened, didn't it?" Her face creased into a delicate frown for a moment, and then she said, "I thought you had died."

"My sister Maggie passed away," Sarah said, choosing not to take offense, as she would have if Mina had said the same thing. Mrs. VanDamm looked as if she might really be confused enough to make such a mistake. The pupils of her eyes seemed dilated, and a glance at the jars on the nearby table told her why. She saw Hood's Pills and Buffalo Lithia Water and Ripley Brom-Lithia and Warner's Safe Cure, among other brands of patent medicines. Some of these were harmless concoctions, but others contained generous dollops of morphine, which didn't cure anything but usually made the sufferer less aware of her disease—and everything else, for that matter. If Mrs. VanDamm was taking these medications with any regularity, she would do well to remember her own name.

"Your sister, yes," she said vaguely. "I remember now. Tragic. And now we've lost our dear Alicia."

"I'm so sorry," Sarah said. Although she hadn't been invited, she seated herself in the chair placed strategically near Mrs. VanDamm's chaise, close enough that she didn't have to let go of her hand. "I really hate to intrude on you at a time like this, but I did see Alicia right before . . . well, the last night she was alive, and I thought you might like to hear that she seemed well."

"I couldn't believe it when Bridget told me you'd seen her. I still don't understand any of it, and Cornelius is no help. That policeman told us the strangest things, but when I ask Cornelius about it, he keeps saying it's none of my concern, but how could that be? She was my child, after all. Everything about her is my concern, isn't it?"

Sarah nodded, although she couldn't help thinking Mrs. VanDamm didn't look as if she'd concerned herself with much of anything outside of this room in quite a while. "What don't you understand? Maybe I could help."

Sarah figured that enlightening Mrs. VanDamm on any subject might earn her the wrath of the rest of the family, but she was willing to take the chance if she was able to get any information at all out of her. Besides, Mrs. VanDamm might not even remember her visit an hour from now.

"I thought Alicia was at Greentree," Mrs. VanDamm said plaintively. "That's where we sent her. Or where Cornelius sent her, I should say. He didn't consult me. He never does, not anymore. Alicia was always high strung, and lately she'd been very nervous. Crying for no reason, that sort of thing. I told him she was just at that age when young girls become emotional, but he thought she would do better away from the city, where things were quieter. She loved Greentree, and she had her horse there, so I saw no harm in it. But now they say she was living in some boardinghouse. I don't believe it. I'll never believe it. Why would she go to a boardinghouse when she had two perfectly fine homes of her own?"

"Alicia *was* living in a boardinghouse," Sarah assured her. "That's where I saw her, although I didn't know who she was at the time. I noticed her because she looked so much like Mina did at that age."

"Oh, yes, she did. Alicia was the very image of Mina at the same age. Sometimes I even called her Mina by mistake. I know she didn't like it, but she never let on. She was so sweet." Her eyes filled with tears, and for a moment, Sarah regretted causing her such pain, but then she realized that Mrs. VanDamm was unable to hold onto that pain for more than a moment. Her watery gaze drifted, and along with it her attention. "Oh, I saw you admiring my bed. It's Marie Antoinette's."

"I beg your pardon?" Sarah asked, confused.

"It's an exact replica of Marie Antoinette's bed. She used to receive her attendants while she was still in bed. It's a French custom, don't you know? But Marie wasn't French and she didn't like having all those people coming up to her bed, so she had them put up a fence to keep them from getting too close. Isn't that clever?"

Sarah had no idea if it was clever or not, but she nodded and smiled politely and tried to figure out how to turn the conversation back to Alicia. She need not have worried.

Mrs. VanDamm might be vague, but she hadn't slipped entirely away.

"Please tell me, Sarah, how did Alicia come to be living at that boardinghouse?" she asked after a moment.

"I believe she ran away from Greentree."

"That's nonsense. Why would she run away? She had no reason."

Sarah knew Alicia had a very good reason, but she was fairly sure Mrs. VanDamm didn't know it, and even if she did, would never admit it. "I believe she was upset by a marriage her father was arranging for her," she tried.

Mrs. VanDamm frowned as she considered this. "I had no idea she was upset. I didn't think she even knew. Cornelius had talked about it, of course, but I couldn't agree. I thought she was too young, although I wasn't much older than she when I married Cornelius. I think marriage can be good for some girls, don't you? Especially to an older man. Cornelius is twelve years my senior, and he helped me settle down. I remember how proud I was to be seen with him when I was a bride. He was so handsome and tall."

For a moment, she seemed lost in her memories of happier times, while Sarah tried to picture Mrs. VanDamm as a sixteen-year-old bride to her twenty-eight-year-old groom. Although it wasn't the perfect picture, it was still a long way from Alicia and Sylvester Mattingly, who must be over sixty.

"Do you know who the man was?" Sarah asked, hoping against hope Mrs. VanDamm could shed some light on the uneven match. "The man her father was planning for her to marry?"

"Oh, yes, but I don't think Cornelius would have gone through with it. He doted on Alicia too much to let her go just yet. And while I think the husband should always be older than the wife, the man Cornelius had in mind was much too old. Too young and too old, do you see? When I was young, many girls married at sixteen, but nowadays, that's not done anymore. She hadn't even made her debut. She would have missed so much.''

And now she will miss everything, Sarah thought, but of course she didn't say it. ''Alicia must have thought her father would go through with it, or she wouldn't have run away,'' she pointed out instead.

''That's something I still don't understand. How could she have gotten away? How would she have known where to go?''

''Someone must have helped her,'' Sarah offered, remembering Malloy's pledge to keep the groom's help a secret. ''Perhaps a friend. Can you think of anyone who would have done that? A young man perhaps, someone her own age who might have been smitten with her.'' *Someone who could have gotten her with child*, she added silently, praying it wasn't Sylvester Mattingly, as she suspected. The thought was simply too awful to contemplate, although it would have explained Alicia's flight perfectly.

But Mrs. VanDamm was shaking her head helplessly. ''I can't think of anyone. Our neighbors at Greentree had some boys, I think, but they're away at school. I don't believe Alicia knows them, either.''

Plainly, all this thinking was too much for her. She lifted a hand to her head and closed her eyes as if in pain.

''Are you all right? Can I get you something?'' Sarah asked, instantly contrite. Morphine addict or not, Mrs. VanDamm was still a grieving mother.

''My salts,'' she said, motioning vaguely toward the assortment of medicine bottles on the table.

Sarah picked through the bottles, seeing Lydia Pinkham's Remedy, which claimed to cure all manner of female ills but which merely masked them with a morphine fog. After a moment, she located the bottle of smelling salts. Lifting the stopper, she passed the foul-smelling bottle under Mrs. VanDamm's nose until her eyes popped open again and her color returned.

''Oh, thank you, my dear. I get these spells where I get so weak and . . .'' Her voice trailed off as her unfocused

gaze suddenly focused on Sarah. "Did Bridget tell me
that you're a midwife?"

"Yes, that's right. And a trained nurse, as well."

"Why didn't I think of this before?" she asked of no
one in particular. "I've been wasting my time with doctors. The doctors are all men. What do men know about
female problems?"

"Are you having female problems?" Sarah asked solicitously, thinking that she might gain Mrs. VanDamm's
confidence by giving her some medical advice. If she was
consulting with Sarah, she would certainly welcome her
back for another visit if Sarah needed more information
later.

"Oh, yes, for years now, and nothing helps. I have
these spells when I feel weak and I can't get my breath,
and other times my head feels like it's coming off my
body. And sometimes, if I'm very still and quiet, I can
actually hear my heart beating. That isn't natural, is it, to
hear one's own heart beating?"

Sarah thought it probably was if you were listening for
it, but she chose to humor Mrs. VanDamm. Perhaps she
did have some problem that Sarah's training could help.
Sarah began to question her about her symptoms, and
Mrs. VanDamm was only too happy to describe them in
great detail. Apparently, she had nothing more to occupy
her time than to sit here alone in the semidarkness and
concentrate on every sensation of her own body.

She quickly learned that Mrs. VanDamm, who was not
quite fifty, had completed menopause and was probably
just experiencing the effects of it. "Do you find marital
relations uncomfortable?" Sarah asked, ready to give
Mrs. VanDamm some tips on how to alleviate that discomfort, but Mrs. VanDamm was shaking her head.

"Oh, dear, I *always* found marital relations uncomfortable," she confessed, rolling her eyes. "I can't imagine how other women manage. After Mina was born, I
told Mr. VanDamm I couldn't endure his attentions anymore, and to his credit, he hasn't bothered me since. It's

been over thirty years now, and I haven't missed it at all, I assure you.''

Sarah was so shocked that for a moment she couldn't even remember what they'd been discussing. She wasn't shocked to learn that Mrs. VanDamm didn't have intercourse with her husband. Many women of her class felt as she did, which was why so many men of her class kept mistresses. No, what shocked her was the realization that if Mrs. VanDamm hadn't had sexual relations since Mina was born, she couldn't possibly have been Alicia's mother.

12

Frank looked around the VanDamm estate in Mamoraneck with new eyes. He thought of Alicia VanDamm and wondered if she had been violated in this very house. If what Sarah Brandt believed was true, and Sylvester Mattingly had raped her and gotten her with child, then it might well have happened here, far away from prying eyes and ears.

Frank hesitated a moment before knocking on the front door, wondering if one reason he'd been taken off the case was because of his last, unauthorized visit here. But this time when the housekeeper opened the door, she looked more resigned than outraged at his presence.

"Just like a bad penny, ain't you?" she said. "You keep turning up."

"I'd like to look around Miss VanDamm's room again," he said, telling only a partial truth.

"You already did that. What do you think, that she came back from the dead and put something there you couldn't've found before?"

"This time I know what I'm looking for," he replied, concealing his surprise that she didn't seem to be aware that VanDamm hadn't authorized his previous visit. Could the woman have neglected to mention it to her employer?

"And what would that be?" she asked skeptically.

"A diary."

Mrs. Hightower's eyes grew large in her homely face. "What would you be wanting with *that*?" she demanded.

"I think it might give me some clues about the identity of her killer. You knew the girl kept a diary, I take it."

Mrs. Hightower sniffed derisively. "Everybody knew it. She wrote in it all the time. For a girl who never went anywhere or did anything except ride that mare of hers, she sure found a lot to write about, I'll tell you that."

"Did you ever read what she wrote?"

"Of course not!" She was thoroughly outraged at the very suggestion. "Nobody would do a thing like that."

"Not even her personal maid? Maybe Lizzie knows what it said. Maybe Lizzie knows where it is."

"Not likely," Mrs. Hightower insisted, "but I guess we won't see the back of you until we ask her, now will we?"

Frank merely smiled expectantly until Mrs. Hightower finally admitted him.

This time she put him in a small front room where he waited until Lizzie had been summoned.

"Mr. Detective," the maid said in dismay when she saw him. "Have you found out who killed Miss Alicia yet?" She was wringing her hands in her apron and looked on the verge of tears.

"Not yet," Frank said, trying to sound kind while knowing he wasn't being very reassuring, "but I'm hoping you can give me some help. Do you know where Miss Alicia kept her diary?"

"Oh, cor, she kept it locked up, nice and safe, because she didn't want anybody never to read it but her, but it ain't there now."

"How do you know?"

"Because they sent me to look for it right after she disappeared."

"Who sent you?"

"Why, Mrs. Hightower, who else?"

Who else, indeed. Frank could think of many possibil-
ities, but the truth was probably that Mrs. Hightower
would only have acted on orders from the VanDamms.
This meant they knew what the diary must contain, and
that would explain why they'd ordered Sylvester Mattingly to find it. Now if only Frank could find out what
it said, too.

"Can you show me where she kept it?" Frank asked.

"I can, but only if Mrs. Hightower says it's all right,"
she said, glancing nervously toward the door, at which
Mrs. Hightower might well be listening.

Mrs. Hightower seemed willing to do anything if it
would get Frank closer to leaving, so Lizzie escorted him
upstairs to Alicia's room. She showed him a small chest
which he'd searched on his last visit. It held mementos
of Alicia's childhood, awards won in school, some trin-
kets that had probably held some sentimental value, but
nothing that could remotely be called a diary.

By now Lizzie was openly weeping, not making a
sound but allowing the tears to flow freely down her face.
Frank felt a twinge of guilt and wondered when he had
become so sentimental. In other days, he would have been
jubilant at the sight of those tears, knowing they would
make the person he was questioning more open and forth-
coming.

"Lizzie, Mrs. Hightower said Miss Alicia wrote in her
diary a lot. Do you know what she wrote about?"

The girl shook her head in silent despair. "Sure and I
don't. She wouldn't let me see it, not ever. I couldn't've
read it, even if she did, of course, but I'd never of wanted
to. She wrote in it all the time, and sometimes she cried.
I don't want to know what made her cry. If she had secrets, she should be allowed to keep them, don't you
think?"

Frank *didn't* think, so he ignored the question. "Did
she have any other place she hid her diary?"

"Oh, no, sir. This was the place. She could lock it up,
and she carried the key around her neck so nobody could

find it accidental. But when she disappeared, the chest was open and the key was on the table there.'' She pointed to the dressing table. ''She must've took her diary with her. That's the only other place it could be.''

Frank sincerely doubted this, since Ham Fisher hadn't found it when he searched her room at the Higgins house, either. He started to ask her if there was anyone else who might know or to whom she might have entrusted her diary when he realized he didn't have to ask. He already knew: the groom, Harvey.

The stables were dim and strangely silent when Frank entered. He gave himself a moment for his eyes to adjust from the bright sunlight outside. The familiar and comforting scent of horses and straw and manure assailed him, swamping his senses at first so that he didn't notice it. But the silence was too great, too complete. Oh, he could hear the horses shuffling in their stalls and the hum of swarming insects and the scurry of rodents in the hay, but something was missing. The place was too still, as if its life force had been sucked out. As if it was empty of human habitation.

Except the other servants had told him Harvey was in the stables. No one had seen him come out, and he didn't appear to be anywhere else, so he had to be here. Except Frank knew he wasn't.

''Harvey!'' he called into the void. A horse knickered, but no one else responded.

Frank's nerves tingled as his body prepared instinctively for whatever he encountered. ''Harvey!'' he tried again, making his way farther into the stable. He glanced into each stall as he passed, seeing nothing amiss. Everything was as it should be except for the oppressive silence that seemed to muffle even his own footsteps. The little mare that Alicia had ridden peeked out at him, blinking her sad, brown eyes. A bay gelding stamped his hoof in the next stall but offered Frank no comment as he walked by.

One by one, he passed each stall until he came to the

last one, and that's where he found Harvey, hanging by his neck from the rafter.

SARAH SHOULD HAVE expected her mother to be entertaining at this time of the day, but she never would have imagined the scene she encountered. The maid hadn't seemed surprised to see her this time and conducted her to the dining room without even being asked. When she saw who was there, she realized the girl must have simply thought she was another invited guest to the elaborate formal tea party her mother was hosting.

The group of ladies sitting around her mother's enormous table represented some of the oldest families in New York, and all of them had known Sarah since she was a babe. If that wasn't bad enough, she saw Mrs. Astor—Mrs. William Backhouse Astor, Jr., matriarch of the Astor clan and designated as "the" Mrs. Astor to distinguish her from the less important Mrs. Astors in the family.

Every instinct warned her to flee, but it was already too late. She was well and truly caught, and couldn't leave without embarrassing her mother.

"Sarah, dear, what a surprise," Mrs. Decker said, hurrying to meet her. She did her best to conceal her shock, but only partially succeeded.

"Sarah, is that you?" Mrs. Astor asked. "How delightful to see you! Elizabeth didn't tell us you were coming."

"She didn't know," Sarah said, smiling as graciously as she could while grinding her teeth in frustration. She needed to speak to her mother alone, not spend hours in meaningless small talk with a group of ladies whose interests were limited to the weather and the foibles of their neighbors.

By then, her mother had reached her and was staring at her anxiously, obviously sensing her agitation. "What is it, dear?" she asked in a near whisper. "Has something happened?"

"No, nothing," she assured her just as quietly. "I just needed your advice on something."

Her mother's lovely eyes lit with surprise and pleasure, but she kept her voice even when she said, "Won't you join us for tea? I think you know everyone." Sending Sarah a silent apology that reminded her that her family's lives were still bound by strict social conventions, her mother reminded her of everyone's name as the maids brought another chair and laid a place for her with the gold-edged china.

"Tea" was really a meal, served with pomp and ceremony on the best china and silver. The tea itself was poured from a large silver pot into dainty white and gold dinner teacups. Trays of sliced cold chicken garnished with nasturtium leaves, daintily cut slices of ham, and strips of tongue were passed. The bread was cut in thin strips and already buttered. Around the table stood small silver pots of preserves of strawberry and gooseberry and orange marmalade and honey in the comb. Silver baskets covered with lace held slices of golden sponge cake and rich, dark fruitcake, and on another silver tray stood Dresden china cups filled with custard and garnished with a generous amount of grated nutmeg.

Sarah managed to sample each treat as it went by her, but she really wasn't hungry. She just wanted all these people to be gone. Sarah was seated too far from her mother to even whisper anything about the purpose of her visit, but her mother knew what she was concerned about these days.

After Mrs. Astor had held forth on the advisability of traveling abroad so early in the season—an inordinate number of icebergs had been spotted recently in the North Atlantic in spite of the unseasonably warm weather—Mrs. Decker brought up the subject nearest to Sarah's heart.

"What a tragedy about the youngest VanDamm girl," she remarked with creditable nonchalance.

"Oh, yes," said one of the other ladies. "I heard Francisca is prostrate with grief."

"She's been prostrate with something for the past ten years," Mrs. Astor said. "And I suppose anyone would expire if her parents were going to marry her off to Sylvester Mattingly.''

"It's true then?'' Sarah couldn't help asking. "They really intended such a match?''

"Oh, I heard the same thing,'' someone else offered. "Although I could hardly believe it. If they were in a hurry to marry her off, they should have sent her to England. My son-in-law, Lord Harpster has several quite eligible kinsmen who would be happy to make the acquaintance of an American heiress.''

"Where she could buy herself a penniless nobleman?'' another woman scoffed.

While the women debated the merits of marrying off wealthy American girls to poverty-stricken English noblemen just to have a titled lady in the family—a practice that had become so widespread it had a name: Anglomania, Sarah considered what she had heard. Apparently, her mother was correct. The VanDamms really had considered marrying their daughter to the elderly attorney, and no one could quite understand why.

After what seemed an eternity of clanking silver and china and meaningless conversation, her mother's guests were finally forced to take their leave, albeit reluctantly. They obviously sensed Sarah had come for something important and were hoping to catch at least a hint of what that might be. In spite of their best efforts to draw her out, they left disappointed.

When the last guest had gone, Sarah's mother took her into the parlor, slid the pocket doors closed and turned to face her. "Now tell me what's happened. Something *has* happened, hasn't it?''

"I'm not really sure, Mother,'' she said as her mother sat down beside her on the sofa and took her hand. "I heard something today that upset me, and I'm wondering if it might be true.''

"Something about our family . . . ?'' she asked with a worried frown.

"Oh, no, of course not,'' she assured her hastily, and

for a second wondered if her mother knew of something she might have heard. "It's about Alicia VanDamm."

Her mother frowned in disapproval. "Oh, my, I was afraid you'd still be worrying yourself about that."

"I noticed you managed to confirm that rumor about Mattingly for me. Thank you."

Her mother frowned. "I'm not sure I should be encouraging you in this, and I'm sure I shouldn't be helping you, but I can't seem to stop myself. Now tell me, what have you learned?"

"I went to see Mrs. VanDamm today."

Her mother didn't bother to hide her surprise. "She received you? You heard Mrs. Astor, Francisca Van-Damm hasn't been out of her bedroom in a decade!"

"She didn't come out today, either. I think she agreed to see me because I'm a midwife, and she wanted some medical advice."

"She can't think she's with child!" her mother exclaimed. "She's much too old for such a thing!"

"Of course she is, but she thought I might be able to advise her on her various ailments, so she allowed me to see her. And while I was there, she told me something very disturbing. She said she hasn't had marital relations with her husband since Mina was born."

Her mother gaped at her, as shocked as if Sarah had slapped her, and for a moment she didn't even breathe. Finally, she managed to gasp, "Sarah, really, I can't believe—"

"Oh, mother, don't be prudish," Sarah said, impatient as her mother's attempt at maidenly modesty. "I deliver babies for a living. Do you think I don't know how they get made?"

"I'm sure you do, but I simply can't believe you would discuss such a thing in my parlor!"

Sarah really had been gone too long from this world. She'd forgotten that women of her mother's station in society might live their entire lives without ever acknowledging the intimacies between husbands and wives. Whatever had made her consider confiding such a thing to her mother, much less expect to receive counsel? And how could she have ever been so inconsiderate?

"I'm sorry, Mother. I don't know what I was thinking." She rose, preparing to take her leave, ashamed of herself and anxious to be on her way. She knew now to whom she should have gone. Malloy would probably be just as shocked as her mother at her references to intimate relationships, but he wouldn't let that stop him from helping her figure this out.

But she'd underestimated her mother.

"Don't go!" she pleaded, capturing Sarah's hand when she would have gone. "I didn't mean . . . I'm afraid I'm just having a little trouble thinking of you as a grown woman. You're right, of course. I *am* being prudish. Please stay, and tell me what it is you need advice about, and I'll try not to be shocked again."

Her mother looked almost desperate in her need to keep her there, and perhaps she was. Probably she thought that if Sarah left feeling her mother had failed her in some way, she would never return. Sarah didn't want to believe herself so vindictive, but she *had* disappeared from her family's life for years the last time, so perhaps her mother was right to want to keep her here now.

Sarah sat down again, still holding her mother's hand. "I'm afraid I forget that other people aren't quite as . . ." She searched for the proper word. ". . . as *familiar* with the more intimate acts of other people's lives as I am. I'm very sorry that I shocked you, Mother, and hope you won't take offense."

Her mother sighed her relief. "I'm really not so prudish as all that, really. It's just . . . You are my little girl, you know, and always will be, no matter how old you get. Or how experienced. Now tell me, what is it you think I can help you with?"

Sarah took a moment to gather her thoughts and re-phrase them in a way that would least offend her mother. "I'm sure you know women who, after they reach a certain age, no longer fulfill their marital obligations to their husbands.''

Her mother nodded, determined not to take offense. "Many women find those duties . . . unpleasant,'' she decided after some thought. "Or even uncomfortable. And others simply decide they don't want any more children, and abstaining from . . . from intimacy is the only sure way to avoid having them.''

"Mrs. VanDamm said she hadn't had relations with her husband since Mina was born,'' Sarah reminded her. "If that's true, where did Alicia come from?''

"Perhaps she was confused,'' her mother suggested. "She would have been in her early thirties when Alicia was born. She married very young, if I recall. Conceiving Alicia so long after Mina would have been embarrassing. Indeed, I remember how surprised we all were at the time . . .''

"What is it?'' Sarah asked when her mother's voice trailed off. "What are you thinking?''

Her mother was staring at something across the room but not really seeing it, because her thoughts were far away. "I was just remembering what people were saying then. We all thought . . . I mean, when there were no other children after Mina and from what Francisca said . . . I believe we thought that what she told you was the truth, that she had stopped . . .'' She gave Sarah a beseeching glance.

"Sharing her husband's bed?'' Sarah offered.

"Yes,'' her mother agreed gratefully. "And she seemed so smug when she told us she was expecting another child, as if she were . . .'' She shrugged helplessly, once again at a loss for words.

"As if she were what?'' Sarah prodded. "Guilty, perhaps? Do you think she'd taken a lover, and that's how—?''

"Heavens, no!'' her mother scoffed. "Francisca was much too dull to even think of something like that. No, it was more as if she were sharing a delicious secret with us. She was delighted with herself and with us for being surprised. She thoroughly enjoyed all the attention she received from it, which is why I was surprised when she withdrew to the country shortly afterward. We didn't see her again until after Alicia was born.''

"I remember that," Sarah said. "Mina went with her. They took her out of school so she could be company for her mother during her confinement. Mina was terribly angry about it at the time. I thought she was just embarrassed about her mother having a baby, and that perhaps she was a little jealous, too. She always resented Alicia, and I guess that's why."

"How odd," her mother said, considering.

"Do you think so? I'd expect her to be resentful of the new baby who got all the attention, especially since she was just approaching womanhood herself. And for her parents to have produced offspring at that stage in their lives must have been mortifying to a girl her age."

"No, I mean how odd they took Mina out of school and sent her to the country with Francisca. You said Mina resented the new baby, and in any case, I'd think they'd want to shield a girl of that age from the . . . the realities of her mother's condition."

It took Sarah a moment to understand what her mother meant, and when she did, she had to agree. In a society where pregnancy was barely acknowledged, it seemed unlikely a family would force their adolescent daughter to confront the reality of it at close quarters when she could have been left at school and remained ignorant.

"What could they have been thinking?" she asked aloud. "Could they have been trying to protect Mina from teasing or from being asked embarrassing questions?"

Her mother looked away, as if unwilling to meet Sarah's gaze.

"You know something, don't you?" Sarah asked.

Her mother bit her lip and sighed. "Not really, but I can think of one possible explanation, although it does no one credit, not even me."

"Mother, what are you talking about?"

Mrs. Decker sighed again. "I feel like the lowest gossip to even think such a thing, but it wouldn't be the first time it happened." Her mother turned back to her, her eyes bleak with despair and remembered loss. "We sent Maggie to France when it happened to us, or at least we tried to."

As Sarah met her mother's tortured gaze, all the awful memories came flooding back. Maggie angry and defiant, refusing to bend to her father's will, refusing to be hidden away until her baby was born. Maggie, pale and dying, making Sarah promise to take care of the child who was already dead. The pain of her loss was still raw, and she saw her mother felt it, too. Her eyes had filled with tears, and she held herself stiffly, as if the slightest movement might shatter her.

That was when the question formed in Sarah's mind, the one she'd never allowed herself to consider, the one she would never have dared to ask all those years ago. "What would you have done with Maggie's child if she'd gone to France the way you'd planned?"

Even though Mrs. Decker resolutely refused to blink, still one tear escaped and cascaded down her pale cheek. "I wish I had thought . . ." she whispered, her voice ragged with the agony of her losses.

"You wish you had thought *what*?" Sarah demanded, clutching tight to her fury because she knew she'd never be able to endure the pain if she allowed herself to feel it.

"I wish I had thought to pretend I was with child myself. I could have gone with her. We could have brought the baby back and . . ."

"And pretended it was our baby sister," Sarah said, finishing the thought her mother couldn't.

Her mother covered her mouth to hold back the cry of anguish propriety forbade her to utter.

Sarah felt as if someone had clawed her heart out. Maggie, Maggie, Maggie. Was that what had driven her to flee? The thought of having her child torn from her, taken away, never to be seen again? No wonder she had been so desperate. Sarah had blamed it on passion, but she hadn't understood that Maggie had made the only choice she could if she wanted to keep her child.

Mrs. Decker drew a ragged breath and turned back to Sarah. "I would have done it. I would have done anything to save her. You must believe that, Sarah."

Anything except let her marry the man she loved, Sarah thought, but she didn't say it. Recriminations wouldn't bring Maggie back, and in all fairness, her mother hadn't been the one who decided what would become of Maggie and her child. Someday she would have to face the person who had, but not today. Today, she had to comfort her mother and herself.

"I believe you, Mother. Any woman would, to protect her child."

Even a woman as shallow and self-centered as Francisca VanDamm, she realized as she watched her mother's lovely face crumble beneath the weight of her grief.

FRANK DOVE FOR the body, grabbing the dangling legs and lifting, relieving the pressure of the rope around the neck, but even as he did so, he knew he was too late. The body was already stiffening, and he could feel the chill of death even through the man's clothes. After a moment, he let go and stepped back in defeat, looking up into the face of death.

Harvey had not gone peacefully. Frank could see the scratch marks on his throat where he had clawed at it while it choked the life out of him. The reaction was instinctive, no matter how much someone might want to die. No matter that he had been despondent enough to make a noose and tie it securely and mount the stool and slip the rope around his neck. Still, when the stool tipped over and the rope cut into the living flesh, the will to live overtook the will to die for at least a few seconds, no matter how futile the effort.

Frank wanted to cut him down. That was always the first thing anyone wanted to do, and Frank felt the urge especially strong when he remembered Harvey was a man his own age, a good man whose only sin had been trying to help a girl he loved. But Frank knew that before he cut Harvey down and afforded his body some measure of dignity, he had to look at everything first to make sure it was as it should be.

The stool was there, turned over just as it would be if he'd kicked it. The rope was tied securely to a hook on the wall, then dropped over an exposed beam. The bloated face and bulging eyes told of death by strangulation. Frank could even imagine a motive or two. Harvey might have blamed himself for Alicia's death and been unable to bear the guilt any longer. Or perhaps he and Sarah Brandt had been wrong, and Harvey really was the father of Alicia's child. Perhaps he was even her killer, although Frank was almost certain he wasn't. Still, he'd been wrong before, and any one of those explanations would have accounted for Harvey taking his own life.

Except he hadn't taken his own life.

A less skilled investigator might not have known that, of course. A less skilled detective, someone who would be investigating a death in the country for example, might have missed it completely. But Frank saw it at once, the first clue that didn't fit. The rope mark on Harvey's throat. The rope mark that went straight around his neck, the way it would if someone came up behind him and put a garrote around it and twisted and twisted until he was dead. The rope from which he was hanging would have left a completely different mark at a completely different angle, and Frank was willing to bet that when he cut Harvey down, he would discover no mark at all underneath it, because Harvey had already been dead when he'd been hoisted up over that beam. And when he turned the stool upright and set it beneath Harvey's feet, he was certain of it, because there was a good six inches between Harvey's dangling toes and the stool he had supposedly stood on when he put the noose around his neck.

Frank spent most of the next hour summoning the other servants, questioning them about what they had seen and heard, and sending someone to fetch the local police, such as they were. Frank figured his own investigation would be the deciding factor in the case, since the local authorities might have never encountered a murder, so he made it as thorough as he could. None of the servants had seen or heard anything untoward, but one of the gardeners had noticed a young man riding by earlier in the day. Why he thought it was a *young* man he couldn't rightly say, except that was the impression he got. All he could really be certain of was that it was a man. Since Frank had already decided Harvey's killer was a man, this was hardly startling news.

When he'd finished with the servants and laid Harvey's body out decently, Frank remembered his original reason for wanting to see the groom in the first place. He could no longer question Harvey about Alicia VanDamm's diary, but he could at least search the man's room to see if his theory was true.

Harvey slept in a room adjacent to the stable. It was remarkably neat, just as the stables themselves. Harvey's meager possessions were hung and stacked and stored, each in its proper place, and his bed was tightly made, blankets tucked just so. Searching the place was the work of a few minutes, since the furnishings were so sparse. And just as Frank had suspected, Harvey hadn't been very imaginative about selecting a hiding place. A loose floorboard underneath the bed came up when Frank pried it with his pocket knife, and beneath it he found the book that Sylvester Mattingly had hired Ham Fisher to find.

It was a slender volume, bound in red leather with gilt edges. Frank only had time to open it and recognize the girlish penmanship inside when he heard the local police arriving outside. He hastily slipped the book into his coat pocket and went out to meet them.

• • •

Wʜᴇɴ ꜱʜᴇ ꜱᴛᴇᴘᴘᴇᴅ out of her mother's house onto Fifty-Seventh Street, Sarah was surprised to see how late it was. She'd wasted most of the afternoon taking tea with her mother's friends, and then she'd spent the rest of it salving old wounds with her mother. At least she finally felt at peace with one of her parents. She hadn't been able to ease her mother's grief at Maggie's death, but they'd been able to share it for the first time without recriminations, something they'd never done before.

If she felt better about her own family's relationships, she was more confused than ever about the VanDamms'. Sarah had known instinctively that her mother would be able to understand Francisca VanDamm. They had been born and bred in the same world, so their values and beliefs would be similar. What Sarah hadn't counted on was having her mother suggest such a horrible possibility for Alicia's existence.

As she reached the corner, Sarah looked for oncoming traffic, and only then did she notice how dark the sky had become, much darker than it should have been for this time of day. As she marveled, she heard the rumble of distant thunder. A storm was brewing off the ocean. Mrs. Elsworth had been right, and here was Sarah, on the other end of town with no umbrella and an even bigger mystery to solve than she'd had this morning.

She thought of Francisca VanDamm and wondered if going back to question her again would be a waste of time. Most likely, especially because she probably wouldn't admit Sarah again. The midwife in her had served the woman's purpose in giving Mrs. VanDamm medical advice, so what possible interest could she have in seeing her again?

But someone else in that house also knew what had happened sixteen years ago and how Alicia had come to be born. And that person probably also knew how Alicia herself had come to be in the same situation, the bastard child sent away to the country to bear her own bastard child in secret. Sarah was sure that if she could just find out how all of this had happened, she would know who had killed Alicia and why.

As thunder rumbled overhead, Sarah turned her steps up Fifth Avenue, back to the VanDamms's town house.

Frank waited on the train station platform while the well-dressed passengers from the city disembarked. They carried newspapers and umbrellas and looked around for the carriages that were to meet them. Not many people were returning to the city at this time of day, so Frank had a car practically to himself, except for a couple of ragged, barefoot boys.

"Candy, mister?" one of them asked, offering him an unappetizing bit of sweet. The boys boarded the train in the city, usually sneaking on without paying the fare, and sold candy to the wealthy men traveling to their homes in the country.

Ordinarily, Frank would have refused. These boys were the worst guttersnipes, homeless ruffians who were always in trouble with the law. Frank certainly had no reason to show one of them a kindness. And he had absolutely no intention of eating anything they sold.

But then he looked into the boy's eyes, something he never allowed himself to do, and he saw the vacant hopelessness of a child abandoned by his family and tossed away like so much rubbish. Alicia VanDamm's diary weighed heavily in his pocket, and perhaps that was what made him pull out a nickel and toss it to the boy. That and the memory of Harvey's body hanging from the rafter.

The boy gave him a gapped-tooth grin. "Thanks, mister," he said, handing him a grimy sweet and scurrying away. The boys would probably curl up on an empty seat at the back of the car and sleep, enjoying the rare opportunity to be warm and dry and unmolested for however brief a time. Life on the streets seldom afforded them such a luxury.

As he heard the two boys whispering at the rear of the car, Frank shook his head in wonder at his own generosity. Sarah Brandt would probably have given the boy her last penny. Her influence would ruin Frank if he wasn't careful.

The train started with a lurch, and the station house receded as the train moved forward into the growing twilight. Frank noticed a flicker of lightning on the horizon. A storm was moving in off the ocean, the perfect backdrop for the reading he had to do.

He reached into his pocket and pulled out the book he had found beneath the floor in Harvey's room. Just as he had suspected, it was Alicia VanDamm's diary. She'd written her name in the front, along with the date, January 1, 1893. He checked the last entry. March 6, 1896, probably the day she'd run away.

In between, she'd written sporadically. Some days she wrote only a line or two. Others she skipped altogether, but sometimes she went on for pages, and those were the ones marked with the blots of her tears. He remembered Lizzie telling him how she'd cry when she wrote in this book, and when Frank read her words, he wanted to weep, too, at least at first. But soon the rage took him, welling like a tidal wave of fury until he wanted to commit murder instead.

As the rain began to lash the windows of the car, Alicia's words began to lash Frank's soul, and when he read her final entry, just as the train pulled into Grand Central Station, Frank knew the truth. He knew that Cornelius VanDamm had killed his own daughter, and even worse, he knew why.

13

By the time Sarah reached the VanDamms's porch, the thunder was louder, and the sky had turned an alarming shade of purple. While she waited for someone to answer her knock, the first fat raindrops began to fall, splatting rudely on the pavement.

"Mrs. Brandt," Alfred said in amazement. It was long past normal visiting hours, and she certainly had not been invited for supper. "I'm sorry, but—"

Sarah never learned whether she could have convinced him with her charm to admit her because at that moment, a streak of lightning split the heavens, releasing a torrential downpour.

Crying out in surprise, Sarah instinctively bolted for the safety of the house, and Alfred's instinct to protect a lady in distress prevailed. He swept her inside and slammed the door against the terrifying onslaught of the storm.

"Good heavens!" she gasped, astonished at how wet she had gotten in just those few seconds. Outside the storm roared with a ferocity that rattled the door.

Alfred looked shaken himself, and he pressed a hand against the panel, as if assuring himself it was securely closed and would hold against the assault.

"Alfred, what's going on?"

Sarah looked up to see Mina VanDamm emerging from the parlor. She stopped short when she saw Alfred was not alone.

"Who's there?" she demanded, squinting to make Sarah out in the darkness.

"It's Sarah Brandt, Mina," she said, stepping into the light of the gas jet. She was unable to believe her good fortune. Mina must have just returned from her trip. She still wore her traveling suit. "I'm sorry to intrude, but I was walking back to the el from visiting my mother's house when the storm broke. It came on so suddenly, I couldn't think of anything else to do but seek refuge here, and Alfred was kind enough to let me in." The best part of the story was that it was almost true.

"This is extraordinary," Mina exclaimed, far from pleased. "We're in mourning, and we aren't receiving visitors, Sarah. I must ask you to leave."

A gust of wind rattled the windows.

"Miss Mina, the storm is frightful," Alfred protested.

For a second the room lit with a blinding flash as lightning split the sky again, and the crack of thunder followed almost immediately.

Sarah saw Mina look up in alarm, but her reaction lasted for only a second. Then her expression hardened again. "Alfred, send for the carriage to take Mrs. Brandt home."

"They can't take the horses out in this, Miss Mina," Alfred said. "They'll bolt for sure."

Surely, she could see Sarah *had* to stay here, at least until the storm had blown itself out. But she didn't have to like it. "Well, I suppose we have no choice. Come into the parlor, Sarah, but don't expect me to be much company. I've only just returned home, and I'm much too tired for conversation."

Without waiting for Sarah's reply to the ungracious invitation, Mina turned and went back into the parlor. Feeling slightly less fortunate than she had a few moments ago, Sarah gave Alfred her thanks and followed Mina.

The room looked even worse in the gloom of the storm than it had the last time Sarah had seen it in broad daylight. Now the heavy furniture seemed to loom forbiddingly, and the heavy draperies plunged the room into near darkness. Even the next flash of lightning could hardly penetrate their folds.

Mina hadn't turned on the gas jets, either, and the day had been much too warm for a fire, although the storm would probably change that. Mina waked to the fireplace and stood by the cold hearth, staring down at it as if she were watching an actual fire.

"I called this afternoon, and Alfred said you were visiting friends," Sarah tried, hoping to engage her sullen hostess in a conversation that she could somehow turn to the subject of Alicia's parentage.

"Alfred had no right to say anything about me at all," Mina snapped, not bothering to conceal her anger or even spare Sarah so much as a glance.

"I'm afraid I pestered him until he admitted you were away. I was afraid you'd just decided not to receive me anymore after my last visit."

Mina gave her a withering look that told Sarah she probably had, then turned her attention back to the fireplace.

Mina hadn't invited her to sit down, but Sarah took a seat on the nearest sofa, looking askance at the water spots on her new suit and hoping they'd dry without leaving marks. For a minute, she debated what to say next, deciding against asking how Mina had enjoyed her trip, figuring that would simply provoke her hostess needlessly. If she was going to provoke her, she could think of a much more productive approach.

"I had a lovely visit with your mother this afternoon," she said.

"*What*?" Mina asked, whirling to face her. "You must be joking."

Sarah wasn't sure if Mina thought she was joking about visiting her mother or about the visit being lovely. She chose not to inquire. "Not at all. She was most anxious to find out how Alicia had seemed that night before she died. I was able to reassure her that Alicia didn't seem frightened or upset."

"You actually *spoke* to my mother?" Mina asked incredulously, as if she hadn't heard anything else Sarah had said.

"Yes, she seemed very well, under the circumstances."

Mina pulled herself up to her full and very imposing height. Sarah wondered that she had never really noticed what a large woman Mina was. But perhaps it was only an illusion since Sarah was sitting and Mina was standing over her.

"I didn't want to believe it of you, Sarah, but I'm very much afraid that your reduced circumstances have made you common. I don't know how else to account for your lack of finer feelings, and nothing but a lack of those feelings could account for the way you imposed upon my mother in her time of grief."

Sarah wondered if she should be insulted, but she didn't wonder long. Since Mina already believed her devoid of any finer feelings, she might as well prove she was. "Your mother told me something very disturbing, Mina. Ordinarily, I wouldn't think of mentioning such a painful subject, but it was so strange, I feel I must tell you so you'll know her current state of mind."

"I know her state of mind," Mina said in disgust. "She hasn't had a coherent thought in ages."

"Then perhaps that's why she told me that you're Alicia's real mother."

For a heartbeat, Mina stood frozen with horror, and then she howled. Threw back her head and howled in agony. There was no other word for it, a sound Sarah would never forget as long as she lived, as if someone had torn loose Mina's very soul. And then she lunged.

Sarah understood her intention with only an instant to spare, and she threw herself off the sofa just as Mina would have landed on top of her. Their skirts tangled, sweeping Mina's feet out from under her, and she went sprawling over the arm of the sofa, knocking over a table covered with bric-a-brac that crashed to the floor in a shower of splintering glass.

Sarah scrambled to her feet, cursing her heavy skirts but knowing she must be ready to defend herself against another attack. Before she was fully on her feet, however, the parlor doors slammed open and Alfred rushed in. He took in the scene with one swift glance, his aged face chalk white as he saw the overturned table and the smashed figurines and Mina VanDamm struggling up out of the mess.

"Don't just stand there, you idiot! Help me up!" she cried, galvanizing the ancient butler who hurried to do her bidding.

Outside, the rain slashed at the windows, and from the hallway came the sound of running footsteps. In another moment, Cornelius VanDamm appeared. He wore a smoking jacket, and his expression was alarmed.

"What on earth happened?" he demanded of Mina, who had struggled to her feet with Alfred's assistance. "I thought the storm had broken a window."

"She attacked me!" Mina shrieked, pointing at Sarah.

Mr. VanDamm stared at Sarah in surprise, having failed to notice her standing there, since the room was so dark.

"Sarah, is that you?" he asked, even more amazed. "What are you doing here?"

"I came . . . the storm . . ." she tried, but Mina gave her no chance to explain.

"I said she attacked me! Aren't you going to do something?"

VanDamm looked from her to Sarah and back to Mina again. "Mina, I think you should go to your room. You aren't yourself."

"Then who am I?" she challenged, lifting her chin defiantly. "I told you she attacked me! Look what she did!" She gestured to the overturned table and the resulting mess.

"Alfred, you may go," VanDamm said, using a softer tone, to show the servant he didn't hold him responsible for what had occurred.

Alfred fled, although he was much too dignified to actually hurry. When the doors had closed securely behind him, VanDamm turned to Sarah. "Mina is upset. She hasn't been herself since her sister died."

"Stop it, Father. She *knows!*" Mina shrieked.

"Mina, there's no reason to shout," VanDamm admonished her.

"I tell you, she *knows*! She knows about Alicia! *Mother* told her!"

He needed a moment to absorb the truth of it, and as he did, his face grew slack from shock. Stunned, he turned back to Sarah, his eyes were terrible. "What did she tell you?" he demanded. "What exactly did she say?"

For a moment, Sarah didn't know how to reply. VanDamm's face seemed carved from stone, and his eyes reflected a torment she could only imagine. "She . . . she told me that Mina is Alicia's real mother," she lied reluctantly, having gone too far now to back down, and braced herself for his fury.

But instead of anger, she saw only . . . relief? Why would he be relieved to learn that Sarah knew their terrible family secret? Unless he'd been afraid she knew Alicia's other secret, which of course she did.

"I'm afraid Francisca has grown quite unreliable in recent years," he said, making his voice quite reasonable, as if he were merely explaining a difficult geometry problem. "She hardly ever leaves her room anymore, and she spends her time weaving elaborate fantasies. You would be foolish to credit anything she said, Sarah."

Sarah felt her hackles rising. She hated being patronized, and she hated the way he patronized his wife, too. Her anger made her reckless. "Mr. VanDamm, I also know why Alicia ran away."

He stiffened again, and this time his expression closed, as if a shutter had been drawn to conceal whatever emotion he was experiencing. "And why do you think she ran away?"

"Because she was with child. I told Mina when I was here before, and I'm guessing you already knew, which is why you sent her to the country in the first place."

"Nonsense," he said, trying for outrage and falling a little short. "That's ridiculous. If that's what Francisca told you—"

"She didn't tell me. I'm not sure she even knows. I guessed it when I saw Alicia the night before she died, and the police confirmed it."

"The *police*," Mina scoffed.

"And we also know that an abortionist visited her right before she died," Sarah said, stung by Mina's contempt and wanting to sting back.

"*We?*" VanDamm echoed. "Who else is involved in this with you?"

Sarah realized she'd said too much, but it was too late. "The authorities. They've been investigating her death, as you well know."

"They aren't investigating it anymore," VanDamm said with a certainty that told her he *had* been behind the decision to take Malloy off the case.

"But they're still investigating the death of the *abortionist*," she countered, determined to best him in this battle of accusations. "She was murdered before the police could question her."

She saw at once that she'd won. His surprise was apparent, and his glance at Mina, telling. What else did they know? And how could Sarah get them to reveal it?

"I told you, she knows all about us," Mina reminded him with satisfaction. "And she'll tell everyone. You know what a gossip her mother is. We can't let her leave here. She'll ruin everything."

"Mina!" VanDamm gasped, but Sarah hardly noticed. She was too busy gasping herself.

Good Lord, what did she mean? It sounded as if Mina was threatening her life, and plainly Mr. VanDamm thought so, too. Outside the thunder roared again, reminding her of the storm that had stranded her here. But as dangerous as it might be outside, she knew she had put herself in even more danger inside. Someone closely connected to the VanDamms had killed two people already to protect Alicia's secret, and if that someone was in this room, Sarah might very well be next.

"Detective Sergeant Malloy knows I'm here," she lied. "And he knows everything that I do."

"She's bluffing, Father!" Mina cried.

He ignored her. "I can pay you," he said to Sarah. "Anything you want. I know your family cut you off when you married. I know you've had to work to support yourself, but I can take care of you. You'll never want for anything again."

"*Stop it!*" Mina screamed. "She won't keep our secret! Don't you understand? She hates us! She wants to ruin us!"

He hardly seemed to hear her. "And if you insist on being stubborn, I can make your life very uncomfortable, too," he continued, not missing a beat and not even bothering to change his tone. "If you choose to ruin us, you will regret the day you were ever born."

"*Father!*"

At last he turned back to Mina, his expression livid. "She's Felix Decker's daughter!" he reminded his daughter coldly. "Do you expect me to have her killed?"

Sarah decided not to wait for her answer. Storm or no storm, she slipped out the door and into the hallway. Just as she reached it, she realized that someone was pounding on the front door. They hadn't been able to hear it in the parlor above the noise of the storm, but whoever was knocking was determined to get in. Perhaps it was just another passerby, desperate for refuge, but Sarah didn't care who it was. She was going to let them in.

"Don't open the door!" Mina shouted behind her. "Stop her, Alfred!"

The ancient butler had just entered the hallway, but he

wasn't quick enough. Sarah pushed past him, nearly knocking him over. She'd just turned the lock when Mina collided with her, determined to bar the way, but whoever was on the other side of the door wasn't going to be denied. The door burst open, slamming the two women against the wall behind the heavy oaken door.

The storm washed in on wind-driven waves, carrying their visitor with it. He was drenched and buffeted, but in the split-second of the next lightning flash, Sarah saw his face.

"Malloy!" she cried, unable to remember being so happy to see anyone in her life.

Behind her, Mina swore a colorful oath, shocking Sarah, but only for a moment. Galvanized, she instinctively tried to shut the door against the storm again, pushing with all her weight. Suddenly, someone was with her, and between the two of them, they got the door closed again. Glancing up, she saw it was Alfred who had rushed to assist her. Everyone else remained where they had been as if frozen.

When Sarah turned, Malloy saw her for the first time. "What are you doing here?" he snapped as water ran from his clothes, pooling on the polished floor at his feet, and she heard Mina's cry of triumph at the evidence of Sarah's lie. Not that it mattered now.

"I found out something about them," she told him with a triumph of her own. She wasn't going to let him know that just moments ago she'd feared for her life and especially not that he had probably rescued her.

Malloy removed his bowler hat and shook the water from it. "Do you know who Alicia's lover was?" he asked with mild curiosity, eliciting another cry from Mina, this time of protest.

Sarah felt her blood quicken. Malloy knew. He knew who the killer was.

"It was Mattingly, wasn't it?" she guessed, almost forgetting about the others in her desperation to know the truth at last.

But Malloy only shook his head and turned to face VanDamm. "I found Alicia's diary," he told him.

VanDamm's face lost every ounce of color, although he managed to hold himself perfectly erect. But Mina gave him no chance to reply.

"He's lying! Her diary was lost! Even Mattingly's man couldn't find it when he searched her room! Don't believe him, Father!"

"Believe me, VanDamm. I know who seduced Alicia and got her with child. I know everything."

VanDamm reached out a hand and braced it against the wall, as if he no longer trusted his legs to hold him steady.

"Father, don't!" Mina cried, rushing to him. "No one will believe him!" She tried to take his arm, but he shook her off.

"They'll believe Alicia," Malloy said, placing his hat carefully back on his head. "I told you, I've got her diary."

Sarah had lost patience. "I don't understand. Who was Alicia's lover if it wasn't Mattingly?"

"It was that groom," Mina insisted. "He was with her every day. I told Father it wasn't right, but he wouldn't listen to me. Harvey was an adventurer who thought he'd make his fortune if he—"

"Stop it, Mina!" her father snapped.

"It's true, I tell you!" she continued, ignoring him. "He's at Greentree. He killed her, too, when he found out he wasn't going to get any of our money!"

"And then he killed himself out of remorse, I guess," Malloy said mildly.

"*What?*" Sarah asked.

"Harvey is dead," Malloy said, still addressing the VanDamms. "Looks like he hanged himself."

"Good heavens!" Sarah murmured, but no one paid her any attention.

"You see," Mina said. "That's it. He killed her, and out of guilt, he hanged himself."

"Except he didn't hang himself," Malloy said, confusing Sarah even more. "And he didn't seduce Alicia. But you already knew that, didn't you, VanDamm?"

VanDamm shook his head. His mouth worked but no sound emerged.

"Then who was it?" Sarah asked, at the end of her patience. "Who fathered Alicia's child and killed her and Harvey? There's nobody left!"

Malloy's face twisted with distaste. "Her father is left. Her own father."

"*No!*" Mina wailed as VanDamm seemed to shrink right before Sarah's eyes. "No one will believe them, Father ! No one will take their word over yours!"

"The diary," VanDamm croaked, as Sarah tried to grasp what Malloy was saying. It couldn't be true. It was too horrible.

"Where is it?" Mina turned on Malloy like a tigress, as if she intended to take it by force from his person.

"I put it in a safe place," he said. "You didn't think I'd bring it here, did you?"

VanDamm seemed to be having trouble breathing. "If it's money you want . . ."

"We'll pay you," Mina finished for him. "We'll make you a wealthy man. Just give us the diary."

"And let him get away with incest *and* murder?" Frank scoffed.

"I never killed anyone," VanDamm insisted. He was gasping for breath.

"You're wasting your time," Frank told him. "A witness saw you coming out of the house after Alicia was killed."

"No, that's impossible!" he insisted weakly.

"Who is this witness?" Mina asked disdainfully.

"Someone very reliable," Malloy said.

"It must be a cat, if he was able to see in the dark and identify my father," Mina said. "No one will believe him."

"What about this abortionist that you say was there?"

VanDamm asked, rallying a bit as he grasped at this straw. "Couldn't she have killed Alicia?"

"If she did, then why did someone kill her?" Malloy countered. "No, I think she went there with the man who killed Alicia, and then he killed her to keep her quiet. Mr. VanDamm, you've been very busy."

"I didn't . . . I wasn't . . . I was at my club that night," he finally managed, his hand pressed to his heart as if he was in pain. "Playing whist with Sarah's father."

He looked at Sarah as if for confirmation, but she could only stare back at him, seeing him now for the very first time as what he truly was.

"A dozen men saw me there," he added when he received no help from Sarah. "They'll tell you. I didn't even know where Alicia was until the next morning."

Malloy glanced at Sarah. "Would your father lie to protect him?"

"No." Her father had many faults, but he valued his reputation as a man of his word, and he certainly wouldn't protect a killer.

"Then that's a foolish lie, VanDamm," Malloy tried, but VanDamm didn't blink.

"It's the God's truth, I swear it. I'd never hurt Alicia."

"You'd never hurt Alicia!" Sarah echoed horrified. "You raped her and got her with child! Your own daughter!"

"It wasn't rape!" he cried in anguish. "Alicia was willing. She loved me, and I loved her. She was everything to me." His voice broke, and he covered his face with one hand, still supporting himself with the other.

"Father, don't!" Mina pleaded, wrapping her arms around him. "You still have me!"

He tried to push her away, his discomfort obvious. "Mina, please," he tried, but she clung to him fiercely.

"I love you, too!" she insisted. "I've always loved you! We still have each other, and now it can be just like it was before she came!"

Sarah watched in horrified fascination as the father and

daughter each struggled to prevail, but before the battle
could be decided, a voice said, "Can't you see he doesn't
want you?"

They all looked up in surprise to see Mrs. VanDamm
on the stairs. She wore a frilly dressing gown which she
clutched to her throat with one of her clawlike hands.
With the other, she held onto the banister, as if afraid she
might pitch headlong down the stairs if she let go.

"He doesn't want you anymore, Mina," she told her
daughter again. "He hasn't wanted you for a very long
time. You're too old. When are you going to accept that?"

"Shut up, Francisca," VanDamm said, a little more
vigorously. "Go back to your room."

"What do you mean, he doesn't want her *anymore*?"
Malloy asked before Sarah could.

Francisca VanDamm lifted her chin, savoring the novelty of having such a large audience. She had probably
not enjoyed this much attention in years. "You didn't
think Alicia was the only daughter he used, did you?"

Plainly, Malloy hadn't thought of this, and Sarah hadn't
had time to. She needed only another moment to determine something else. "Did he get Mina with child, too?
Is that how Alicia was born?"

"What are you talking about?" Malloy asked.

"She's crazy!" Mina cried. "Don't listen to her!"

"He told me I'd have to pretend she was mine," Mrs.
VanDamm said, "or else he'd give the baby away to
strangers. Now I realize he was only trying to frighten
me. He had no intention of giving her away. He wanted
her for himself, especially when he saw how beautiful she
was. He used to stand over her cradle and unbutton his
pants—"

"*Stop it, Francisca!*" VanDamm shouted. "Have you
no shame?"

"Have *you* no shame?" she countered. "You're the
one who used your own children like whores!"

"And when you couldn't pass off Alicia's baby as your
wife's the way you did Mina's," Malloy guessed, "you

hired an abortionist to get rid of it. Except she refused to operate because Alicia was too far along.''

"That's a lie! I told you, I wasn't even there!'' Van-Damm insisted. ''I have witnesses! Sarah's father—''

"And when you realized she was going to leave you and take the child with her,'' Malloy continued, ''you flew into a jealous rage and strangled her!''

"No! No!'' VanDamm was gasping again, clutching his chest. ''I'd never hurt her! I swear it! How can you even think such a thing?''

"Stop it!'' Mina cried. ''Can't you see you're killing him? Father, you must let me take you to your room. I'll take care of you, just like I used to. You'll see, it can be just like it was before! I won't let them bother you any-more. I'll take care of everything.''

"The first thing you'll need to take care of is finding out who killed Alicia,'' Malloy reminded her. ''A man went to the boardinghouse that night with Mrs. Petrovka, the abortionist. That man killed Alicia, and the same man killed Mrs. Petrovka and Harvey. If it wasn't you, VanDamm, who was it? Someone you hired? Was it Mat-tingly? Or his man Fisher? Who was it? Don't you want to see the person who killed her punished?''

"Not if it would cause him embarrassment,'' Mrs. VanDamm said from the staircase. ''His good name is all he has left since he lost his soul the first time he used his baby daughter for his pleasure.''

"Don't listen to them, Father,'' Mina said, reaching up to stroke his face. ''They can't make you say a thing. Come with me. I'll make you forget she ever existed! I can be your little girl again just like it was before she came!''

He stared at her for a long moment, and Sarah watched in amazement as his expression slowly changed from dis-taste to disbelief to horror. ''It was *you*!'' he said, his voice a hoarse croak. ''You killed Alicia!''

"Don't be ridiculous!'' she scoffed, thoroughly offended. ''You heard him. The witness said it was a *man*.''

"It *looked* like a man. But it was you, wasn't it, Mina?"

"I don't know what you're talking about! You've had a shock, Father. You aren't yourself. Mother has a sedative that will help you—"

"I know about you," he said, silencing her.

The two of them stared at each other as if they'd completely forgotten about the others, and in that moment, Sarah had a chance to figure it all out.

"*Mina* was the man with Emma Petrovka!" she told Malloy, whose expression told her he doubted her sanity.

"What are you talking about?"

"Look at her!" Sarah said, pointing to where Mina stood beside her father, shorter by only a few inches and almost as tall as Malloy. Her body was sturdy and angular beneath the flounces of her dress. "If she were wearing men's clothes, and it was dark, she could easily pass for a man."

Malloy couldn't believe it. "Why would she want to—?"

"For the freedom!" Sarah explained, unable to believe he couldn't comprehend it at once. "As a man, she could go wherever she wanted and do whatever she wanted."

"And she did."

This time the voice came from behind them, from someone they'd completely forgotten was there. Alfred's face was gray and slack, but his eyes burned with a righteousness Sarah would never have guessed he possessed.

"Alfred, if you want to continue in our employ . . ." Mina began, but he simply shook his head.

"No one will work for you when they know what you've done in this house."

"Stop it! Stop it right now!" Mina shrieked. "I won't have it, I tell you!"

"What do you mean, Alfred?" Malloy said, ignoring her outburst. "What did she do?"

"She dressed like a man and went out at night. Been

doing it for years. I don't know everything she does, but someone saw her going into an opium den once, wearing her man's clothes, or that's what I heard.''

''There were prostitutes, too,'' her father said, his voice hollow. ''Women she would pay for God knows what.''

Distracted by the shock of it all, Sarah had lost track of what she should be surmising, but Malloy hadn't.

''You dressed like a man,'' he said to Mina, ''and hired Emma Petrovka to get rid of your sis—'' He stopped himself and made the correction, ''. . . of Alicia's baby. And when Petrovka wouldn't operate and left, you killed Alicia to get rid of both her and her child.''

''Lies! It's all lies! Father, don't believe them!''

But he *did* believe them. ''You killed her,'' he murmured incredulously. ''You killed my darling girl!''

On the staircase, Mrs. VanDamm cried out like a wounded animal.

''*No!* No, I didn't, I swear it!'' Mina screamed.

''How did she know where to find Alicia that night?'' Malloy asked.

''I didn't! I couldn't have!'' Mina insisted.

''The report,'' VanDamm said. ''Sylvester had sent it here to the house. We'd been trying to find her diary before we brought her back, and he had a man in the boardinghouse with her, looking for it. But I was out and didn't see his report until the next morning. Mina could have read it, though. She would have known where to find Alicia that night.''

''And when she realized Mrs. Petrovka could implicate her, she killed her, too,'' Malloy reminded them.

''I don't know who you're talking about! I never saw this person!''

''And poor Harvey,'' Sarah remembered. ''Did she kill him, too?''

''Yes. She was dressed like a man again,'' Malloy said. ''One of the servants saw her riding away. She must have come up behind him and strangled him with a piece of rope. He might have even known she was there. He wouldn't have considered her a danger, so she could pretty much do whatever she wanted. Then she somehow got him up and hanging from a rafter. How did you do it, Miss VanDamm? You must be much stronger than you appear.''

"Father, you can't believe this . . . this bogtrotter over your own daughter!" Mina grabbed him by the lapels, clinging when he would have pulled away. "Have you forgotten Alicia left you? She ran away, but I stayed! I've stayed with you all these years! That must count for something. I love you, Father! You must love me, too. That's what you said! That's what you told me all those times when you—''

"*No!*" VanDamm roared as thunder shook the house. "You killed my beautiful girl! Get out! Get out of my sight!''

"Father, *please!*" she begged, but he tore her hands away from his coat and shoved her from him.

"I'll be glad to take her out of your sight," Malloy said. "Would the women's lockup be far enough?"

The look Mina turned on him was pure venom, and Sarah took a step backward just from instinct. "Malloy, I wouldn't try to—" she began, but Mina interrupted her.

"You'll never arrest a VanDamm," she told him acidly. "Tell him, Father. You'd never allow it, would you? No matter what I've done or haven't done.''

Everyone looked at VanDamm, and for a moment, Sarah believed he would forbid Malloy to take her. As much as he might despise her for killing Alicia, he would have to risk losing everything he prized in life in order to see his daughter arrested and tried for murder. But to her surprise, his expression hardened. His dark mustache stood out boldly against his pale skin, and sweat dampened his forehead, but he held his head high as he said, "You killed Alicia. How can you think I would care what happened to you?"

The sound she made was so anguished, it chilled Sarah's blood, and for a moment she thought Mina might attack her own father out of sheer rage. But the balled fists struck his chest in frustration, not fury, and when he grabbed her wrists to hold her, she wrenched free, and with one last shriek, she picked up her skirts and ran.

Malloy would have stopped her if she'd headed for the front door, but she went for the stairs instead, charging up them as if all the devils of hell pursued her, and she surely put Malloy into that category.

She slammed past her mother, and for a second it looked as if Mrs. VanDamm might go toppling over the banister, but before anyone could think to catch her, she'd grabbed hold and clung as Mina ran by her up the stairs.

"Can she get out that way?" Malloy asked Alfred.

"Not unless she jumps out a window," the old butler replied.

"Mr. VanDamm," Sarah asked in alarm. "Are you really going to let Malloy arrest her?"

"Of course not," Mrs. VanDamm said unsteadily as she sank down onto one of the steps. "He was only trying to frighten her. They'd throw him out of his club if his daughter was hanged."

"Shut up, Francisca," VanDamm said wearily. He was still rubbing his chest absently, as if the pain had vanished but he wanted to be ready in case it returned. Sarah could literally see him gathering the remnants of his pride and self-confidence around him again as he struggled to regain his dignity.

Why this should be so important to him when she and Malloy now knew the filthiest secrets about him, she had no idea, but it was, as evidenced by the power he still seemed to believe he possessed.

"You've done your job, Detective Sergeant," he told Malloy. "You found Alicia's murderer, and now you may go."

"I have to arrest her," Malloy said, stubborn to the last. "She killed three people. No one who knows that is safe now, not even you."

Whether VanDamm believed him or not, they never

learned, because the sound of running feet upstairs distracted them.

"Mr. VanDamm!" a voice cried from abovestairs, and in another moment, a maid appeared on the landing. "Mr. VanDamm! Miss Mina went up on the roof! I tried to stop her. The storm's that bad, I told her, but she wouldn't listen. She just opened the door and . . ."

By then Malloy was halfway up the stairs, taking them two at a time in determined leaps. Sarah started after him, but VanDamm almost knocked her over as he rushed past, pushing her out of the way. Outside, a flash of lightning lit the room as bright as day, illuminating Mrs. VanDamm's fragile features. Sarah knew she would never forget the expression on that face.

She would have expected fear or shock, or even horror and disbelief. Instead she saw pure, naked triumph as she raced up the stairs behind the men.

14

SARAH WAS CURSING THE TIGHTNESS OF HER COR-sets by the time she reached the dark, narrow stairway to the roof. Gasping for breath, she stared up at the gaping doorway above her. For an instant, another flash of lightning revealed the raging storm through the opening. The driving rain had washed halfway down the stairs, and the cold, damp air swept past her to invade the rest of the house.

Thunder cracked, making her jump. Only a fool would go out into this.

Then she heard a shrieked, *"No!"* and she was galvanized.

Gathering her skirts in both hands, she clattered upward, sliding and nearly losing her balance on the wet steps but finally launching herself out onto the roof. The storm attacked her, lashing at her hair and her face and her clothes, trying to tear her apart, and for a second she was blind. The darkness and rain and wind obscured everything, but then, in another flash of lightning, she saw them.

They were standing at the edge of the roof. Mina was on the low ledge that encircled it, holding on to some pole for balance while her father pleaded with her. "This is crazy, Mina! Get down from there! You can't believe I'd let them take you to jail!''

"You're just worried that I'll embarrass you if I jump!'' she accused, clinging tightly to the pole but perilously close to being swept over the ledge by the force of the wind. "If I kill myself, you won't be able to explain it to your friends!''

"Is that what you want? To become an ugly piece of gossip that women whisper about over afternoon tea?'' he shouted.

"I won't care what happens when I'm dead!'' she cried, throwing back her head as if daring the storm to take her. The rain had drenched her, turning her hair into a sodden mass and molding her dress to her body.

It drenched Sarah as well, drowning and stinging and chilling her, but still she inched forward, compelled to get closer. Perhaps if she could sneak up unnoticed, she could grab Mina and . . .

"Don't come any closer!'' Mina screamed, halting Sarah in her tracks, but she wasn't even looking at Sarah. In fact, she probably hadn't even noticed Sarah, who was still in the shadows. Malloy was the object of her warning. He'd been edging around, working his way up behind Mina, but now he stopped, too. They all stood like statues, frozen in the darkness for that awful moment in time.

"Mina, give me your hand!'' her father commanded. "Let's go inside where we can talk this over like civilized people!''

A lightning flash illuminated them, bleaching all the color from their faces but starkly revealing the expressions on those faces. Mina still clung to the pole as the rain and wind tore at her. VanDamm stood tall and straight, looking powerful enough to force her down using his will alone. He reached out confidently, as if he could not imagine her refusing his order.

"Come here, Mina,'' he said. "You're making a fool of yourself.''

That was when Sarah realized Malloy had moved. He

was closer now. Mina hadn't noticed because she was watching her father, but Sarah saw he was going to be close enough to grab her in another few steps. Forgotten, Sarah stole through the shadows, ready to help him when he made his move. He'd need that help. If Mina decided to jump, Malloy wouldn't be able to hold her alone.

Her sodden dress weighed her down as she tried to hurry, but at last she was close enough to smell the wet wool of Malloy's suit and to hear Mina's frightened animal sounds above the roar of the storm. She must have finally realized her peril. If she let go of the pole, the wind might sweep her off the wall and over the side of the house where she would be dashed to her death on the cobbles below.

"Father!" she cried, her anguish as raw and cold as the wind.

"Give me your hand!" he said, shouting above the storm.

Slowly, painfully, still clutching the pole with one hand while reluctantly letting go with the other, she reached out to him while behind her, Malloy reached out, too, ready to grab hold and haul her down.

And just in that instant when VanDamm's hand met Mina's, the sky exploded in a blaze of light as lightning struck the pole to which Mina clung.

Afterward Sarah remembered it all in minute detail, right down to the color of Mina's eyes as the electricity jolted through her and into her father, and sparks flew everywhere. Although it seemed to last a lifetime, the scene took no more than seconds, and then they were plunged into darkness again.

"Mina! Mr. VanDamm!" Sarah cried as the smell of burnt flesh filled her nostrils. Then she tripped over an obstacle she hadn't expected, and she saw that there were *three* bodies down, not two. *"Malloy!"*

She practically fell over him. Had he been touching Mina when the lightning struck? Was he hit, too? He'd been flung on his back, and Sarah dropped to her knees beside him. "Malloy! Malloy! Can you hear me?" she screamed, slapping his wet face with both her hands. She was rewarded with a moan. She laid her palm on his chest and felt a heartbeat through the soaked wool, weak but regular. He was alive!

Then she turned to Mina and VanDamm, but she saw as soon as the next flash of lightning that they were both gone. The rain slashed down at their staring eyes, and neither blinked. And their hands, Sarah saw, were still touching, melded together by a force neither of them could deny.

SARAH FOUND THE apartment without any trouble at all. She was a little surprised by the neighborhood, but then she shouldn't have been. Nothing about Malloy should surprise her.

She hefted the basket she carried higher on her bent arm and lifted her skirts with the other while she climbed the stairs to the second floor where the boys playing outside had assured her Malloy lived. Outside the door, she hesitated for a moment, entertaining doubts for the first time. She still wasn't sure what had compelled her to find him. But then, what did it matter? She'd found him, and unless she wanted to turn around and go home, carrying her basket of cheer with her, she'd better knock and deliver it so she could clear her conscience once and for all.

A woman's voice answered her knock, telling her to wait a minute, which she gladly did. She wasn't sure what she was expecting. She hadn't thought about it, but she was fairly certain Malloy wasn't married. Had he told her that or was it just her general impression of him? Then she saw the woman and knew he wasn't.

She was small and round and wore her graying hair pulled tightly into a bun. Her plain face was as wrinkled as a prune, and she seemed as surprised to see Sarah as Sarah was to see her. "What is it, now? We've done nothing wrong," she said with a fierce frown.

Sarah wondered who the woman thought she was. "I'm

Sarah Brandt. I came to see Detective Sergeant Malloy. To see how he's doing, that is.''

The woman's suspicion turned instantly to surprise. ''You're here for Francis? Whatever for?''

''I . . . I was with him when he . . . when he was injured the other night. I called at the hospital, but they said he'd only stayed a little while. He was gone by the time I got there.''

''That's been three days ago,'' she said, suspicious again. ''If you was so concerned, what took you so long to get here?''

Sarah smiled. ''I had no idea where he lived, and it took me that long to find out.''

''Did it now?'' she asked, crossing her arms over her chest in a gesture designed to be intimidating. ''And why would you go to all the trouble?''

Sarah was beginning to wonder herself. ''I was worried about him, and I . . . I felt a little responsible that he was hurt.''

The door to the next apartment opened and another old woman stuck her head out to peer curiously at Sarah.

''Maybe you'd better come in then,'' the woman Sarah had decided was Malloy's mother said. Mrs. Malloy gave her neighbor a haughty glance before ushering Sarah into the apartment where they could have some privacy.

The place was crammed with knickknacks and plaster saints, just as Sarah would have expected from a woman of Mrs. Malloy's age and class, but it was neat as a pin nonetheless. Also what Sarah would have expected.

''Now, how does a woman like you know my Francis?'' she challenged, looking Sarah over thoroughly, as if considering withholding her approval if Sarah didn't have a reasonable explanation.

''I met him when he was working on a case. A girl I knew was murdered.''

Plainly, she doubted this very much.

Sarah wasn't about to attempt to convince her. ''Is Malloy here?'' she tried.

"He stepped out for a while."

"He must be feeling better then," Sarah guessed.

"He wasn't hurt much. The doctor said he was just stunned. His head aches, though he won't admit it. Never would give in to being sick, not even when he was a boy. At police headquarters, they told him to take a few days off to rest."

"Which he doesn't appear to be doing," Sarah pointed out.

Mrs. Malloy ignored her. "What's that you've brought?" she asked, nodding at the basket on Sarah's arm.

Now she felt a little foolish. "Some food. I thought he lived alone and might appreciate something homemade."

Mrs. Malloy carefully digested this information, her pinched expression pinching even tighter. "And what would your husband be thinking of you traipsing all over town taking homemade food to other men?"

"I'm a widow," Sarah said and watched understanding brighten the old woman's faded eyes.

She sniffed her disapproval. "In my day, a woman didn't go calling on a man. It wasn't proper. Still isn't, so far as I know."

Sarah couldn't help smiling. "I'm not calling on him, Mrs. Malloy. I just felt sorry because he got hurt and I was partly to blame. If you'll just tell him I came by—"

"Frank's not a free man," Mrs. Malloy told her. "If that's what you're thinking, that he's just got his old mother, and he'd leave her quick enough for a young, buxom widow like yourself, then you've got it wrong, my girl."

Sarah could hardly keep from laughing aloud at the notion that she might have set her cap for Frank Malloy. Or even more preposterous, that he might be the least bit interested in her in return. Somehow managing to keep a straight face, she said, "I assure you, Mrs. Malloy, I'm not—"

"Because he's got his boy to think of, he has, and he's

got no time for the likes of you or any other female.''

"His *boy*?" Sarah echoed in surprise.

"Yes, his boy," Mrs. Malloy confirmed smugly. "Or didn't you even notice him over there?"

Sarah looked where she was pointing and realized she *hadn't* noticed the child playing in the far corner of the room, his back to them. For a second she marveled that a child could play so quietly she hadn't even been aware of him, and then she marveled that he hadn't come over to inspect their visitor the instant she entered the room, as any child would have done. From here, she could only see the red-gold curls his grandmother must be reluctant to cut, even though the boy was out of diapers.

Mrs. Malloy strode over to where the child sat and at her approach, he turned and finally noticed Sarah. His small face lit up with a glorious smile, and he dropped the toy soldiers he'd been carefully arranging and hitched himself around to face her.

He was beautiful. There was no other word to describe him, and Sarah was so taken that for a moment she didn't register the fact that he was crawling toward her instead of walking as a child his age should have been. That was when she noticed his twisted foot, and her heart broke. How tragic that a child so winning should be crippled.

She still couldn't stop smiling at him, though. He was simply too sweet. "Hello, young man," she greeted him, stooping to be closer to his level. "My name is Mrs. Brandt. What's yours?"

The boy stopped when he reached her and reared upright on his knees, holding out his arms to be picked up.

"He don't talk," his grandmother said before Sarah could reach for him. "He's simple, too."

The words were like a knife in Sarah's heart. He's simple *too*. In addition to being a cripple. The tragedy of it was too horrible to contemplate as she stared down into the cherubic face. She had just set her basket down and reached out to him, instinctively wanting to take him into her arms, when the door opened behind her, distracting them both.

Malloy came in, seeming to fill the crowded room with his presence. He took in the scene with one glance as Sarah rose to her feet. He did not look pleased.

"Malloy," she said by way of greeting.

He looked at his mother, as if seeking some unspoken message. Sarah couldn't tell if he received it or not, but when he looked back at Sarah, he was glowering. "What are you doing here?"

"She brought you some food," his mother said, as if it were an accusation.

The boy had lost all interest in Sarah and now was waving his arms and trying to jump up in an attempt to get his father to notice him, but Malloy didn't take his gaze off Sarah. He was furious.

"I was worried about you," Sarah tried. "They took you away in an ambulance," she added when he looked as if he was going to scoff.

"How did you find me?" Plainly, he wasn't pleased that she had, so she decided to irritate him even further.

"Teddy got me your address."

"Teddy who?"

Sarah smiled blandly. "Teddy Roosevelt. Commissioner Roosevelt to you."

The boy was pulling on Malloy's pant legs, demanding to be noticed. "Mum, take care of him, will you?" he said impatiently, barely sparing the boy a glance. His face was scarlet.

The old woman pried the boy's hands loose and scooped him up, showing a strength that surprised Sarah. He looked far too heavy for her to manage, but she held him easily.

"There's some cookies in the basket," Sarah offered. "Maybe he'd like one."

The old woman gave her a withering glare before turning away. The boy was struggling, reaching for Malloy who continued to ignore him, but eerily, the child made no sound. Not speaking was one thing, but he appeared to be completely mute.

"Take him next door," Malloy told his mother before Sarah could puzzle it out.

"And leave you two alone?" she said, pretending to be shocked.

"*Just go.*"

Not even Sarah would have disobeyed him when he used that tone, and the old woman was no braver than she. The boy tried to grab Malloy as she carried him past, but he failed. His face was tragic with disappointment, but for all his frustration, he still uttered not a sound.

"Very nice to have met you, Mrs. Malloy," Sarah called as they walked out the door. The old woman merely grunted.

Neither Sarah nor Malloy spoke until they heard the door to the apartment next door closing.

"Now, what are you *really* doing here?" he demanded wearily.

Sarah let out a sigh long-suffering sigh. "I told you, I was worried about you. I went to the hospital that night, when I was finally able to get away from Mrs. VanDamm, but you'd already gone home. I tried at police headquarters, but no one would tell me how to find you."

He muttered something that might have been a curse.

Sarah grinned with satisfaction. "A very nice gentleman named Brogham said it would be worth his life—or words to that effect—if he told me where you lived."

"He was right about that."

"It took me three days to think of it, but I finally realized I could ask Teddy, and he was *dee*-lighted to find your address for me," she said, mimicking Teddy's favorite phrase.

"You *know* Roosevelt?" he asked incredulously.

"Of course I know him. All the Knickerbocker families know each other."

"Why didn't you say so before?"

"You never asked."

The look he gave her was meant to curdle her blood, and it very nearly did, although she tried not to let on. "You appear to be doing well," she ventured.

"I'm fine."

"You didn't look too fine the last time I saw you."

Plainly, he didn't want to remember. "I just got the wind knocked out of me is all. And I hit my head when I fell, I guess." He reached up to rub the back of his head but stopped when he realized what he was doing and adjusted his hat instead.

She decided not to mention what his mother had said about his head hurting. "Your son is a very handsome child." His expression was a warning not to trespass, but she ignored it. "What's his name?"

For a second she thought he wouldn't answer, but then he said grudgingly, "Brian."

"And his mother?"

"Died when he was born. A midwife killed her."

His bitterness scalded her, and she almost cried out from the shock of it. "Oh, Malloy, I'm so sorry!"

Of course, Sarah couldn't be sure that's what had caused his wife's death. Women died in childbirth every day, and it was nobody's fault. But obviously, Malloy believed the midwife had been at fault, or at least he needed to blame her for it. And that explained so much of Malloy's attitude toward her. She must bring back terrible memories for him.

If so, he didn't want to dwell on them. "You still haven't told me what you're doing here. And don't give me any more stories about how you were worried about me."

Sarah sighed in defeat. "I guess I'll have to confess, then, before you use the third degree on me. I called on Mrs. VanDamm the other day. The experience was absolutely extraordinary, and I wanted to share it with someone, but I couldn't think of anyone else who would really appreciate it except you."

If he was surprised she'd sought him out just to gossip,

he didn't mention it. Instead, he was as interested as she had expected. "You called on her? What happened?"

Apparently, he wasn't adverse to a little gossip himself.

"She was sitting in the parlor, wearing a new gown that someone must have spent an entire night making to have it ready so quickly, and she was receiving every visitor who came to the door. A lot of them were coming, too, because nobody had seen her in years and because the deaths of her family were so shocking."

This time Malloy scratched his head in bewilderment. "Was she telling people what really happened?"

"Of course not. Alicia's death is old news by now, since people believe she'd died a natural death at their country home, so it was Mina and Mr. VanDamm's deaths they were concerned about. Everyone knew they had been struck by lightning, but nobody could imagine what they'd been doing on the roof in that terrible storm in the first place. She'd made up a story for them, though. Mina, it seems, was distraught over her sister's death, and she'd decided to do herself harm, being unable to bear the tragedy of Alicia's loss. Her father had rushed to save her, and they'd both been struck down."

Malloy shook his head. "Did anybody believe her?"

"I doubt it, but they pretended to, which is all that matters. And you can't imagine the change in her. I expect she still takes her 'medicines,' but she's completely different in every other way. She's actually lively and interesting. And she's thoroughly enjoying being the center of attention of every person whose opinion matters in this city."

"Every person whose opinion matters *to her*," he corrected her.

"At any rate, she's turned Mina and VanDamm into tragic martyrs, and poor Alicia is very nearly a saint."

"And she's the star in her very own melodrama."

"Savoring every moment."

Malloy shook his head again and pushed his hat back to express his disgust. "I wish I still believed in hell. I'd like to think of VanDamm and Mina burning in it.''

Sarah had to agree. ''I've never been able to understand what makes a man do the things he did. Mina may have killed Alicia, but he was the one who twisted her and made her so evil in the first place. He ruined both his daughters, completely and utterly.''

As she might have expected, he picked up her one betraying remark. ''Have you met men like VanDamm before?''

Sarah managed not to shudder at the memories. ''I've delivered their daughters' babies. Most of the time they deny it, of course. Sometimes everyone denies it, but I always know. The way they act gives them away. The only difference between them and VanDamm is that VanDamm had enough money to keep his sins a secret for over thirty years.''

For a long moment they both contemplated those sins. Then Sarah remembered something else.

''Did you get in any trouble for being there that night?'' she asked.

He tried to pretend he was angry again, but this time Sarah saw through him. ''You didn't have to say that you'd sent for me.''

''I was afraid it would be a black mark against you otherwise. VanDamm did have you taken off the case, remember?''

''It doesn't matter now that he's dead. Besides, Superintendent Conlin—he's the one who ordered me off—is going on a long vacation to Europe, and rumor has it he'll retire when he gets back. I doubt he even remembers my name, so I'm not too worried he'll go to the trouble of booting me off the force or even reporting me.''

''That's a relief, since Teddy only promotes men whose records are clean,'' she added sweetly.

''I'm surprised you didn't tell *Teddy* the whole story.''

''I did,'' she said, horrifying him. ''I wanted him to know how honorably you behaved even when Alicia's own father didn't want her murder solved. You deserve a lot of credit.''

"I don't want any credit for this case.''

Sarah remembered what she'd thought of Malloy when she first met him. She'd thought he was as corrupt as most policemen were. She'd assumed he wouldn't be interested in solving Alicia's murder unless he'd get a reward for it. Then he'd gone on to solve it even at the risk of losing his job. Once she'd believed him selfish and even cruel. What other kind of man would become a policeman? But now she'd met his son, and she knew the answer.

"That's why you do it, isn't it? Because of your son.''

"What do you mean?'' he asked, instantly defensive.

"That's why you work for the police. Why you want to be a captain. So you can support Brian.''

She could almost see his hackles rise. "I'd be a poor excuse for a man if I didn't.''

"I wish I believed more men felt that way. I've seen too many abandoned children, though. Especially when the children are less than perfect.''

"Don't make me a hero, Mrs. Brandt,'' he warned. "I'll only disappoint you.''

Sarah was no longer sure of that, but she decided not to argue. "Another reason I came here was to thank you for not giving up and for finding Alicia's killer.''

"And for bringing her to justice?'' he asked bitterly.

"I don't think we can take credit for that, although they both certainly got what they deserved. The State of New York couldn't have done a better job of it in that new electric chair of theirs. And now neither one of them will ever hurt anyone again. If that isn't justice, it's the next best thing.''

"If you say so.''

Sarah looked at his rough Irish face and realized that at some point she had begun to respect him. Meeting his son had helped her understand him, too. They would never be friends, of course, but together they had accomplished something unusual and amazing, which gave them a bond she'd never experienced with anyone else. Perhaps in time . . .

But they wouldn't have that time, and neither of them really wanted it. The case was solved. The reason for them even to know each other was gone, and they never need encounter one another again.

"I guess this is good-bye, then," she said, offering her hand.

He wiped his own on his pant leg before taking hers. His grip was strong and warm through her glove. "If the department had female detectives, you could've been good at it."

Absurdly pleased by the unexpected compliment, Sarah felt herself blushing for the first time in years. "Well, if you ever need help on a case again, you know where to find me."

As if he ever would. They both smiled at the thought, and Sarah took her leave. Out on the street, she looked up and thought she saw him watching her through the window. Then she looked again and decided it had probably just been a trick of the sunlight on the glass.

Feeling the odd mingling of satisfaction in a job well done and regret that the job was over and her mundane life beginning again, Sarah made her way back into the life of the city.